SPECIAL MESSAGE

THE ULVERSCROFT FOUNDATION
(registered charity No. 264873 UK)
was established in 1972 to provide funds for
research, diagnosis and treatment of eye diseases.
Examples of major projects funded by
the Ulverscroft Foundation are:-

- The Children's Eye Unit at Moorfields Eye Hospital, London
- The Ulverscroft Children's Eye Unit at Great Ormond Street Hospital for Sick Children
- Funding research into eye diseases and treatment at the Department of Ophthalmology, University of Leicester
- The Ulverscroft Vision Research Group, Institute of Child Health
- Twin operating theatres at the Western Ophthalmic Hospital, London
- The Chair of Ophthalmology at the Royal Australian College of Ophthalmologists

You can help further the work of the Foundation by making a donation or leaving a legacy.
Every contribution is gratefully received. If you would like to help support the Foundation or require further information, please contact:

THE ULVERSCROFT FOUNDATION
The Green, Bradgate Road, Anstey
Leicester LE7 7FU, England
Tel: (0116) 236 4325

website: www.foundation.ulverscroft.com

1 3 1538227 4

A member of the Sherlock Holmes Society of Scotland, Séamas Duffy lives and works in Glasgow. He has written for *London Fictions*, and is currently working on a historical crime novel, *The Tenants of Cinnamon Street*, based on the Ratcliff Highway Murders of 1811.

SHERLOCK HOLMES AND THE FOUR CORNERS OF HELL

In *The Adventure of the Soho Picture Gallery*, three people are murdered, their corpses showing unmistakable signs of ritualism. As Holmes unearths a web of vice, deception, and intrigue, the trail leads to the upper echelons of society. *The Adventure of the Edmonton Horror* causes the wildest speculation — is it a matter for a detective, a clergyman, or an occultist? Finally, *The Adventure of the Rotherhithe Ship-Breakers* sees Holmes tracking down a would-be assassin — although no-one is certain of the intended target. The investigation will lead him to one of the foulest, most dangerous corners of riverside London, which even the locals call 'the Four Corners of Hell' . . .

SÉAMAS DUFFY

SHERLOCK HOLMES AND THE FOUR CORNERS OF HELL

Complete and Unabridged

ULVERSCROFT
Leicester

First published in Great Britain in 2015 by
Robert Hale Limited
London

First Large Print Edition
published 2016
by arrangement with
Robert Hale Limited
London

A catalogue record for this book is available
from the British Library.

ISBN 978–1–4448–2797–2

Published by
F. A. Thorpe (Publishing)
Anstey, Leicestershire

Set by Words & Graphics Ltd.
Anstey, Leicestershire
Printed and bound in Great Britain by
T. J. International Ltd., Padstow, Cornwall

This book is printed on acid-free paper

For Carol

Acknowledgements

My sincere thanks to Judy Fisher for her assiduous and cheerful assistance with the editing and proofreading of this book.

Table Of Contents

Foreword

Doctor Watson's delineation of the Dartmoor landscape in *The Hound of the Baskervilles* is rendered in such fine detail as to be able to paint a picture from it. He captures every nuance of the bleak, inhospitable moor topography: the tors, goyals, and granite peaks; the bogs and wetlands; the gorse and rolling pastures; from the Bronze Age Grimspound and the treacherous sphagnum moss of Fox Tor Mires, to the 'dripping moss and fleshy hart's-tongue ferns' on the high banks of the green lanes through which the wagonette, bearing the new tenant of Baskerville Hall, is driven.

It is perhaps the most powerful description of any landscape in the Holmesian canon, yet it is in his depiction of the London streets, I think, that Conan Doyle excels. The reason for this is contained in G.K. Chesterton's observation that 'a city is, properly speaking, more poetic . . . than a countryside, for while Nature is a chaos of unconscious forces, a city is a chaos of conscious ones.' One thing that Conan Doyle did for Victorian crime fiction was to create the atmosphere of gaslight and fog that is forever associated with Sherlock Holmes and London. Dickens, it may be argued, had already done it in the fields of both mainstream fiction and documentary writing; Robert Louis Stevenson did it for what might be called the urban Gothic; but Conan Doyle's rendering of the murky, vaporous, lamplit streets of the capital in *The Adventure of the Bruce-Partington Plans* (where 'the fog was so thick that a cab was useless') remains in the memory long after the culprits have been led away by Inspector Lestrade. There are a number of such instances in the canon where the cityscape overwhelms the reader so powerfully that it compels us, if only momentarily, to forget about the plot and the obscure motives of the characters. There is a scene in the *The Sign of the Four* where Holmes and Watson are following the trail of the creosote barrel with the mongrel, Toby, through the back streets of south London as the city is beginning to wake up. It is a very fine piece of atmospheric writing. Conan Doyle does it again, twice, in *The Man with the Twisted Lip* where he brings to life the east end of London around Paul's Wharf with its opium dens, dark alleys, and cargo of bodies — and he does it with only a very few deft strokes of the pen, he doesn't pile on the detail; then he repeats the trick as Holmes and Watson drive back through the sleeping suburbs to Lee, where Holmes points out that:

'We have touched on three English counties in our short drive, starting in Middlesex, passing over an angle of Surrey, and ending in Kent.'

There are a number of instances in the canon where this strong sense of place floods the foreground with colour: the goose chase in *The Adventure of the Blue Carbuncle* down through Bloomsbury and Covent Garden; the ramble along Fleet Street and the Strand in *The Adventure of the Resident Patient*; the drive from the Lyceum to Thaddeus Sholto's house in the company of the mysterious coachman as the lamplights are coming on (again in *The Sign of the Four*), where Holmes intones the names of the nine streets along which they pass like the runes of a secular litany. But the poetry of this particular cityscape is partly hidden: 'there is no stone in the street and no brick in the wall that is not actually a deliberate symbol. The narrowest street possesses, in every crook and twist of its intention, the soul of the man who built it. Every brick has as human a hieroglyph as if it were a graven

brick of Babylon; every slate on the roof is
. . . a document' (Chesterton again).

In the Holmesian canon, Conan Doyle continues what has been called a 'great tradition of ambulatory writing' through London and the scenes described above reveal strong elements of what would today be recognized as psychogeography. He is one our first Londonists, a term currently undergoing a notable, and welcome, renaissance. *The Four Corners of Hell* invites readers to lose themselves in the London streetscapes, and to savour those moments when, as Chesterton puts it, 'the eyes of the great city, like the eyes of a cat, begin to flame in the dark.'

Séamas Duffy
Glasgow

The Adventure of the Soho Picture Gallery

Prologue:
From the Diary of Doctor John H. Watson

Looking back on the century which drew recently to a close, I take up my pen for the hundredth time and reflect that the most exhilarating years of my life have undoubtedly been those spent in collaboration with my friend, Sherlock Holmes. Those decades were more eventful than even my youthful escapades amongst the wild, lawless settlements of the Australian gold diggings, and no less perilous than my luckless stint in the second Afghan war, in which I was badly injured and narrowly escaped death, for there were many occasions when my friend and I braved the gravest personal danger with little compunction — indeed occasionally with wilful recklessness — in pursuit of the ends of justice. For it is now public knowledge that Holmes was himself quite ready to render the ultimate sacrifice to bring the arch-criminal Moriarty and his heinous gang to the gallows: 'He promised me inevitable destruction and it has not happened yet!' my friend would afterwards privately boast.

As Holmes's chronicler, I attained a position of modest, albeit vicarious, fame to which I must confess that my own unexceptionable abilities would never have led. In the case which I now bring to public attention, I was privy to the inner history of a remarkable series of events which seems destined to keep schools of historians, not to mention a legion of obscurantist theoreticians of conspiracy, well occupied for many a decade to come. For perhaps there is no single individual in possession of all the facts of what was undoubtedly one of the most convoluted problems ever laid before Holmes. Since the events first came to light, a cloud of opprobrium had hovered over many an exalted reputation and so, at the conclusion of the case, I prudently placed these papers in the safekeeping of Cox & Co., for the guardians of our libel law, as we may discover herein, are as capricious and cruel as the deities of Greek myth. It is only with the passing of the last of the principal actors in the drama, and the retirement from public life of one who held high office at the time, that I considered it appropriate to publish the present account.

That these papers form part of that secret history of the state, over which much effort was exerted to ensure its remaining concealed from public view, is undeniable. It will doubtless be questioned by some whether these papers should ever be permitted to enter the public realm, but the accession of a new monarch to the throne has brought with it a fresh spirit. Besides, I remain firmly of the view that the case will be of enormous interest to the historians and criminologists of the future; as for the general reader, I fear he will be startled out of his well-worn grooves of contentment and his habits of complacency by the story of this extraordinary chain of events, the climax of which saw the defenestration and public disgrace of a Privy Councillor, continued with the fleeing of a belted earl to France to avoid a scandalous prosecution, and concluded with a successor to the Crown blowing his own brains out in a Rhenish sanatorium. Free of the constraints of English law to which I allude above, certain elements in the French and the American press speculated freely upon the matter (the former with lubricity, the latter with *schadenfreude*), and used the affair as the pretext on which to cast ridicule upon the entire system of constitutional monarchy.

If I have been fortunate in my long years of association with Sherlock Holmes to witness the many triumphs of that great intellect, his impeccable reasoning, the subtle power of inference and remorseless logic brought to bear upon problems which defeated the capabilities of lesser men, I have also been afforded more than a glimpse of the sorrows, the miseries, the cruelties, and the raw injustices of this world, and it is to that darker side that these pages tend. Moreover, in the course of re-examining this disturbing case, I was reminded in the most salutary manner that the story of criminal detection is but rarely conducive to happy endings.

John H. Watson, M.D.,
Marylebone,
London,
August 1902

1

I have recorded elsewhere in my reminiscences that the year 1895 had been marked by the continuation of a spate of robberies which had begun the previous winter. The nature of these crimes had given rise to serious concern on the part of the authorities, for they were apparently well organized and were often aggravated by an assault upon the victim. More importantly, none of the culprits had been brought to book, for although both the general press and the *Illustrated Police News* carried details of the attacks and made constant appeals for witnesses to come forward, none did so; and thus no criminal was ever apprehended.

However, by the middle of June, even these disquieting felonies faded from prominence due to a series of ghastly murders of street women in the City and surrounding districts, which began to fill the headlines and letter columns alike. There had been three murders within ten days, or rather ten nights, for they all appeared to have been committed under cover of darkness, a fact which brought back to many Londoners vague, disturbing memories of the terrifying autumn of 1888. The police authorities, however, went out of their way to assure the public that it was not the same hand at work this time, and there appeared to be some substance to this claim, for none of the crimes were coloured by the extreme brutality which characterized the gruesome killings of that year, where the almost inhuman savagery which had followed the murders gave rise to conjecture regarding the mental as well as the moral state of the assailant. Inexplicably, Holmes's assistance had not been requested by Scotland Yard in the present series of incidents, which led to my presumption that they were pursuing some definite direction of their own. It was my friend's invariable custom not to interfere without invitation; from the few remarks he had made, I could tell that although he was puzzled by the murders, he had neither propounded a theory as to their possible solution, nor had he expressed an opinion as to the conduct of the case by the police. In fact, he had been kept occupied for several weeks by his retention, at the behest of one of the oldest and most respected families in Somersetshire, in the case of the Peasedown Claimant. The story of this complicated affair, which was brought to Holmes by one

12

of our neighbours — the proprietor of the Baker Street Bazaar — I may one day lay before the public, but in consequence of the law's relentless delay it remains, as I write these words, *sub judice*.

As I pored over the newspapers one morning before Holmes appeared for breakfast, I seemed to detect a strange facet of our London mentality: for whilst the press reports contained the most disturbing allegations, emanating from the Aborigines' Protection Society, of the most appalling cruelties — widespread murder and mutilation — practised against tens of thousands of natives in King Leopold's Congo, these largely bypassed the public's interest as did, it must be said, a report of thirty coal miners killed, and several hundreds injured, by the ignition of fire-damp in a Durham colliery. I recalled Señora Durando's words from a few years ago that, to the English public, these things were like happenings on another planet, for an examination of the correspondence columns of *The Times* and the *Morning Post* showed that the attention of Londoners was riveted on the sensational reports of what had been called 'The City Murders' — a phrase which conjured up to me the image of an outbreak of internecine warfare amongst the stockbroker fraternity. In point of fact, the

13

third murder had occurred just outside the City boundary though it was the City police who were the first to attend the scene. There abounded in the newspaper columns a profusion of opinions and speculations as to the motives and possible identity of the killer; comminations of the incompetence and impotence of the police authorities; indignant, if predictable, remonstrances by a certain Irish playwright, all accompanied by insolent cartoons in *Punch*. There were also inevitable calls for vigilance committees to be formed, as well as stern advice, no doubt well intentioned, to this class of unfortunate women of the streets to remain indoors until the murderer had been caught.

As it happened, I had been to my club the previous evening to play billiards with Thurston, and we ran into McKenzie, who had been a fellow student of ours at London University and was now employed as a police surgeon. Soon enough, the small talk ran out and before long, the conversation edged round to more professional matters as McKenzie, who boards near Smithfield, had been called out to conduct the post-mortem examination of the first victim. McKenzie's friend Philips had officiated in the second murder and they had naturally compared notes. In fact, although the police authorities had stated that they were not certain that all three murders were the work of the same man, both McKenzie and Philips had heard rumours through the usual professional channels that there were similarities in the patterns of the injuries, and more importantly, in the size and spacing of the murderer's fingers which were demonstrated in the bruise marks on the corpse. They had come to the distinct conclusion that the assailant must have been the same in all three cases. Of course, as far as any conclusion drawn at the inquest was concerned, it would have been the legal prerogative of the coroner to sum up the case, and in my experience, doctors' opinions were routinely disregarded or discounted. I was musing over this fact when my friend's voice broke in on my thoughts.

'Well, Watson, have they solved it yet?' he asked, as he rang the bell impatiently to signal his appearance to Mrs Hudson.

'Far from it, Holmes,' I replied, looking up from the newspaper, 'it is one of those exasperating cases where the motive seems to be as impalpable as the culprit,' and I concluded by telling him of my conversation from the previous evening.

'I am sure your colleagues' opinion will turn out to be the correct one, but I did wonder why the police seemed to be so irresolute on that particular point. They make mountains out of molehills, of course, and yet ignore the most blatantly obvious. As for their hesitation,' he shook his head in displeasure, 'wasn't it the great Augustine who said, 'God grants forgiveness to your repentance, but not to your procrastination'? You know, I rather think I could express their method as an exact mathematical formula: $D^2 \times P = R$: dither, dither, panic, repent — for they usually conclude in these cases by jumping in with both feet and arresting everyone within a quarter of a mile and then find they have to release them without charge.'

Holmes's musing was cut short by the sound of the front doorbell ringing, followed by a heavy, well-known tread upon the stair. Presently the door opened and in stepped the dapper figure of Inspector Lestrade of Scotland Yard. He bore the air of a man at the limit of frustration.

'A fresh pot of coffee is imminent if you will take a cup with us,' said Holmes, as the visitor drew up one of the chairs to the table and sat down with a deep sigh.

'No doubt you can guess the reason for my visit,' the Inspector remarked.

'I have read the headlines, at any rate,' replied Holmes.

'Have you given any thought to the case?' Lestrade continued.

'Very little, apart from noting your lack of progress in determining a motive or in obtaining even the vaguest description of the killer. I have just been remarking to Watson on the Yard's deplorable tendency to dawdle on the job.'

Lestrade winced as Holmes continued, 'As you know, I usually await your summons unless I have information which gives me some anticipatory knowledge of a crime about to be committed, or information to which I consider you may not be party. In any case, most of the newspapers, even the less bad ones, tend to give the sensational details and omit the important facts, so it is generally impossible to form even a preliminary opinion on the basis of a press report. However, Watson and I were just discussing the particular point of whether this recent campaign is the work of one man or two. The authorities seemed to be unsure of this, and I am unable to see why.'

'Well, I can tell you that,' replied Lestrade, as Mrs Hudson arrived with the coffee tray.

'I would certainly like to hear the official account of all three murders from your own lips; leave out nothing, however trivial it may seem,' said Holmes, once our housekeeper had left the room.

'For once, the facts are pretty much as they have been stated in the press, though some of the papers have gone a bit hysterical over it, especially the ones which pander to the cruder tastes. That's quite surprising, since to be honest — and I know this does not reflect any credit on the Yard — the murder of a streetwalker anywhere in London is not particularly uncommon, nor does it normally make the front page. There are more than a thousand working around Spitalfields and Whitechapel, and this year alone we had one killed on the very last day in March . . . then two in April; we had another suspected case about a month ago, let me see . . . the week after the Brixton Tramway accident. Admittedly she was never identified — a particularly gruesome affair where the torso was found in the Thames with the head and limbs missing. There was another a week later in Green Dragon Yard — twenty-two stab wounds, and according to the police surgeon at the inquest, not all from the same knife. Now as to the recent spate of murders: at least two of the three seem to have followed more or less a pattern, but here's the strange thing — the victims all lived in the West End; they were all well-dressed, respectable-looking young girls

18

who worked around Soho and the Haymarket. They managed to keep their occupation concealed from their neighbours and families, and they catered for a much higher class of client, if you know what I mean: *toffs*. As far as we know, they had no connection at all with the places where they were killed. None of them was known in any of the public houses nearby, and we have no idea what they were doing there.'

'It is possible, is it not,' asked Holmes, 'that they may have been frequenting premises there that are used for purposes for which they are not, shall we say, licensed?'

'It *is* possible, but generally the beat men in the divisions know all the dives and shebeens and kiphouses. I knew most of them myself when I worked there, and I'll wager some of them are hardly changed. None of the victims has any record, nor were they known to us.'

Lestrade took out his notebook and continued: 'It all started on the twelfth of June when the body of Jane Smart, twenty-seven, was found at about a quarter-past four in the morning in Falcon Lane, just off Falcon Square, by two tradesmen passing on their way to work. She had been seen drinking champagne with a client, 'a real toff' her friend said, at a posh hotel in the West End around half-past ten the previous evening: she was never seen alive again. She had been strangled and the body was left underneath one of the windows of a terraced house, yet nobody in the house or the street heard or saw a thing. The time of death seems to have been during the early hours of the morning. There was no robbery, and the girl's purse contained four pounds and some change. We thought nothing of it at the time, but when we lifted the poor girl's body to remove it to the mortuary, we found a five-shilling piece lying on the ground beneath the body. As the girl had been carrying a fair amount of money, we assumed that it had fallen out of her pockets or purse, or had been dropped by her assailant as he was making his getaway. The strangest thing, though, was that the dead girl was clutching in her left hand an ear of corn!'

'Most remarkable.'

'How she came to have this is a complete mystery, and, though we had hoped it might give us a clue as to her attacker, we have drawn a blank. As you know, there was a second murder five days later at St Clement's Court: the first we knew of this one was on the Monday morning about six o'clock. Constable Chandler, a City man, had been on fixed point duty at the junction of Cannon Street not far from the

Monument Underground Station when he saw two men running towards him. One of them cried, 'Another woman has been murdered in the lane!' so Chandler followed them back to the passage where he found the body of a young woman lying on the ground; she had been strangled, as had the first victim. The time of death seems to have been about the same as the first victim. She was Patsy Harvey, an Irish girl from Limerick, twenty-four, and again her purse contained a decent sum of money; likewise, when Chandler bent to examine the body, he found a five-shilling piece, and in her left hand she grasped on this occasion not one, but *two* ears of corn.'

'This was not mentioned in the public reports of the case,' I said.

'No, that's right, Doctor. In cases like these where we have a series of murders, we often hold some of the minor details back from the press and public. The official force is not only deluged by hoax letters in these matters, but often also beset by numbers of quite innocent but deranged persons, who, from some unfathomable motive, claim to have committed the deed themselves. It is a strange sidelight on human nature, gentlemen; we know for certain that in a rare number of cases, some of these people have actually died on the scaffold, their innocence being afterwards established by almost chance discoveries. If some of the small, but significant, details of the crimes are held back, any impostors can be eliminated by close questioning.'

'Excellent,' said Holmes. 'Are you sure, though, that neither you, nor any of your men on the case have said a word about the ears of corn at the moment?'

'As certain as I can be about anything.'

'You ought to have come here straight away after the second murder; precious time has been lost. Any further details?'

'This girl had last been seen in the Haymarket about ten o'clock, where she had been waiting for a client to pick her up in a cab.'

'I don't suppose anyone knows the name of this client?'

'We have no names. No one saw her leave the street on Sunday night. As with the first case, no one in the vicinity where the body was found had heard anything. Our conclusion is that both victims must have been killed very quickly and noiselessly — it looks like the work of a professional killer, almost certainly the same person in both instances. Now, the third one was slightly different, and a particularly bold one, too, because it was discovered just after midnight on Friday the twenty-first, when there were still quite a few stragglers around. It was just outside the boundary of the City, near Petticoat Lane, that a railway porter coming home from Liverpool Street Station saw the figure of a young woman lying apparently comatose at the corner of the alley. She was well-dressed, which marked her apart from most of the local inhabitants, and when the man bent over her, he suddenly realized that she was dead. She was Rosemary Carden,' Lestrade continued, 'twenty-two. She had been seen earlier in the day coming out of the Duke's Head public house in Frith Street, then later in the evening she was seen waiting outside the Half Moon near Piccadilly. No robbery, but again a five-shilling piece was found under the body. Now then, gentlemen, how many ears of corn do you think this time?'

'Three,' Holmes and I replied, almost in unison.

'None at all!' said Lestrade, relishing the effect of his words. 'That's the difference with this one, you see, that's why we're not sure that it is the same bloke. This murder certainly took place earlier in the night than the others had done, for both the porter and the policeman who first attended the scene depose that the woman's body was still warm. And that's what caused us to wonder if it was the same person.'

'But the five-shilling piece? That is obviously part of the killer's ritual,' I said.

'Yes, but to return to the point about the details which we give to the press,' said Lestrade, 'it occurred to us that someone may have read about the five-shilling piece, and may have copied the pattern of the murder, without knowing about the ears of corn that had been left in the girls' hands.' Lestrade shook his head sadly. 'As well as people admitting to crimes they never committed, we suspect that in other cases there are those who go out and copy murders that they've read about; it's a strange world and no doubt.'

'Nevertheless, on the balance of probabilities, I think it is likely that the murders were carried out by the same person,' said Holmes, 'and I shall take that as a working hypothesis. The absence of the ears of corn in the third case may or may not be significant; they may have been placed there and then subsequently knocked out of the woman's hand by the porter when he disturbed the body.'

'Yes, but we searched the area thoroughly afterwards.'

'Well, who knows what might have been

overlooked in the dark,' said Holmes diplomatically. 'It is not impossible that someone else may have disturbed the body before the porter arrived, and then was too frightened to report the matter. Then again, perhaps there is some reason for the third victim not having it.'

'I am certainly keeping an open mind on it,' replied Lestrade. 'To be honest, I am not sure that the coins and the corn are not simply a blind to throw us off the trail, but why they chose them I have no idea. Apart from what I have told you about the five-shilling pieces and the corn, there are really no other clues and no witnesses.'

'You mentioned some letters,' said Holmes.

'Oh, the letters! I wouldn't like to tell you how many hoax letters I have seen in the past ten days or thereabouts, for the guv'nor's desk was covered with them. Between those and the ones the press have passed on to us, I have given up counting. To be frank, I wouldn't want to waste your precious time on them.'

'You think they are all hoaxes?' Holmes asked.

'It is always difficult to tell,' said Lestrade, pausing. 'There were one or two sent to the *Islington Gazette* which were so atrocious that they might well have been written by someone with murderous tendencies, and the ones addressed to me personally certainly made my blood curdle. You may call at the office and view them at any time.'

'I think I shall do so, for one ought not to exclude any data no matter how irrelevant it may seem at the time. There is not a single suspect?' asked Holmes.

'We've interviewed one or two people who were reported as behaving suspiciously on various occasions, but there was nothing at the bottom of it,' Lestrade sighed wearily. 'I'm afraid that's all there is to tell.'

'What about these girls' clients?'

'It is almost impossible to find out who they are, for none of the dead girls' friends would tell us even if they did know. It is likely that there are some very respectable people involved.'

'Therefore it is just possible, is it not, that the victims have been murdered to preclude blackmail or to prevent scandalous gossip leaking out?'

'If that were the case, we'd have a hundred bodies a week. It would be like the plague year.' Lestrade shook his head. 'No, it suits these girls to keep their mouths shut, so I should think there must be more to it than that.'

'All the same, we cannot rule out the

possibility that here has been some blackmail attempt, perhaps involving all three women, which has tragically backfired.'

'As far as we can ascertain, none of these girls knew each other.'

'Dear me, that is stranger still. Well, I had given very little thought to the matter other than to conclude that given the singularity of these crimes, the killer must be some species of madman, who, I believed, would find it impossible to remain at large for very much longer. It is the completely ordinary crime — the matelot knifed in a riverside tavern, the stranger beaten, robbed, and left for dead in one of the rookeries — in which it is more difficult to bring the culprit to book. If this is the same man, why should he stop at three? It is possible that he may strike again.'

'That is the conclusion I have come to. The guv'nor is extremely concerned, too, and that is why I have come here to ask if you would take a look at the case.'

'Yes, I should be certainly happy to do so, but before I can give you even a preliminary view of the case, a visit to the actual scenes of the murders would be very useful, especially in the company of someone who has professional knowledge of the case. I am bound to go out this afternoon on another matter, but if I could prevail upon you this evening, Inspector; and perhaps, Watson, you would accompany us?'

I glanced at the clock with some alarm. It was now well half past eleven o'clock and I recalled that I had a number of appointments with patients — the first at twelve noon — for I had agreed to oversee my friend Jackson's practice, as he had gone abroad. I quickly donned my coat and hat, seized my basket, and dashed for the door. As I rattled off in the cab up through Marylebone High Street towards the Park, I pondered over the strangeness of the case. A less encouraging start to any of our adventures I could scarcely recall. I tried to fathom the significance of the five-shilling pieces and the ears of corn. Were these really a blind, designed to throw the police off the true scent as Lestrade had suspected? Or was the man simply a deranged lunatic whose recklessness must inevitably bring about his capture? I cudgelled my brains and tried to apply Holmes's methods in order to make some sense of the matter, but I confess to no avail; as the cab gained the crest of Primrose Hill, the roaring of a steam engine emerging from the railway tunnel into the cutting below brought me out of my reverie. After a detour to another of Jackson's patients in St John's Wood, I returned to

Baker Street. When the maid brought in afternoon tea, she handed me a note which Holmes had left with her before he had gone out. It was characteristically terse: 'Leave tonight, 8.30.'

2

Our four-wheeler called promptly at the appointed time and very soon we were trundling away through the noisy, crowded thoroughfares of Marylebone. Although the day had been bright and warm, the temperature had dropped sharply, and by sunset a slight evening chill had set in, bringing with it the first slender wisps of mist. We drove along Blandford Street, and as we went down through the junction of Lower William Street and Marylebone Lane, the yellow glare from the windows of the Queen's Arms lit up the street-corner, and we could hear the merry buzz of singing voices mixed with the unmistakeable clatter of the piano resounding through the street. Crossing Wigmore Street, into Oxford and Regent Streets, we went down the Haymarket, past Trafalgar Square and into the Strand, through Covent Garden and on towards Fleet Street. Although the opera and theatre crowds had disappeared, there was still a milling throng thick on the pavements, and one could hear the hoarse shouts of the hot-chestnut sellers, the shrill calls of the flower girls, and the occasional hum of a barrel organ, whilst a steady procession of hansoms and broughams rattled by on the opposite side.

I was somewhat diverted by this flowing tide of humanity which marked our passage through the beating heart of this magnificent city, though Holmes reclined in the corner, characteristically detached and deep in thought, unmoved and oblivious to his surroundings save for an occasional remark when some familiar sight brought to mind a previous case. By the time we had passed St Clement Dane's, the pavements had grown less crowded, and as we drew by the Temple, thick woolly clouds of vapour were curling up from the steep lanes leading down to the river on our right and were beginning to suffuse the light from the gas-lamps and to deepen the gloom of the quieter streets of that quarter. Past St Paul's, on through the sepulchral City and up beyond Bishopsgate, the breeze had dropped and the haze grew thicker and heavier. By the time we had arrived at our rendezvous with Lestrade in a warren of dismal backstreets in Spitalfields, we were mired in the drab wraiths of a summer fog. It may have been due to the depressing object of our journey, but I recall musing that such a fog as this had shrouded the nefarious activities of London's felons since time immemorial.

Once we had alighted from the cab, Holmes bid the driver wait for us and we followed Lestrade to the scene of the third murder: Frying Pan Alley, a dark, narrow, evil-smelling cobbled lane off Sandy Row, barely wide enough for the passage of a cart. Even in daytime, the tall buildings would have rendered the place sunless, and within a few yards of the opening, the shadowy passageway made a dog leg, which threw the corner into complete darkness. The foggy atmosphere and the footpath lit only by the single gas lamp at the end of the street gave the whole place an impression of brooding melancholy. Lestrade halted at the corner and, indicating a spot on the ground, began his explanation.

'I thought we should begin with the most recent one and work backwards to the first. This is where Rosemary Carden, the third victim, was found. The woman who owns the house here,' he pointed to a low window a few yards beyond the angle of the wall, 'a widow, Mrs Greenbaum, describes herself as a light sleeper, and has two sons and a daughter who live on the premises, too. She deposes that they were all in bed by eleven o'clock and remained there undisturbed by any sound until the body was discovered and the police arrived.'

Holmes surveyed the scene, taking in everything. He scrutinized the corner where the body was found, walked along to the window of the house, then gazed at the pavement, the high walls of the passage and the houses opposite, then back toward the entrance to the lane. By now, more than three days had passed, and it was beyond all hope that my companion would be able to glean any material evidence from the scene; not once did I see that spark of illumination in his features which would show that he had discovered anything of importance.

Finally with a shrug he remarked, 'Your assumption seems to have been that the deceased was murdered *in situ*. It seems barely credible that someone could have been murdered within yards of these houses without letting out a single sound and without putting up any kind of struggle.'

'It is technically feasible to commit a murder of this kind without the victim making any sound,' I replied to Holmes. 'However it would have to be done very quickly, with precision and sudden great force; if it were botched in any way, it is obvious that the victim would scream out in terror and so alert the local populace.'

'No, it simply won't do,' retorted Holmes. 'I'm afraid, Lestrade, I find it quite impossible to credit that this woman was murdered under the windows of houses in which whole families were sleeping. The only alternative explanation is that the victim's corpse must have been conveyed here and dumped after the murder.'

'But why would anyone want to do that?' asked Lestrade incredulously.

'Once we have discovered why they were murdered in the first place, perhaps we can come to a view on that question,' replied Holmes. 'There is nothing more to interest us here, now let us make our way to St Clement's Court.'

We returned to the waiting cab and proceeded through a succession of narrow, muddy streets of dirty, smoke-blackened two and three-storied brick tenements, some of the houses so narrow that they suggested stables built for human beings. The dour monotony of the entire district was relieved only by the gaudy street stalls in the lanes with their babble of quaint guttural tongues, riots of brightly-coloured fabrics lit by the flaring lamps, and the miasma of exotic odours. Finally we arrived at the spot off King William Street where the third murder had occurred. St Clement's Court was at the confluence of a warren of alleyways which retained their mediaeval aspect, and which wound back to the rear of the parish church — two men could barely have passed side by side in the extremely constricted passageway.

'It's very quiet here in this part of the City, almost deserted during the night, and as you can see, there are few houses in the area,' explained Lestrade. 'Nothing was seen or heard until two fish porters heading down to the Billingsgate market happened to notice what they thought was a bundle of clothing, went to investigate and raised the alarm. The body was found right here at the mouth of the passage. It is at least possible in this case that the victim could have been murdered on the spot, for the nearest houses are a long way off from where the girl's body was found.'

'Yes, I suppose so,' replied Holmes, 'but what on earth would she be doing wandering about the deserted streets of the City at that time of night?'

Lestrade shrugged.

'Where does the passage lead?' asked Holmes.

'Only to a disused churchyard.'

'And you have searched it?'

'Yes, we found nothing.'

'Well, let us pass on, then.'

We set off again towards Moorgate Street and then turned west through the labyrinth of another slum quarter. We came to an ill-lit square, straggling a junction of four deserted streets, which seemed to hold an even more malevolent atmosphere than Frying Pan Alley. The area was not as densely inhabited, but was suffused with the smell of fried fish, sawdust and rotting vegetables overlaid with the sharp reek of hops from the Angel Brewery nearby, save where the pungent odour of tomcats emanated from the side courts and yards. Lestrade once again guided us to the actual site of the murder. Falcon Lane was another narrow, dingy passageway, which led from Falcon Square to a quadrangle where the buildings were mostly offices and tall warehouses. There were few dwellings, however Lestrade pointed across the street to a tall, narrow, red-brick house.

'On the opposite side of the passage from where the body was found, lives the warehouse manager of the Enfield Electric Company, a Mr Walter Davies, and his family and servants,' he said. 'The family had been wakened at various times during the night, due to one of the children being taken unwell; at least one adult in the house was awake all through the night and a light would have been burning.'

'And they heard nothing?' asked Holmes.

'Not a sound.'

'Then that settles it. It is perfectly inconceivable that any murderer would have struck here, so close is it to the door of the house where a lamp was burning through the night. It would be madness to try to commit a murder here. You cannot have failed to notice the marked similarity in the three locations we have seen: each one is dimly lit, or in a locality with few residents, and in each case a spot has been chosen a few yards from a main street — why? To make it easy for the assailant, or an accomplice, to bring the body in a cab, drag it out, and dump it there. There can be no doubt about that.'

'Nothing came out about that at the inquests,' said Lestrade.

'What do you think, Watson?' said Holmes, turning to me.

'I had come to no firm conclusion on it,' I replied. 'The question of *where* the murders were committed was not mentioned in any of the police surgeon's reports.'

'No, but then my frequent remarks about the official police lacking imaginative powers can equally be ascribed to the medical profession, who have a similar predisposition to accept things at face value,' said Holmes.

'But why should the murderer wish to

move the bodies at all?' the Inspector went on doggedly.

'To conceal the true place of murder is the most obvious reason, as it may give a clue to the residence or the habitat of the assailant,' I said.

'I think it is pretty obvious that the victims may have been lured into a cab on the prospect of conducting business,' replied Holmes. 'But the question is, why not simply dump the bodies in some vacant ground, or in open spaces such as railway goods yards which abound, or drop them into one of the many waterways? Instead the hypothetical assailant carries them, at enormous risk, through some of the most densely-populated areas of the city, which can only multiply his difficulties one hundredfold. Consider the mere practicalities of conveying a body through the streets of London, even under the cover of darkness, at one or two o'clock in the morning. There are the usual loafers and idlers abroad at such an hour, and constables on the beat and on fixed point duty. One would require a good knowledge of the city streets, and also of the habits of its denizens and their guardians, in order to evade all of these. The assailant would almost certainly have needed a four-wheeler and that would put him in the power of the cabman. One may consider the jarveys of the city to be an amenable lot; however, I can scarcely imagine one willing to risk his neck by becoming an accessory after the fact of murder for the sake of a few sovereigns.'

'Of course, he may be a cabman himself,' I suggested.

'It is not impossible, but the fifteen shillings which have been left at the scenes of the murders would represent a couple of days' wages for a cabman,' replied Holmes, 'and then every cab is recognizable by its number too, which would make it very risky.'

'The bodies could just as easily have been transported in a gentleman's private coach,' I said, recalling Lestrade's words.

'But then such a coach might equally be recognized by the livery,' said Holmes, 'which would make it every bit as risky, especially after the second murder when, presumably, the constabulary would have been more alert.'

'At least that would eliminate the jarvey,' I said.

'But only at the price of putting him in his own coachman's power,' said Holmes.

'Unless he has some hold over the man,' I replied.

'Or pays him very well for his silence, I suppose,' said Holmes.

'He may drive his own coach when on

these expeditions,' Lestrade interjected.

'It is an interesting hypothesis,' answered Holmes, 'but on the whole, an unlikely one.'

'If it is not a jarvey in his own cab or a gentleman's private coach, what then?' the Inspector asked.

'An idea is forming in my mind, but do not ask me to elaborate at this stage until I have more data. Whatever the method of disposing of the bodies, we must not lose sight of the question of the killer's motive. We must look for some common link, someone who knew all three victims; our chief difficulty here, of course, is that it will be impossible to get anyone to admit to knowing this class of person.'

'You have put your finger on it as usual, Mr Holmes,' Lestrade replied, 'for in cases like these, the success of the police depends very much on information supplied by the public. Even if there are no witnesses, sometimes people report that they have heard or seen something out of the ordinary. If you look at some of the neighbourhoods we have just come through, there are some of the vilest and lowest dens of crime and vice in the city; places that defy our notion of civilization: thieving, murder, and worse. Most of the beats in the area are double beats, for even our uniformed men daren't walk through some of these places at night save together in an armed group. Most of the lowlife beggars here would cut their tongues out rather than speak a word to the official police; they have their own unwritten laws, and they avenge their wrongs by their own hands. You also have a lot of foreigners in these parts, the outcasts of Europe — mostly Jews from Poland and Russia, some of whom have had a pretty bad time of it at the hands of the Czar's police. They will have nothing to do with any person in uniform, which is one reason why we can't act against the protection rackets that go on. So you see, between their fear of the official police and concern for their own skins, I doubt that we shall get any help from that quarter.'

'Yet they cannot all be bad,' I said. 'After all, what is the risk of collaborating with the police to help capture such a desperate character compared with the chance of having the life choked out of you?'

'But you see, Doctor, so far it's only these poor streetwalkers that have been attacked, and there are plenty respectable folks, though they might be alarmed by it all, who probably feel that the victims are only getting what they deserve; self-righteous is what I would call them. Ah, that reminds me, you wanted to look at the hoax letters, Mr Holmes.'

We drove back through the misty gloom to

Scotland Yard. Lestrade brought us into his office and laid a pile of papers before us, which he had drawn from his desk. Holmes began to read them, and after a few minutes, shook his head in a mixture of wonder and amusement.

'For sheer variety,' said he, 'this beats the marble rink dalliances and lost feather boas of the agony columns any day!'

He passed them across to me as he finished reading them. The assortment was indeed a remarkable one: letters, postcards, notes — in one case the words were scribbled across the back of a music-hall bill; another was written on a scrap torn from the back of a man's, not entirely clean, shirt.

'At least half of them,' I remarked, 'claim either to have committed the crimes themselves or to be offering to supply the identity of the culprit for a sum of money ranging from a few shillings to a hundred pounds.'

'Now, if a reward was to be offered that might be different,' Lestrade smiled ruefully, 'for the very same people would sell their own soul for the price of a half pint of gin! The first pile of letters I have shown you are the ones that we are fairly certain are either hoaxes or have been sent by near lunatics. This one here, for example, is from a chap we know as 'Head First'. Bert Slater is his name, and he has admitted to nearly every murder that has happened in the last three years. Just dying to meet Jack Ketch face to face! Constable Adams knows the man quite well; an insomniac, perfectly harmless, and wouldn't hurt a fly. He was a lighterman once — won the Doggett for Horseleydown — fell off a planking in the East India Dock one day, got a knock in the head, and was never the same again.'

'It is also not unknown for an unscrupulous journalist or a sensationalist editor to add some fuel to the fire in order to keep a good story moving along; it has happened before,' I remarked.

'That's right, do you remember the Ansell case of '92? Stanbridge of the Eastern Argus got three months for wasting police time,' Lestrade replied. 'This collection here,' he continued, taking out another envelope and laying it at Holmes's elbow, 'is a bit more sinister.'

Lestrade was right: some of the writers warned darkly, and ungrammatically, that further outrages were to be expected without providing any details, but one batch of letters stood out from the rest. There were three of them, which had come in pale green envelopes, and were laid out with great precision; the contents consisted of scriptural texts carefully pasted on to the pages with annotations typed very neatly below in red ink. Holmes glanced over these very keenly.

'There are a few slim clues which may guide us to the identity of the sender,' he said. 'Expensive typing paper and envelopes; the typewriter is fairly new — no sign of wear on the keys. American machine undoubtedly . . . almost certainly either an Underwood No. 2 or a Remington No. 6, I should say. These are recent models, so there cannot be too many in circulation.'

Holmes held a sheet of paper to his nose. 'Keys recently cleaned and yet it is a new machine; therefore, someone who is rather fastidious to the point of obsession; written by a man, I believe, for no educated woman would use such language. There are several other minor indications, but those are the principal ones. Now let us take a look at the envelopes: the address is typed — to 'Inspector Lestrade', so someone has gone to the trouble of finding out who is in charge of the case. Postmark the same in all three: Kensington. Of course, many people think that a typed note is less likely than a written one to give a clue to their identity because a strictly graphological examination is not possible. Nothing could be further from the truth, for each typewriter — even a new one — has an almost unique set of characteristics.'

'I was not aware of it,' said Lestrade.

'It is a curious thing, you know; a typewriter has really quite as much individuality as a man's or a woman's handwriting — a fact which helped me to trap that devious swine Windibank in '89. No two of them produce exactly the same effect.'

'Then we ought to have a fair chance of tracing the machine to the buyer?' asked Lestrade.

'I should think so, providing it was bought in this country. I should begin by checking all the shops in the Kensington area which sell typewriting machines — try Meredith & Dodds in Kensington Church Street and Wright's in the High Street first; those are the biggest suppliers to the private market. Failing that, try the Atlantic Typewriter Company, a few doors along from Wright's, who supply mainly offices and banks. Find out how many people have recently purchased either model, along with a red ink-ribbon. As both models are fairly new, the number is likely to be small, and you ought to have your man.'

'I shall get someone on to this right away,' said Lestrade, making a note.

'Have a look at these, Watson,' said Holmes. I opened the first one, which contained the following:

'HARLOTS AND ABOMINATIONS OF THE EARTH, 12th June 1895
Revelation x: 5 — Blessed is he that watcheth. Revelation xvii: 1 — The angel said 'Come hither; I will shew unto thee the judgment of the great whore.''

Under these passages, the writer had added:

'*Serviam: I shall serve the Lord.*'

The second letter read:

'THE WRATH OF GOD, 17th June 1895
Revelation xviii: 1 — It has become the habitation of every foul spirit and the cage of every unclean and hateful bird.

Again there was a postscript:

'I shall choke the breath from the unclean bird of the night.'

'They are all postmarked on the afternoon of the days of the murders,' said Holmes, 'which makes it well-nigh impossible to determine whether they were sent by the actual killer, for the news would have been made public by that time. That means that they could have been written by anyone who had read of the murders in the papers. Notice that the writer does not make any mention of the details of the crimes.'

'I noticed that,' said Lestrade. 'And this one here arrived after the third murder.' Holmes glanced over it and handed it to me. It ran:

'HIS SWORD SHALL PIERCE, HIS FIRE SHALL BURN, 21st June 1895 Revelation xvii: 4 — I saw a woman sit upon a scarlet coloured beast, full of names of blasphemy; and the woman was arrayed in scarlet colour having a golden cup in her hand full of the filthiness of her fornication.'

This time the writer had typed as an addendum:

'I shall empty these vessels of sin, full of the tainted money of harlotry.'

'They send a chill of horror through my spine,' I said.

'Bad as it has been,' replied Holmes, 'I feel sure that there is more to come.'

3

It was quite an hour or more before my usual breakfast time when I rose next morning, but Holmes was already up and about.

'Well, last night's fog has dissipated in more ways than one,' said he, lighting his pipe as the bright summer sun streamed through the window, 'and I was in some ways indebted to our correspondent with the new typewriter.' I noticed that he was surrounded by a pile of papers, and a map of London lay open beside him.

'I have been thinking about those letters,' I replied. 'Even if they were not the work of the murderer, that anyone should glory in this . . . this cold-blooded slaughter is perfectly inhuman. You know, Holmes, even the most battle-hardened soldier I ever came across, from a rifleman up to a general, would occasionally reflect with some sorrow on the human loss of war.'

'Indeed, Watson, one recalls the Iron Duke's words about there being nothing half so melancholy as a battle won, except a battle lost.'

'And to use scripture to justify such savage

darkness of the human mind seems the grossest and most wicked blasphemy.'

'You put it well, Watson; 'savage darkness' indeed. When I had begun to consider the question of motive in this case, I was forced to acknowledge that there is a psychological element missing from our present forensic sciences. Even the French, who are leagues ahead of us, have a tendency to look at criminology from the point of view of the natural sciences: chemical science, projectile science, document examination, the analysis of fingerprints, and so on; whereas the study of the criminal mind, *per se*, is a subject which remains virtually unexplored. It has been left largely to the novelists to attempt speculation upon it. It occurred to me that Dostoevsky, for example, is in his own way as pertinent as Vidocq or Bertillon, for he is just as adamant that 'trifles are important' as the Frenchmen, and his exposition of the workings of the disturbed criminal mind is exquisite and persuasive. In his best work, he shows how the criminal, Raskolnikov, does not set out to do wrong; on the contrary, he set out to do *right*, or at least what seemed to him to be morally justified within the grander scheme of things. That was the important point to grasp. The entire series of events which ensued were almost an object lesson in the operation of the law of unintended consequences. In the complicated way of things, he ends up in fact committing with great compunction a deed which he knows to be morally wrong, purely from force of circumstance and as an expedient and instinctive act of self-preservation. The detective who began to suspect Raskolnikov did so for purely psychological reasons; his trifles were traits of character, based upon the most infinitesimal scrutiny of his suspect's behaviour, not a trail of material clues.

'Most cases call for keen scientific analysis and razor-sharp logic, particularly in reasoning in reverse from effect back to cause; whereas others require a more subtle psychological approach to the problem. A tiny minority, perhaps especially those perpetrated by the complex mind of a master criminal, entail both. We have, in the present case, the practical question of method — how the murderer conveyed the bodies to the sites. But more important is the question of motive: what does this man intend to achieve? Does he wish to rid the streets of these poor daughters of Eve? Does he believe that creating a panic in the streets may frighten them away from their iniquitous careers?'

'He appears to be some loathsome zealot of the Puritan stamp.'

'The writer of the letters undoubtedly is. But, it is a leap from that to believing that the writer of those letters must also be the killer.'

'But he may be the killer's amanuensis.'

'Very good, Watson! But, you see, the killer has left his mark with what would appear to be symbols of ritual murder and so, even if the message is intended to mislead, where is his need for an amanuensis? Whatever is behind the campaign, we are forced to ask why he began with these three. You recall the scientific kernel of your medical training.'

'Analyse, explain, predict.'

'Exactly. I think I may have been able to do that to some extent, for the pattern of these murders, had we only known it, seems to have been quite straightforward.'

I looked up sharply in astonishment. '*Straightforward!* Come, Holmes, you cannot be serious.'

'I said the *pattern* of the murders, not the motive, which, as I suggested, calls for a mind capable of quite extraordinary sagacity and invention. My discoveries thus far have rather led me to think that there is some greater design behind this campaign than the ravings of a fanatic.'

'You implied that there was some clue in the letters,' I went on. At this point our discussion was interrupted by the appearance of Inspector Lestrade, looking dishevelled. His grave countenance did not portend well.

'Dear me,' said Holmes to our visitor, shaking his head, 'so soon?'

'Yes, I am afraid so. Your prediction of last night was correct,' the Inspector replied grimly. 'There has been a fourth murder.'

'At Bunhill Fields, I suppose?' asked Holmes.

Lestrade looked dumbfounded. 'Why, right beside it,' he stammered in incomprehension, 'just across the road from there in a place called Cromwell's Yard.'

'Hmm, that is irritating; my calculations must have been out by a few yards,' Holmes muttered enigmatically.

'Calculations!' repeated Lestrade in astonishment. 'What on earth . . . '

'Just before you arrived, I was giving Doctor Watson a demonstration of my chain of reasoning — '

'And you told him the exact place where the murder was committed?' Lestrade asked incredulously.

'I had not got quite that far with my explanation, but I had already deduced it from the evidence of the three previous murders.'

'*Deduced* it!' the Inspector said.

'My theory also leads me to the supposition that the dead girl would have been found clutching five ears of corn as well. Is that correct?'

'Yes,' he stammered, 'that is absolutely correct, a five-shilling piece on the ground and five ears of corn in her hand. Come, Mr Holmes, you could not possibly have worked all that out by theorizing alone. Someone must have given you the tip-off.'

'I assure you, Lestrade, that until you walked through the door, I had no idea that any crime had been committed, although as I told you yesterday, I had begun to entertain a strong suspicion as to what was to come.'

'If I didn't know you so well, I'm not sure you wouldn't fall under suspicion of having committing the murder yourself! But why did you not warn me?'

'I said I had worked out the place, not the time. In fact, as you can probably see, I had only just arrived at my conclusions this morning. I made a detailed analysis of the evidence of the previous murders, then I perused a map of London, and concluded with a most instructive lesson in the more esoteric points of seventeenth-century church building history.'

Lestrade reeled in bafflement, though I confess I was no less astounded than he was at my friend's words. 'Now really, Sir, I know you enjoy your little jokes, but this is hardly the time or the place. You are surely taking a rise out of me now.'

'Am I? Well, we shall see. The explanation had better wait until I have visited the scene of this latest outrage.'

'If you would come with me immediately, I should be greatly obliged.'

Once we had settled in the cab, Lestrade described what had happened. 'I have left Mr Gregson in charge at the scene of the murder. I must apologize for the few hours' delay in reaching you, but I was obliged to seek the guv'nor's express permission to bring you along in this case.'

'Were you indeed? That is most interesting in the light of the direction which my inquiries have taken. Pray continue.'

'We had to search the place immediately in the unlikely event that the assailant may have still been hiding there, but aside from that, my colleague has strict orders to ensure that nothing is moved until you have had an opportunity to inspect the area. There is a builders' depot just off the City Road, called Cromwell's Yard, located behind a working men's club and a public house, the Trafalgar, both of which were practically full last night. The yard is owned by Jones & Wragge, a respectable firm of coach and van builders. The manager, Arthur Tilson, hires it out to general collectors and rag-and-bone men who use it for the safe keeping of their vans and carts at night. The yard can also be entered from both the rear of the club and the tavern, for there is an outside privy there for the use of the clientele of both establishments by arrangement with Tilson. The place is unlit at night and at about 1.30 in the morning, one of the club's customers, a George Woods, went outside to use the privy and in the dark he practically stumbled over the body, which he thought might be a drunk. It was lying face down just inside the doorway from the street. He says that he thought at first the woman was so inebriated that she was unable to stand up, so he then went back into the club to get some help, and when he returned with two of the customers, they realized she was dead. Woods and his cronies say they were too frightened to touch her, and by the time they raised the alarm and went to look for a policeman, there might have been as much as an hour's delay. The body was stone cold by the time the first constable arrived on the scene. What with the noise going on inside the club, a shout or a scream from the victim may not have been heard in this case. I know your theory, Mr Holmes, about this killer moving the bodies about, but it occurs to me that Woods going back into the club to seek help may possibly have given the man the chance to escape,' said Lestrade.

'Until we are able to examine the evidence in greater detail, we should be unable to say with any certainty,' replied Holmes. 'No witnesses, as usual?'

'None. I know it's a case of shutting the stable door and all that, but when I spoke to the Commissioner last night, he mentioned something about a reward of one hundred pounds.'

At the City Road, a couple of uniformed constables were attempting without much success to disperse the knots of neighbours and onlookers who had gathered at the street corner. Lestrade's colleague, Inspector Gregson, hailed us as we alighted from the cab and introduced Dr Knowles, the police surgeon.

'It is comforting to see that Scotland Yard is pulling out all the stops,' remarked Holmes to Gregson.

Gregson smiled bleakly. 'We are waiting for an identification to be made. That can't be done until the body has been removed to the mortuary, and we were waiting for your arrival before we did that. Here's where it happened.'

The yard itself bore a most bleak aspect: it was situated in the middle of a terraced row of mean-looking, cramped, two-storied houses between a pawnbroker's and a cats' meat shop. From the pavement, we went through a narrow wooden doorway which was set into a larger door built to slide on casters to permit entry to wheeled traffic. Gregson pointed out in turn the rear exits from the club and the dingy tavern, which led to the unlit yard, and added that the doorway from the street was never locked. The corpse had been covered with a sheet which Knowles now pulled back: it revealed the figure of a young woman, respectably dressed. The bruising around the neck was evident; a silver coin lay on the ground beside the body, and in the victim's hand could be seen five ears of corn.

'Strangulation; no other injuries from what I can tell; no smell of poison or strong drink,' said Knowles. 'The time of death is difficult to state accurately: the body is quite stiff although it has not attained maximum rigidity, and as the temperature had dropped sharply during the night, this would slow the process down to a considerable degree. I should say death occurred between eight to ten hours ago, which would put it at between eleven o'clock last night and one o'clock this morning.'

'The question of whether the murders have been committed *in situ* is one we have been turning over in our minds since yesterday,' I said in reply to the doctor. 'In the three previous cases, it was too late to determine this with any degree of certainty, as my friend and I had not been called upon. Inspector Lestrade, you said, did you not, that Woods had deposed that he found the girl face down?'

'Yes, Woods signed a statement to that effect. He certainly sobered up pretty quick after what happened! The other two fellows who were with him at the time said the same. What difference does it make?'

'It may make all the difference in the world, for I believe we may now have an opportunity to test my friend's theory in the present instance,' I said, turning to my medical colleague. 'It is sometimes possible to tell whether a body has been moved after death by the pattern and extent of *livor mortis*.'

'Yes, indeed. Now that you mention it, I was slightly puzzled when the Inspector had said the deceased was found lying face down, for I discovered during my examination that the dead woman's blood had pooled on the back — my apologies for talking in what must seem like jargon to the rest of you, but this would show that the body was in a supine rather than a prone position for a period immediately following death. There was an unexpected absence of discoloration in the areas adjacent to the spine of the corpse. That is a most likely indication that parts of the deceased's back had been in contact with the ground, or some other hard object, for a period immediately following death. That would be unlikely if the murder had been committed here and the body left in the position in which the man found it.'

'Which would accord with my theory of the murder having been committed elsewhere, and the body having been brought here in a cab?' asked Holmes.

Knowles nodded. 'That is one possible explanation, providing the body were laid on its back during the journey. Of course, Woods could have moved the body and then later denied it.'

Holmes nodded appreciatively. 'I believe that is unlikely. Now, if you give me ten minutes, gentlemen,' he continued, 'I will look over the yard.'

My friend tiptoed back and forwards a number of times, with concentration upon his features. Then he knelt by the corpse with his back to us, and scribbled something in his notebook. He returned to us within half the time stated.

'I have seen nothing to conflict with

Woods's account of what happened,' my friend remarked. 'He seems to have lingered for a short while before going back into the club and probably stopped to light this.' Holmes passed a muddy vesta to Gregson. 'It is natural that he would seek to throw a light upon his discovery. You had better add it to your collection, just in case. Now, as to the five-shilling piece and the corn, there is nothing very remarkable about either. The coin is dated '1892', and I should imagine the corn — it is barley, in fact — was probably very easily obtained from any of the corn chandlers in the immediate district who supply the breweries. Let us have a closer look at the roadway. It is simple enough from the marks of the horse's hoofs to determine that a cab has come down the road from the direction of Old Street. It stopped here briefly — you can see where the hoof marks indicate this, and it was a four-wheeler, for here is the track of the second set of wheels in the dust. There are the abrasions where a wheel has grated against the edge of the kerb. Then the cab went on down the hill towards the City. The trail will now have been lost in the traffic which has long since passed over it. However the murderer, or at least his accomplice, has left his spoor. Now look here, what do you see?' he asked, pointing to vague footmarks at the edge of the pavement.

'Very little,' Lestrade replied; Gregson likewise shook his head.

'You can just about make out the footprints on the flagstones going from the edge of the pavement to the opening of the yard, and then those returning. What is the difference between those two sets of prints? Look again very closely.'

'Why, the ones going towards the yard are more closely spaced than those coming back,' I replied.

'But the first set is more distinct,' said Lestrade.

'He seems to have dragged his feet here and there,' added Gregson.

'Inference, possibly, that whoever it was may have been carrying a heavy load,' said Holmes. 'The shorter stride corresponds to extra weight the man had to carry, and once he had dumped the body, he then reverted to his normal stride, which was quite lengthy going by this.'

'Big feet, too,' Lestrade said.

'As large as my own, I should say,' Holmes agreed, putting his foot in the indentation left in the gutter, 'only narrower. Yes, size ten.'

Holmes took out and applied his tape measure. 'Going by the gauge of the wheels, it was almost certainly a four-wheeled public cab. The horse's shoes are well-worn too, which you wouldn't find on any gentleman's coach. It strengthens all the points of my supposition.' My colleague, Knowles, had been standing watching and listening to my friend's performance, nodding appreciatively at each point made as though he were seated at a lecture.

'No one actually saw a carriage, I suppose?' my friend continued.

'I was coming to that. I don't think it bears any relation to the case,' said Gregson, 'but PC Hewlett, who was called to the scene by Woods and his friends, came on at midnight. He was on the Finsbury Square beat, and just after one o'clock he was detained briefly by some trifling incident relating to a cab. It was nothing of any import; the cabman had some trouble with a loose fastening on one of the doors, so Hewlett stopped to ask the driver if he needed any assistance. Had he not delayed thus at the corner of Chiswell Street, it is possible that he may have been here in time to catch the culprit red-handed. He did, however, discover a bloodied knife in the doorstep of a shop nearby and became suspicious, as there had been several murders — '

'Dash it, man, the victims had all been strangled — what can a knife have had to do with it?'

'But this has been the biggest manhunt for years, and the beat men had all been sternly warned to keep a look out for anything unusual; when he saw that the blood on the knife was still wet, he hardly knew what to think.'

'Still wet?'

'Yes.'

'Hmm, that was very clever.'

'Clever?' repeated Gregson, looking puzzled.

'Yes. Where is Hewlett now?'

'Over there with Constable Lamb, trying to keep that crowd at bay.'

'Ask him to step this way, *tactfully*, now; do not suggest to him that he is any kind of trouble.'

The Constable was sent for and Holmes continued the interrogation.

'Can you describe the coach which you saw during the night?' he asked the young, eager-looking Constable.

'It was just your standard London growler, Sir,' replied Hewlett.

'You're certain that it was not a private coach or a hansom?'

'Absolutely sure.'

'Did you get the number?'

'Of course I did, Sir,' Hewlett bristled indignantly in front of his superior, 'we are required to pay special attention to the plates and report anything amiss. It was 9435.'

'I sent a man down immediately to the Public Carriage Office to attempt to trace the owner of the cab,' interrupted Gregson.

'My attention was then distracted by the cabman,' Hewlett continued, 'who pointed out that there was a knife lying in the shop doorway.'

'Did you not think it a most implausible coincidence that the cab had stopped exactly where the knife had been left?' said Holmes drily.

'Not at the time. Soon after that I was called here, and when I discovered that the girl had been strangled, I could find no explanation for the knife. I asked the Inspector if there had been any other incident during the night involving a knife, and there wasn't. By the time I'd gone over to pick up the knife and examine it, the cab had started away.'

'Yes — to take the killer home from the City.'

'You don't think that was the killer — '

'No, that was his accomplice; the killer was inside. Dear me, Constable Hewlett, to think that you fell for a schoolboy trick like this. There can be little doubt that the knife was placed there as a ruse to distract your attention and make a getaway. By the time the alarm was raised and the body was found, that cab would have been half a mile away or more. With some little presence of mind you might have earned your share of the reward.'

Lestrade grimaced. 'Our public reputation was bad enough before this, Mr Holmes: if the papers found out, we should have a riot on our hands . . . '

'They shall hear nothing from me, Inspector, it is not my game to embarrass the official force — you can usually achieve that yourselves without my assistance,' he added acerbically. 'Still, at least we have the cab number. Now, Hewlett, what about this cabman's appearance?'

'He was a fairly young chap, well built, around medium height, blond hair sticking out from under his cap and a beard, though I didn't pay any particular notice to him.'

'Recognize him again?'

'Yes, I think so.'

'Good. Anything else?'

'Nothing I can think of.'

'Come, Hewlett, you are a trained police-man; was there no trifling detail that you noticed?'

'Well there was one thing: I couldn't put my finger on it at first, but now that I think about it, he seemed rather very well-dressed for a jarvey. That's all I can say.'

'There was an occupant in the cab, was there not?'

'Yes, he was as drunk as a lord, Sir. I saw him lying in the corner of the cab snoring his head off. The jarvey said he was bringing the gentleman back home from his club in Shoreditch.'

'Can you remember anything about him?'

'Not much: dark hair, sallow complexion, foreign-looking.'

'How tall?'

'Hard to say, Sir, as he was reclining at the time. He was not small, though.'

'Large boots?'

'I think so.'

Holmes permitted himself a glimmer of satisfaction at this reply. 'Constable Hewlett, you have been most helpful, and I must commend your attention to detail, for though you may have let this man slip from your grasp, you have given us one or two of the only real clues we have as to the suspect.' As he spoke, a uniformed constable rushed up breathlessly from the direction of Finsbury Square and handed Lestrade two envelopes. He tore open the first and uttered an exclamation under his breath.

'According to this,' said the Inspector, handing the note to Holmes, 'there is no cab registered as 9435!'

'I had begun to suspect that,' my friend replied. 'There is a subtle, scheming brain behind this.'

The Inspector took a brief look at the second envelope, and I noticed his expression change from annoyance to alarm. I glanced over his shoulder and observed the green envelope with his name typed in capitals in red ink. On this occasion the envelope was not postmarked Kensington, but 'E.C.' — the City, whose precincts began a mere two hundred yards from where we stood.

'Look at this,' the Inspector said. 'Not a word of the murder can possibly have reached the papers yet.'

'Open it,' said Holmes. The letter read:

'BABYLON HAS FALLEN, 25 June 1895 *Revelation xvii: 16. When the righteous man cometh he shall hate the whore, and shall make her desolate and naked.*'

Then, typed by the sender, one single word:

'*Servavi*'.

'Past tense,' I said.

'Yes, it will be his last. I had already come to that conclusion before I saw the letter,' said Holmes.

'It's but little consolation, I can tell you,' said Lestrade glumly. 'You still have not explained to me, Mr Holmes, how you came to know the place of the murder.'

'You had better come back to Baker Street with us,' Holmes replied.

4

Tobias Gregson had been left to attend to the disposal of the body and supervise the dispersal of the crowd. Once Holmes, Lestrade, and myself were seated comfortably in the sitting room, my friend waved us to the cigar box, lit his pipe, and looked at us through the smoky haze.

'Mrs Hudson will have the kettle boiled in no time,' he said, 'but now to business. 'Straightforward' was the word I used when describing the pattern of the murders to Doctor Watson this morning, and I may say that he fairly jibbed at the word. Nevertheless, once I have explained it all, I am convinced you will both agree with me. It came about this way: as you know, my knowledge of London topography is fairly precise, and an idea had entered my head regarding the locations where these bodies were found. When I looked at the street map of London, the suspicion became a certainty. I plotted the sites and discovered that the locations where the first three bodies were found were almost exactly the same distance apart.'

'I was not aware of that,' said Lestrade.

'Attention to detail combined with the faculty of imagination,' replied Holmes. He rolled out a plan of the area, which showed three crosses placed on it in red ink.

'I had got this far when you arrived this morning,' he continued. 'These crosses are almost exactly one thousand yards apart. Now that seemed far too round a number to be a coincidence, but it was the language used by the writer of those letters we read yesterday, which set me thinking. A thousand yards corresponds to two thousand cubits, if you know what a cubit is.'

'I have a vague memory of it,' I said. 'It is one of those archaic words from scripture which calls to mind linen ephods and vases of manna, though I fail to see the relevance.'

'In order to understand that, I spent an hour or two reading up on the subject, where I discovered that two thousand cubits has a very powerful historical significance. It is known as 'the hallowed distance'. I think you will find the precise quotation somewhere in Joshua — and it is enshrined in the rituals surrounding the Ark of the Covenant in King Solomon's temple. This 'hallowed distance' has a more recent resonance and one that is rather closer to us. It is an established fact that the rebuilding of the City of London following the great fire was entrusted to Freemasons, such as Sir Christopher Wren and Nicholas Hawksmoor, who employed this symbolism to scale their chief works. There is a profusion of Hebraic, pre-Christian symbolism in the obelisks, eyes, and pyramids, and an obsession with the motif of death and rebirth — hardly the stuff of traditional Anglican ecclesiastical architecture, where, you will admit, cherubim and seraphim tend to predominate. For example Hawksmoor's design of St George's in Bloomsbury is a precise replica of King Solomon's temple in Jerusalem, a fact which did not escape the notice of the Puritans at the time, many of whom condemned the building as pagan. The entire City of London was rebuilt to oblique variations on this geometry, which was not only hallowed but also covert: at least, it was understood only by members of the Craft. Two thousand cubits from St Paul's to the western boundary of the City at Temple Bar; two thousand cubits to the eastern boundary; two thousand cubits from St Mary Woolnoth to Christ Church and so on.'

'We are getting rather off the track, are we not?' interrupted Lestrade impatiently.

'Not at all; we are very hot upon it, as I hope to show. You see, I grasped the obvious fact that unless this was an elaborate hoax — a possibility which I had by then begun to discount — one is forced to adopt the hypothesis that the locations of these murders had some veiled significance, perhaps known only to those who can decipher the code. That is what enabled me to predict the location of the fourth murder. If the first three murders were two thousand cubits apart, it followed that the fourth would be as well. It was also likely that the sites would form some covert pattern, and so they do. If I place the fourth cross on the map at the place where the body was discovered last night, it makes the arrangement complete. I was absolutely certain, too, that I had solved the mystery of the five-shilling pieces left at the murder sites: the five-shilling piece is supposed to represent a crown, and the realization of this together with my research had served to strengthen my pessimistic assumption that there was more to come.'

'But how?' asked Lestrade.

'To discover the significance of the coins, it was simply a matter of being literal. At that point three crowns had been left at the murder sites; a much more likely number would be four crowns, would it not? The gnomon, so to speak, was the fourth crown, and it was rather obvious how and where we should find it, was it not?'

'And so you guessed where the fourth one would be?' asked Lestrade.

'It was hardly guesswork; I reasoned it out. Though once I had plotted these first three,' Holmes said, pointing to the map, 'it was not difficult to extend the pattern to place the fourth point in or near Bunhill Fields, though due to the small scale of the plan, I seem to have been out by a few dozen yards. But I have told you only half of the story, for I further discovered in the byways of ancient Masonic lore that 'Four Crowns', or rather its Latin equivalent — *Quattuor Coronae* — was the name chosen by a Lodge which was founded a few years ago by a branch of the Freemasons in London. You will hardly be astounded to learn that its seal is four crowns set in a diamond shape. The Lodge, incidentally, has some very esteemed and respected members — quite a few peers of the realm, a smattering of government ministers, but also a former Metropolitan Police Commissioner and a remarkable number of senior Scotland Yard men. The significance of the corn in the victims' hands seemed quite prosaic at first, for every Masonic temple is adorned with the symbol of a sheaf of corn representing the fruits of labour, but it was the variation in the numbers that was puzzling. The first victim had one; the second had two; the third, none; the fourth, five. The number of the Quattuor Coronae Lodge is 1205 — one, two, nought, five!'

'Brilliant!' I said.

'But what does it mean?' asked Lestrade.

'You will agree that the ritualism is unmistakeable? The obvious implication is that the members of this Lodge are in some way responsible for, or have some connection with these outrages. One might speculate that they have been initiated by the Quattuor Coronae, either as some form of retribution for breaking the rules or for some injury to one or more of its members. The situation manifests to me many parallels with the infernal persecutors of the innocent John Openshaw some years ago. Of course, it occurred to me that it was equally possible that the entire scheme had been invented by the murderer as a blind in order to throw the police off the trail, or to deflect the guilt upon the Lodge, which may, after all, have absolutely nothing to do with it. I have by no means discounted that possibility yet, but it certainly disposed of any theory that the killings were the work of some deranged homicidal lunatic. It now appears to form part of a definite campaign, the precise motives of which are yet unclear to me.'

'I find it very hard to credit,' said Lestrade.

'The most difficult part,' I remarked, 'is in understanding how these unfortunate women come into this conspiracy at all.'

'One might speculate that their profession brings them into contact with the upper classes, and this Lodge caters primarily for the upper classes,' said Holmes.

'Then the most obvious explanation is a blackmail attempt,' I said.

'I am struck by the fact that it seems rather too obvious. If the persecution emanates from there, it may not be retribution for transgressions; it may be the price of guilty knowledge, perhaps innocently discovered, of the secrets of its some of its members. It may be a sign that the punishment has been meted out, or it may be a warning to others not to meddle with such forces.'

'But surely,' Lestrade went on doggedly, 'if they were responsible, they would hardly advertise their guilt?'

'That is a much more difficult question. The ritualism may be designed to throw guilt on the Lodge unjustly. Equally, the Quattuor Coronae may have adopted the stratagem of 'concealing by not concealing' — a very clever double bluff. To return to the point about Hawksmoor: the six churches and two obelisks he built stand upon the London topography for all to see; yet they combine clandestinely and at the same time overtly to form the 'Eye Of Horus' of Masonic lore.'

Lestrade shook his head in disbelief. 'I cannot deny that this is very clever of you, Mr Holmes, but your secret codes and evil eyes — '

'If you wish to disregard my advice and work independently, that is no concern of mine, but there can be no doubt that the Craft glories in its arcana, and revels in its puzzles and subtly adroit double-negatives, its mysteries and its symbols — 'veiled in allegory' to use their own chosen phrase.'

'It all seems quite fantastic,' the Inspector went on.

'To the modern scientific mind, perhaps: but the belief that mystic shapes combined with sacred words or numbers can work primitive magic is a potent one; it persists even in our own day within the body of established religion. These paraphernalia of the Craft were not fashioned purely for the adornment of their temples and for the embellishment of their regalia. These sigils, which date back through the Crusades to the sands of ancient Egypt, have carried with them for thousands of years a timeless, universal power; a power which mere words cannot convey; a power which in the right hands may transform the mind and the soul of man for great good or for terrible evil.'

I must confess that a thrill passed keenly through me as my friend spoke these words, for his eyes had that faraway look which I had often seen, and his voice had a peculiarly ethereal cadence.

'These codes and sigils are all around us,' he continued in the same vein, 'we simply never notice them: look closely at a dollar bill the next time you see one; think of London's memory as held, not in any library or museum, but in its ancient stone, bloodied soil, and turbid waters; finally, reflect upon the palimpsest which has been inscribed through the ages upon the City of London, for it is one of the most potently and most mysteriously coded precincts in the western world.'

Then the severely pragmatic Holmes seemed to come back down to earth.

'I also intend to set in train some practical lines of inquiry of my own,' he said.

'By the four-foot-nine brigade?' Lestrade laughed. 'I'll admit privately that they're better than a whole division of flat-footers, though I'm never sure that their activities are strictly legal, and I certainly wouldn't like to think of them turning on the other side of the law. Mind you, I've often thought the same about yourself, Mr Holmes: no offence, of course.'

My friend chuckled noiselessly. 'Yes, the Irregulars will have a part in it, but I shall also employ some of my contacts in — well, perhaps I should hardly say any more about that in front of yourself.'

'No, I should prefer to be without the guilty knowledge. I'll turn over in my mind what you have told me, though my head is still spinning. I should be obliged if you'd let me know if anything further turns up,' Lestrade said as he picked up his hat to leave. 'I must be off to a meeting with the guv'nor. As you know, the papers are full of talk of setting up vigilance committees — it's the last thing we want.'

'They would be wasting their time: there will be no more murders, and in any case, this man is too clever to be caught by the official police. He would merely amuse himself with these vigilance men.'

'Yes, I remember the last time. Every crank within five miles . . . ' He shook his head in despair.

Once the Inspector had left, Holmes remarked, 'I am not sure how much longer I can retain our friend's confidence in this matter.'

'You are irritated by his scepticism?'

'Not at all, Watson; a healthy scepticism is a most necessary character trait in any detective, official or otherwise — if only it were balanced at times by a bit of imagination. No, it is Lestrade's loyalty which concerns me.'

'My dear Holmes, I confess that I am mystified by this remark. Whatever can you mean?'

'As I pointed out, some very senior City and Metropolitan Police Officers are members of this Lodge. A Police Commissioner was formerly the Lodge Grand Master. If these murders are somehow related to a decree emanating from that organization, no one would be in a better position than these men to frustrate the pursuit of justice, should they so wish. And what would Lestrade, a mere Inspector, do if that were found to be the case? It would place him in a very difficult position indeed. I think we shall keep our own counsel in this for the moment.'

'I must confess, I would be shocked to find that anyone of Sir Edward's standing . . . '

'I have no doubt that you would be, Watson. However, you make a rather unjust implication there, which is that wrongdoing is the monopoly of the lower classes. What about the dreadful child murderer whom we helped send to the gallows eight years ago, was there ever a more respectable individual?'

'Stevens? Yes, as I recall he presented an amiable appearance and demeanour, and was in the employ of one of our offices of government. A man who held an honourable army record, and a lay preacher to boot.'

'And collusion, not to say outright corruption, within the official force, even at such exalted levels as Sir Edward's is, sad to say, hardly unknown. I can recall several cases both at home and on the continent: there was the Eveline conspiracy in Bruges in the year '84 which resulted in scores of resignations from the Belgian police force; some years ago, 1877 to be exact, Lestrade's predecessor, Inspector Meiklejohn, and two Chief Inspectors — Palmer and Druscovitch — received two years' hard labour apiece as a reward for their own extramural activities. Several other higher-ranking officers were brought to trial, but were subsequently acquitted solely due to the lack of evidence. The scandal completely discredited the entire Metropolitan Detective Force, which was abolished. Most interestingly, in the light of our present researches, it emerged later that many of the protagonists in the case were members of the somewhat ironically-named Three Grand Principles Lodge.

'There is a further consideration, Watson. It is a matter of fact that the oaths of the Freemasons' initiation bind all of its members, and I quote with authority, ' . . . to conceal all crimes of your brother Masons, and should you be summoned as a witness against a brother Mason be always sure to shield him. It may be perjury to do so but you must remain true to the binding oath you have sworn.' This loyalty supersedes that of the ordinary citizen towards the common good — indeed, towards the law of the land; the oath of secrecy applies to all of its members regardless of whether they are doctors, policemen or jarveys. The motto is 'Aude, Vide, Tace.' Listen, Watch, Be Silent; and the greatest of these, Watson, is 'Tace' — be silent!'

The front doorbell was ringing as Holmes continued, 'As you know, I had already established as a working hypothesis that the assailant had employed a cab, and the evidence of this morning confirmed that. I have reverted to my usual method for finding needles in haystacks; I assume that will be my man now.'

Presently, a smartly-dressed, alert-looking young man appeared at the door of the sitting room.

'Ah, Cartwright, Mr Wilson tells me that

you have been promoted.'

'Yes, Sir, and a rise of wages too,' he smiled.

'Well, I trust that you are neither too busy, nor too proud, to undertake private commissions.'

'Not at all, Sir. I'm always very glad to help. So is Mr Wilson. He loves to boast how often he has been able to assist Mr Sherlock Holmes in his cases.'

'Excellent. Now, this errand may take up the rest of the day and most of the evening as well. Here is a list of the cabmen's shelters in the West End: start at Half-Moon Street and work your way out through Paddington to Westborne Grove. I am looking for a jarvey who owns his own cab and hires it out privately. That's to say, one who hands his cab over for a period of time to an unlicensed driver — a 'buck' as they call them. Ask very discreetly, though. A hansom is no use; it must be a growler. If you can find such a man, then there is a half sovereign waiting for him on application at 221b Baker Street. I would be also obliged if you could call in to Bradley's in Oxford Street and ask the proprietor to send up a half-pound of his best, strongest Balkan. This should be enough to keep you going,' he said, handing the young man a heap of coins.

Holmes glanced across at me as Cartwright's steps faded on the staircase. 'Yes, a rather paltry stratagem, I know,' he added.

'I did not precisely say so, Holmes — '

'Your eyes said it, Watson. Let me anticipate your objections. This may cause the perpetrator to be more careful — well, one might easily argue that he could scarcely be less careful; indeed, thus far, audacity and recklessness have been his particular hallmarks. It may draw the attention of the murderer to the fact that Mr Sherlock Holmes is on his trail — perhaps, though, it may just be enough to flush out someone whose involvement has been an innocent one, for I have considered the matter and judge that on the balance of probabilities this jarvey is completely ignorant of the purpose for which his cab has been used. Of course, we may be deluged by a score of such fellows, but I feel that I am equal to the effort of separating the wheat from the chaff.'

'I did wonder why you did not send Cartwright straight to the Public Carriage Office to enquire.'

'Ah, that was a mere point of discretion: the hiring out of cabs to another licensed driver to use for hire is permitted, but I suspect this is a different transaction entirely.

Hence my instruction to Cartwright to ask discreetly.'

Feeble as I must confess it seemed to me at the time, Holmes's ploy did bring forth fruit. Just after six o'clock there was knock at the door, and into the room walked a tall, lean, middle-aged man carrying a whip. He wore a waistcoat, muffler, and great-coat with a faded, grimy velvet collar, and the hair brushed back from the forehead framed an honest-looking face. He removed his cap and stood uneasily on the carpet.

'I was told to ask for a Mr Sherlock Holmes,' said the cabman.

'And you are?' replied my friend.

'John Jacobs, cab number 6614 out of Cocker's depot off the Brompton Road. Badge number, 13740.'

'You own a four-wheeler?'

'Yes. And a young gentleman from the messenger's office called at the Pont Street shelter, seems you was wantin' it for the loan of.'

'I did not exactly say so; rather, I wanted some information and I am grateful to you for taking the trouble to come here,' said Holmes, pressing something into the man's hand.

'Oh, ask away,' said Jacobs brightly, looking the shiny coin.

'Have you hired out your cab privately within the last few weeks?'

'Yes, I have that, Sir, on a number of occasions, although it is not strictly, er . . . '

'Yes, I know. Can you say to whom you hired it?'

'To a man by the name of Smith.'

'Do you know the man?'

'No, I don't. I had a feelin' I had seen his face somewhere before, though I couldn't say exactly where. He was coachman for some gentleman, that's all I know.'

'Then Smith may be a false name?'

'I suppose it might, though I can't see why. He seemed open an' honest enough about it all, an' he paid up in advance. A sovereign on each occasion and the same to the long-night man who I normally turn the cab over to, as he lost a night's wages.'

'Did he say what he wanted the cab for?'

'No, but,' the man reddened, 'well, when a gentlemen doesn't want to be seen ridin' in his own coach . . . '

'Did it occur to you at all that the dates coincided with the dates of these recent murders in the City?'

The man thought for a moment than said, 'Ah, but they didn't, Sir.'

'You are certain?'

'Yes. He has hired out the cab quite a

number of times. Let me see now . . . yes, six times in the last few weeks, in fact.'

'Aha, a clever touch, Watson!' Holmes said, glancing across at me.

'You mean he knew that if he hired the cab only on the dates of the murders, it might look suspicious, so he has thrown in a few other dates to put us off the scent?' I asked.

'Precisely. This fellow is no fool. He had it again last night I presume, Jacobs?'

'Yes, he did, Sir. Do you gentlemen mean to tell me that this man might have used my cab for — '

'It is more than possible,' interjected Holmes, 'I am almost certain that he did.'

The man suddenly turned very pale and pressed his hand to his forehead, dropping his whip upon the floor as he did so. I sprang up and grasped him by the arm as he appeared about to collapse.

'Do not be alarmed,' Holmes went on soothingly, 'for I am equally certain that your involvement would have been an innocent one, and the proof of that is that you have come here in the best of faith and told me willingly all that you have done. You may rest assured that no harm will come to you. Now, my good man, sit down for a moment and drink this. Is there anything else you can remember at all about this man Smith?'

'Just below middle height, stocky build, fair hair, beard, age . . . thirty-five I'd say, hard to tell with the beard.'

'Did he come to see you in his master's coach?'

'Yes.'

'Did you notice anything about it — the colour for example?'

'No, he only came in it the first time at night, so it was too dark to see. The coach was a dark colour, that's all I can say. I remember he passed by the shelter, drove on a bit, then stopped by the junction near Sloane Street and then walked back to me.'

'Anything about the livery on the coach?'

'The usual stuff, lions and castles I think. Wait, though; I seem to remember black and white stripes across the door. Yes.'

'You are certain about the colours — black and white stripes?'

'Yes, because the chap had the same device on his uniform coat.'

'Excellent! You have been of immense help, John Jacobs. You are obliged, as you must now understand, to report this to the official police — ask for Inspector Lestrade at Scotland Yard. Tell him the story in your own words, and you may as well say that I sent you. If this man Smith should call again, though I think it is unlikely, please let me know immediately,' said Holmes, handing the man another coin prior to his departure.

'Well, Watson, things are beginning to move in our direction at last!' my friend remarked, rubbing his hands. 'As you know, heraldry is a subject closely related to that of English charters, of which the Magna Carta is itself the seminal charter, and which was the subject of my researches earlier this year. At least, it was until we were interrupted by Soames of St Luke's.'

I recalled very well sitting in our lodgings by the university's library at the time, amazed and fascinated in equal parts, as Holmes rambled on about courts of chivalry, distraints, and rules of tincture.

'You will recall my discovery that of the twenty-five barons who signed the charter, it was possible to trace all but a small number to present-day families in England. In the course of my studies, I became familiar with the various coats of arms of those families as well as their various ancestries. As it happens, the heraldic device which Jacobs described is officially known as 'a baton in bend sinister compony of six, Argent and Sable' and shows that — '

'That the original grantee was related to the sovereign, but born out of wedlock,' I interrupted.

'Excellent! I did not know you were so well up in heraldic lore.'

'I am not, but I am well up in Sir Walter Scott.'

'You are on top form this morning, my dear Watson! Though personally I am inclined agree with the Lake Poet who said he found the madness of Blake more interesting than the sanity of Scott.'

'This one will have descended from Charles the Second's illegitimates, no doubt.'

'Quite probably. More importantly, though, I know of only three titled families in London whose coats of arms bore this device. They are Baron Ampthill, the Duke of Marylebone, and the Earl of Titchfield. The first named left these shores for the dust of Africa in '84 and died there childless some years ago. The barony became extinct upon his death and the estate escheated to the crown. The second is a bedridden octogenarian known widely for his Christian philanthropy; the third, I must confess, is a gentleman with whom I am not so well acquainted. What does the good book say, Watson?'

I looked up the entry, which read:

'*Clermont*, Edmund Algernon, 8th Earl of Titchfield, G.C.M.G, C.B., D.L. Married Lady Georgina Carson-Hayle, daughter of Sir Richard Carson-Hayle, 3rd Earl of Hayle. Five children. Deputy Lieutenant of Hamble and Solent. Grandfather was an *aide-de-camp* to Wellington during Peninsular campaign. Royal Horse Guards, Master of the Bishop's Waltham and the Fareham Hunts. Chief Advisor at the Office of Home Affairs. Address: Deanery Street W1; Clubs: Carlton, White's, Tankerville.'

5

I saw little of Holmes for a while following our interview with Jacobs, for I had been once again occupied in looking after Jackson's practice next door to my own former quarters, a short distance from Baker Street. Save for a scribbled note which told me that he had gone to seek the assistance of Wiggins, I had not the vaguest notion as to where my friend's investigations had taken him, although Mrs Hudson muttered vaguely to me about his 'comings and goings at all sorts of odd hours of the day and night', and remarked knowingly upon the succession of 'very strange characters' who had been frequenting the house. All of which had the effect, needless to say, of causing me to ponder deeply upon the intricacies of the present affair. Truth to tell, I could scarcely recall a case in which there was, to use one of my friend's favourite axioms, such a tangled skein. This coachman must surely be implicated in the crimes, but was it his hand that struck the fatal blow in each case, and was he carrying out these appalling crimes at the behest of an esteemed aristocrat, one of the most respected peers of the realm? Was he also the writer of the letters? And what could explain the involvement of the Freemasons, whom I had always regarded as a semi-charitable institution committed to the brotherhood of man? After what Holmes had said, their Enlightenment appeal to reason seemed to me to be wildly at odds with their mysterious fascination for secrecy, ritual, and pursuit of ancient truths. Was it merely a front for a secret cabal of murderers, with Titchfield at its head? I recalled an investigation some years ago, the effect of which was like ascending a range of hills with a series of false summits. Each time we had gained what we thought to be the peak, there always seemed to be yet a further ridge soaring above us.

Normally I revelled in my short spells of work when I returned temporarily to medical practice as a locum, but on this occasion the hours dragged in the surgery; for once I was greatly relieved when my former neighbour returned from his medical conference in Austria, and I at last found the opportunity to interrogate Holmes on the progress he had made in the case.

'Not a word from Lestrade,' he replied in answer to my query. 'The official forces are out of their depth, as usual.'

'And the unofficial ones?' I asked.

'Hardly much better, I am bound to confess, yet I believe we have made some slight progress. I posted Wiggins and some of his crew in Mayfair to keep an eye on our man Titchfield. He has been followed everywhere and I receive reports at regular intervals. I have discovered that his coachman is one John Henry Thisley. He comes from a family of cabmen, lives in Paddington, and was formerly employed by the Great Western Railway Company as a goods van driver. His description tallied fairly closely with the ones given by Constable Hewlett and Jacobs. Wiggins reported to me that Titchfield is in the habit of leaving his Whitehall office each evening and going straight to his club, and so I sent a note to Jacobs, asking him to be outside the Carlton last night. We loitered on the corner of King Street on the pretext of agreeing on a fare, and when Titchfield arrived, Jacobs managed to get a good look at Thisley as he alighted from the driving seat. He is fairly sure that it is the man who hired the cab from him. Thisley was clean-shaven last night, but had worn a beard when he went to hire the cab, though it was probably a false one, and I feel sure this is our man. Jacobs recognized the markings on the coach too, and the plucky fellow is now prepared to swear to this in a court of law. However, that alone does not take us very far, for I am certain that this Thisley is merely an accomplice.

'To whom, though? Titchfield?'

'Not directly. When Edmund Algernon Clermont descended from his coach, I observed that he did not in any way resemble the occupant of the cab as described by Hewlett. In order to find this other fellow, I have engaged the services of a number of occasional associates, some of whom inhabit the darker recesses of the criminal fraternity. There is one gentleman from Notting Hill who has lately come to my notice. Like Ricoletti and Aldridge, this person has resolved to give up a life of crime and seek redemption on the right side of the law. He is perfectly placed, for there is little wrongdoing that goes on in the criminal sub-strata of the West End that does not come, at some time or in some way or another, within the purview of this lately much reformed, if still somewhat venal, fellow. He has in one or two recent minor cases been useful to me in preventing a crime, and though he has abandoned his former ways since his release from the Isle of Wight, his reputation amongst the criminal fraternity, founded upon his frequent incarcerations there, remains a sound one. Thus he is able to sink down amongst the lowest strata of the underworld, move amongst its denizens, and root around for information without giving the least suspicion, for he has no connection with the official police and will not be called upon to appear in any court.'

'It is reassuring to know that occasionally one turns over a new leaf.'

'Yes, it casts an interesting sidelight on some of the earnest and arrant nonsense which is written, and spoken, on the subject of recidivism. I have another associate in Stepney, one Harry Mercer, a former safecracker and no mean pugilist, who will also make some very discreet inquiries on my behalf in that district. Whilst I think our search lies west rather than east, one can hardly overlook the violent history of that part of the metropolis. Similarly, I have been in touch with Barker, an erstwhile university acquaintance, whose collaboration with me predates even the Reginald Musgrave case about which you produced a most entertaining account some time ago. Transpontine London is Barker's speciality, and he will take a hand on the Surrey side. These three all have a description of the man whom Hewlett saw inside the cab on the night of the fourth murder and will do what they can. In short,

Watson, to use a phrase with which you will be familiar, I have committed every battalion to the field.'

'Indeed, you have left no stone unturned,' I replied with enthusiasm; yet my friend's disappointment was plain to see, and he had begun to chafe a little against the inaction. He decided to put the case entirely out of his mind and took himself off to the Reading Room of the British Museum to bury himself in Thucydides's chronicles of the Greco-Persian war, whilst I went along to my club for a game of billiards, and then on to the Turkish baths in Northumberland Avenue.

His mood was no brighter on my return some hours later.

'Still no news?' I asked.

'Nothing at all,' he shrugged. 'Still, there is a concert at St James's tonight — what do you say to a short course of therapy, Chopin and strings? All four pieces on the programme contain parts for the cello. It is a most magnificent instrument: the ear appreciates the violin as it soars to the lyrical heights, but the rich, sonorous notes of the cello have a tremendous power to assuage the deepest, most melancholy tempers of the human soul. It is a strange thing, you know, but I have always found its particular resonance to have a remarkably soothing effect.'

'It may be something to do with the closeness of its timbre to the human voice,' I replied.

'I have no doubt that that is the reason, for it accords well with my conviction that the power to make music predates the facility for human language. We have just enough time if we leave now.'

★ ★ ★

We found Inspector Gregory Lestrade occupying one of the armchairs in our sitting room when we returned just before midnight.

'We got a visit from the cabman Jacobs whom you managed to find,' our visitor said, 'and he gave us a full description of the man who hired the cab from him. Now if we could only find the owner of this coach with the black and white stripes, but there must be hundreds with that design.'

'Oh, I would not be so sure of that,' replied Holmes evasively.

'We also found the sender of those letters, the ones in red ink. It was exactly as you said, Mr Holmes. I sent one of my plainclothes sergeants out to Kensington. He spoke to the managers at all the shops you mentioned. Meredith & Dodds said they hadn't sold a single new model of the types you mentioned nor had Wright's, but the Atlantic Typewriter Company had sold two: one was a Remington bought by a firm of copywriters in Soho; the second, an Underwood, was delivered to a private address in the Fulham Road, a Mr Obadiah Weaver, a gentleman whom we've had an eye on for a long time. President of the Association for the Suppression of Vice — one of these hellfire-and-damnation types, produces pamphlets in a similar style to those letters, and hands them out by the score in Hyde Park; you know the sort of thing, foredoomed to perdition and predestined to salvation. Well, he is foredoomed to prison now! He turned pale when Sergeant Mellows knocked on the door, but he wouldn't let him enter the house. Mellows threatened to leave a constable and come back with a warrant, at which point Weaver gave in. Strange fellow — he made Mellows take his boots off before he let him across the threshold.'

'I told you the writer had an obsession with cleanliness,' Holmes said.

'There, in his study, was the very machine, an Underwood, and on it was a red ink-ribbon. Mellows ran him in straight away. Mr Gregson gave him a thorough going-over and he admitted sending the letters, but denied he had anything to do with the murders.'

'How did he explain having sent the fourth letter before the reports reached the press?'

'It turns out he had been to the City Press Syndicate in St John Street early on the morning of the murder and got the story from one of the reporters. He explains that was how he was able to send the fourth letter so quickly.'

'But it was sent from the City, not Kensington,' I said. 'He had not the time to get back home, write the letter, and post it.'

'No, that's right; but he said he had worked out where the fourth murder would happen and knew it was only a matter of time. He had written the letter beforehand and kept it in his pocket. It turns out he was standing amongst that little crowd which had gathered. He wanted to see my reaction when I opened the letter,' he said.

'Good Lord!' I expostulated. 'Do you mean to say he was watching us all the time?'

Lestrade nodded, tapping the side of his forehead. 'Come to examine the effect of his handiwork! He said he had only written the letters to make his point about the vice and iniquity in the City, and how the police were not only turning a blind eye to it, but were implicated in it. Raved on about Sodom and Gomorrah, then he actually told me that he was glad that someone was punishing them for their wickedness — I must say it was all I could do to restrain myself. I put the fear of death into him and told him he was the prime suspect for the four murders and he went to pieces. I took a bit of a gamble and asked him straight out about the ears of corn, but he looked completely blank. I don't believe he has anything to do with the murders at all, and I can always tell when that type is lying. He has no record of any criminal activity, though he was one of the suspects in the Whitechapel case.'

'Yes, but so was half of London, if I recall,' replied Holmes.

'Well, he'll get a night in the cells and six months' hard for misleading the police in a murder case,' said Lestrade as he stood up to leave, 'but I think we have to eliminate him as a suspect in our inquiries.'

The daily report from Wiggins lay on the table. 'Not much here,' Holmes said, shaking his head in frustration once he had read it, 'the Earl appears to have spent his time going about some very mundane business.'

'Entirely unaware, of course, that his footsteps are being dogged.'

'Yes, though there is one small point which I may follow up. Wiggins reports that Titchfield had made a visit to an address in Cleveland Street yesterday morning, number nineteen, in fact. It seems to have been the only vaguely unusual departure from the predictable round of Whitehall, his club, his home and church.'

He reached for the trade directory and flicked through the pages. 'This gives the address as the premises of the Soho Picture Gallery. I have told Wiggins to leave a few of his band to keep an eye on the house at Mayfair, whilst he and Simpson have taken up surveillance at Cleveland Street.'

'I suppose in the absence of anything really useful to do at the moment, we really ought to satisfy our curiosity by taking a walk over there after breakfast tomorrow,' I suggested.

A short stroll next morning took us along New Cavendish Street to the corner of Upper Marylebone Street, where we turned right into a narrow thoroughfare of tall, dull-looking, terraced houses leading down from Fitzroy Square. Number 19 stood opposite the Strand Union workhouse, from which the unmistakeable odour of wet laundry wafted across the pavement. The four-storied house was identical to many others in the street. A brass plate bore the name 'Soho Picture Gallery. Private: Members and Invited Guests Only. Prop. Chas Newland.' To the side, was the narrow frontage of a seedy-looking shop, number 19a, around which an enclosure of low railings prevailed.

'We are looking for a painting,' Holmes whispered to me as he rang the bell. We waited some time before a seedy-looking, shabbily-dressed character of late middle-age appeared. He seemed surprised to see us and kept us at the street door.

'Are you Mr Newland?' asked Holmes.

'No, I'm his caretaker,' the man answered gruffly.

'I'm trying to find a — '

'You are not members,' the caretaker interrupted, looking at us suspiciously, 'you can't come in unless you have an invitation.'

'I have a recommendation,' said Holmes brightly. 'My name is Mortimer Harris, and I was advised to try this gallery by a chap I met last week at Christie, Manson & Woods in St James's, you know of the place?'

'Yes.'

'He said that it might just be worth making a visit here. I am looking for a painting by Lusignan called *Phoebe Et Coeus* — I have a client who would be prepared to pay well above the market value to lay his hands on it.'

'What's this chap's name?' he barked. 'The one you met.'

'Dash it, I've forgotten now; he is not a close acquaintance, but a fellow dealer whom I bump into from time to time. You've heard of the painting, I suppose?'

'Yes, of course,' the man stammered, 'we don't have it.'

'Nothing at all by Lusignan?'

'No.'

'My friend here, Mr Grenville Price, is a dealer, too; an agent for Binghams, in fact,' said Holmes, gesturing to me.

'Indeed,' I smiled, 'a collector and a connoisseur. I'm looking for anything at all by the Barbizon school.'

'Perhaps Mr Price and I could come in and have a browse around,' Holmes continued ingratiatingly.

'Not possible.' He shook his head. 'As the sign says, invitation only. If you don't have a card, you can't come in.'

'Oh, I see. That's very disappointing,' replied Holmes. 'How does one go about obtaining a card?'

'By recommendation from an existing member.'

'May I make an application to the proprietor at this address?'

'Yes, that's what to do,' the man said abruptly, closing the door in our faces. Holmes laughed silently as we retraced our steps up the street.

'It's obvious that the fellow knows nothing about art, as I suspected from the moment he opened the door. There is no such painting and no such artist; I simply made the names up. I am intrigued by what it is that brings the Earl of Titchfield to a picture gallery where they won't let you see the pictures. Well, this is hardly the time and place to engage in speculation. Let us go across to the street corner over there — I have had a sudden desire to have my boots polished,' he said.

'But you had them done only this morning, didn't Billy — '

'You may recognize the shoe blacking boy, incidentally,' my friend interrupted.

There was indeed something familiar about the young fellow who had set up a stall at the street corner. 'Why, it's Wiggins!' I said, surprised as he raised his head to greet us.

'No need to shout it all over the street!' Holmes whispered in an amused tone.

'Why, he even has a badge!' I said as I noticed the green and white enamelled numbers on the boy's lapel.

'Of course, Watson, you do not think I am such a fool as to allow our strategy to be scuppered by the mere curiosity of a passing constable!'

'Made one an' six already, Sir,' said Wiggins, grinning.

'Any sign of your aristocratic friend today, Wiggins?'

'Yes, he came about ten o'clock and left about half an hour later, Mr Holmes.'

'Anything else?'

'The place is full o' toffs, not just the one whose coach we're followin'. I seen some o' their faces in the papers. Another well-heeled gentlemen came in just as he left. A couple o' military-looking came yesterday afternoon and Simpson says there was a vicar too, last night. Sometimes they are in and out in a couple o' minutes, sometimes a bit longer. The place gets ever such a lot of mail. There seems to be a delivery wiv' every post, and telegraph boys comin' and goin' all day.'

Holmes thought for a moment. 'Does the caretaker admit the mail boys to the Gallery?'

'Yes.'

'Hm. Strange that he was so insistent on keeping us out, Watson. Do these boys bring any large parcels?'

Wiggins furrowed his brows for a moment. 'Not especially,' he replied.

'Hmm, perhaps that part is done elsewhere,' said Holmes inexplicably.

'Elsewhere? D'you mean the other house?' said Wiggins.

'The *other* house! What do you mean?'

'The one down the street — number thirty-two; Simpson seen it.'

'During the night?'

'Well, about nine o'clock last night, just after he came on, he said.'

Holmes's eyes brightened. 'What did he see?'

'A bloke comes along wiv a handcart an' takes the stuff in, then goes away again. Happened twice. Simpson thought he must be a costermonger comin' home from Berwick Street after the market closed.'

'What exactly is this *stuff* like?'

'Dunno exactly what it is; comes in boxes but Simpson follered him the second time an' says it didn't look like greengrocers' stuff. It was all covered up wiv a tarpaulin so he couldn't see what was inside.'

'Did Simpson say whether the man went to the picture gallery?'

'No, cos I asked him.'

'And you haven't seen anyone going between the two houses?'

'No.'

'Most remarkable. Do you know if the gallery is occupied during the night?'

'Yes, there's quite a few comin's an' goin's, but the old caretaker, the one you spoke to just now, never leaves.'

'And number thirty-two?'

'No, the house is empty most of the time, just the man wiv the cart.'

'Excellent. If anything else comes up, let

me know immediately,' said my friend, as he turned to leave.

'Deeper and deeper, Holmes,' I remarked once we had returned to Baker Street. 'You think there is some connection between the two houses?'

'It is difficult to interpret it as mere coincidence, though one never knows. I am coming round to a view as to the reason for both the exaggerated caution at the gallery and as to the possible contents of the handcart.'

'And that is?'

'I think that it may be a racket in fake art.'

'Forged paintings?'

'It begins to look like it. Perhaps the work is done at number thirty-two and the transactions are conducted at number nineteen.'

'It seems rather exaggerated caution.'

'The stakes are high, Watson, very high.'

'High enough to be connected with the murder of four innocent people?'

'The amount of money which changes hands in that game nowadays would astonish one. The law of supply and demand ordains an enormous financial value for the limited number of the most famously-celebrated works of art, especially those whose creator is dead. You will recall the great substitution scandal, which involved forgeries of works by artists from the

Darlington School, where the judge took a very stern view of the matter, and for which my old friend Matthews ended up doing five years. It hasn't put a stop to it, though: we put that clever young Stamford behind bars; then there was Victor Lynch, and I have heard dark rumours of the Honourable Aubrey Conk-Singleton's collection that defy belief. The situation is, if anything, worse in France and the *Pays-Bas*. In the celebrated Trouillebert case, the forger made his entire living out of making forgeries of one man's work: Jean-Baptiste Corot. Indeed, some wag once said that of the three-hundred-odd paintings which the late Corot made, over a thousand were sold in London! There is great competition amongst auction houses, dealers, galleries and private collectors: the arbiters of taste and judgment. But as long as avarice continues to surpass expertise, the business of forgery will thrive and increase.'

'I seem to recall reading a year or so ago about one of the big Bond Street galleries having failed after they had bought paintings that were later discovered to be forgeries.'

'Yes, that was Cochrane & Mertens' *Salon Parisien* and I think it was some of Van Beers's works which were involved. Now to return to the practical, the immediate priority is to discover what is going on at number thirty-two by the most direct means; that is, by taking advantage of the fact that the house appears to be unoccupied for most of the time. I have my jemmy, my dark lantern and — '

'And you have your faithful Watson!' I added.

'No, my good fellow,' said Holmes shaking his head, 'I should not think of embroiling you in anything which would endanger your life or your reputation. For one thing, there is your neighbour's practice to consider, and your arrest and conviction as a burglar would weigh heavily upon my conscience. After the Drury Lane business, I feel far less inclined these days to expose you to any — '

'I won't hear of it, Holmes!' I interrupted. 'If you are about to step into the gap of danger, I shall be there with you as ever before. Jackson returns tomorrow in any case, and besides, it is merely a spot of housebreaking — nothing that we have not done before; and it is ultimately in the cause of justice.'

Holmes flushed with pleasure and grasped me by the hand.

'Splendid, Watson, there is not one person whom I should rather have at my side in such an enterprise. It is not much more than a half mile or so, though we shall need to be all the more cautious in broad daylight.'

6

We left Baker Street just before midday, our nefarious intentions well camouflaged by loose clothing, for Holmes had his dark lantern, his drill, and his jemmy concealed under his cloak. Inevitably, we took the quieter byways of which Holmes, like his counterparts in the criminal fraternity, had the most intimate knowledge. We crossed Manchester Square and plunged into a labyrinth of empty cobbled lanes — of which the existence I had previously been entirely oblivious, though they were barely five minutes from my doorstep. Indeed after a few minutes, had it not been for the fact that the day had remained bright and clear with a brilliant sun overhead, I could scarcely have told in which direction we were moving, but Holmes enumerated each place as we passed: Bentinck Mews, Queen Anne Lane, Deacon Close, past the rear entrance of the Langham, on through Riding House Passage and finally to a narrow passage leading off Ogle Square, which faced across to the house at number thirty-two.

'Hold on to these,' he said, handing me his

tools, 'until I have had a word or two with Wiggins.' He returned quickly and iterated to me his plans.

'What if our man with the cart should return unexpectedly?' I asked.

'It is highly unlikely: according to our information, nothing happens there during the day. But should the man make an unscheduled return, then *in extremis*, Wiggins will set up a commotion which will delay him until we are safely removed from the scene. The main difficulty will be in avoiding the attention of the inquisitive public or a passing constable whilst getting through the front door, but we shall simply have to take our chances in that respect. In any case, we have a clear view up and down the street and with the aid of these,' he flourished a prodigious assortment of skeleton keys which he had drawn from the voluminous pockets of his cloak, 'we should be able to avoid the use of force.'

The front of the house was recessed slightly from the passageway. Holmes fiddled with the lock for a moment or two as a distant buzz of voices floated over from the open windows of the King and Queen on the other side of the street, then the door slid noiselessly open. We passed inside quickly and saw by what light the grimy windows allowed that the house was in a somewhat dilapidated condition. Even on this warm summer afternoon, there hung about the place the reek of damp and an atmosphere of decay, and some of the wallpaper had begun to peel away below the cracked yellow ceiling. A narrow hall led past two rooms, which opened on the left and right to the foot of the uncarpeted stairs. It did not require my friend's acute powers of observation to discern that a succession of feet had recently worn a path down the dusty stairway towards the lower floor.

'Well, let us see what hidden delights the cellar holds,' said my friend, as we picked our way down the creaking steps. The lantern shone into a corner of the lower area where a number of plain cardboard boxes were stacked. Holmes sprang across the floor, withdrew his penknife and sharply slit the cover of the uppermost box. He pulled back the cover and gave an exclamation. I looked over his shoulder and saw that inside the heavy cardboard box were a number of smaller packages, on top of which a slip of paper bore the legend: 'Handle With Care. Penistone Explosives Company, West Riding, Yorkshire.'

Holmes and I looked at each other in surprise and horror.

'*Dynamite!*' I exclaimed. 'This is what

came in the handcart?'

'This was not at all what I had expected to find, Watson.' I had rarely seen such a picture of bewilderment upon his features. He laid down the lantern and began to pace up and down the floor. Finally he said, 'My chain of reasoning has been faulty, but I think I am beginning to understand now. Let us recall our steps and return to the upper air, for I feel there may be more interesting discoveries ahead.'

Neither of the doors we had passed on the ground floor were locked and we found the first room empty. The second had been a kitchen, where a dusty old dresser, with shelves containing some ancient dusty crockery, and a chipped sink were the only adornments. We went swiftly up the staircase to the first floor, on which there were three further rooms; only one was locked. Holmes produced another key and in a moment we were inside a large, airy single apartment. The room was situated at the corner of the house and its main window, albeit heavily curtained, faced the houses opposite, whilst a narrower side window possessed an unobstructed view northwards along Cleveland Street. It was spare and tidy, and showed some signs that it had recently been used for living purposes. There was a bed, a wardrobe and a dresser in one corner, and in the other a writing-desk with inkpot and pen and three drawers. Holmes walked over to the bureau and in a few seconds had the drawers opened. Two of these were empty, but the third drawer held a stock of writing materials and a large envelope. From Holmes's eager expression, I could tell this had immediately excited his interest. He withdrew the envelope from the drawer, and carefully opening it, he drew from it various slips of paper covered in writing which at first I took to be some foreign language — a European one I hazarded, for I recognized the Latin characters but not the words. The first line read:

ipxw ejex mpse fexb sewx ejfx

Holmes gave a whistle of surprise. I should never have described his temperament as mercurial, but his features now broke out in such an expression of smug delight that it was hard to believe this was the same man who chafed with disappointment and chagrin only a few moments ago.

'I suppose I ought to have expected it the moment I saw the boxes of dynamite. What do you make of it, Watson?'

'I have no idea what to make of it!'

'I think I have.'

'What language is it?'

'One you know very well, Watson,' he said with an enigmatic smile. I took a closer look at the entire list of messages, and still to me the words seemed to be quite unpronounceable in any tongue: many of them had no recognizable vowel sounds.

'No, you must be mistaken, Holmes, for apart from a little military and kitchen Urdu, I speak only — '

'It is a code, Watson,' he interrupted.

'Which?'

'The A for Z cipher.'

'To whom or what does it refer?'

'I am not certain. This first message reads: 'How did Lord Edward die?' '

'Lord Edward *who*?'

'I must confess, I am at a complete loss to say.'

'How many Lord Edwards do we know of?'

'There must be dozens, I am sure.'

'But how many do we know who have died recently?'

'One moment, though, the reply to the question reads: 'Like a man without a sigh.' Aha, I have it now! It is a sign and countersign. Yes, that is the most likely explanation — it is to establish the authenticity of the recipient.'

'But why?'

'Going by the content of the messages I should say this was a code being used by the Irish Republican Brotherhood.'

'The Fenian dynamiters?'

'Yes.

'You mean you have deciphered it already?'

'Of course, Watson. It is a fiendishly simple one, albeit yet ostensibly complicated. The cipher is composed merely by employing the letter occurring in the alphabet after the one intended and grouping the ciphers in sets of four. Any superfluous letter in the set is usually denoted by 'x' or 'z' which are the least used letters in the alphabet and their presence as decoy ciphers are thus easily detected. Thus the recurring word '*jsfm boey*' means Ireland-z. There is also '*bnfs jdbw*' which is America-x, and I quickly recognized the ciphers '*mpse nbzp syww*' and '*qsjn fnjo jtuf syzx*' which are, with superfluous letters removed, 'Lord Mayor' and 'Prime Minister' respectively. This envelope appears to contain messages from one member of the cell to the others, who are presumably conspiring somewhere in London at this very moment.'

'So this is what they would call a safe house?'

'Indubitably,' he replied. 'Now give me a few moments to copy these messages.'

So saying, he whipped out a pencil and notebook and set to work with haste. I saw that he was able to transcribe into English without hesitation straight from the code. When he had completed his task, he very carefully replaced every paper in order and returned the envelope to the exact place in which he had found it.

'As you can see, although the messages are in code, the telegraphic addresses and dates are clear: the first item of correspondence emanates from one 'Cúchulain' and has been sent from the Western Union telegraph office in East 198th Street, New York. I presume it has been routed via that office from Ireland to avoid detection by our agents in England. They have been addressed to 'Sarsfield' in Clerkenwell, and presumably collected from the Post Office there to avoid giving away the address of the recipient.'

He laid them out on the desk. 'Here are the messages in sequence,' he said.

7th May 1895 from Cúchulain, New York to Sarsfield, London. 'How did Lord Edward die?'

12th May 1895 from Sarsfield, London to Cúchulain, New York. 'Like a man, without a sigh.'

21st May 1895 from Cúchulain, New York to Sarsfield, London. 'A will return from America to take command of final stage.'

4th June 1895 from Cúchulain, New York to Sarsfield, London. '32 Cleveland Street.'

5th June 1895 from Cúchulain, New York to Sarsfield, London. 'Sunday evening B3 and C1 arriving from Ireland.'

9th June 1895 from Sarsfield, London to Cúchulain, New York. 'Awaiting further orders from America.'

16th June from Cúchulain, New York to Sarsfield, London. 'Salisbury, Lord Mayor. 29 June. St Mary 25SW, 40NW.'

'A fine haul, eh!' Holmes looked at me, 'Do you see the game now, Watson?'

'I think I am beginning to grasp it,' I replied.

'You must recall some eight years ago the so-called Jubilee Plot to assassinate our reigning monarch was foiled. Thirty pounds of the best-grade dynamite were discovered in the safe house which was in Clerkenwell on that occasion. It was the same crowd behind it.'

'The man with the handcart may be the 'A' referred to as returning from America to take command?'

'It is possible. First there is the arrival of the leader, who will disseminate the orders to strike and presumably co-ordinate the operation; then the safe house is established; then a meeting is called with B3 and C1, whom I take to be subordinates with, I fear, putatively fatal consequences for a certain British statesman. This time they have chosen as their target the Prime Minister — a man who, it must be admitted, is extremely unpopular in Ireland. In time-honoured tradition, he is always the principal speaker at the Bankers' Dinner, which is held in the Mansion House on the last Saturday in June.'

'I am confounded by the reference to St Mary and the letters and numbers, though.'

'I fancy we shall clear that up very quickly. The Mansion House sits in close proximity to the church of St Mary Woolnoth, does it not? That explains St Mary. Having established that, then the letters and numbers must stand in relation to it; I take 'S' and 'W' to mean south and west, and 25 to enumerate yards or paces. From memory, I would say that places us at the opening of St Swithin's Lane. Forty yards north and west from there brings us to the corner of Mansion House Place. I may not be able to recall every lamppost and manhole in the district, but I think I can be fairly certain that that is where the dynamite is intended to be placed.' He smiled grimly. 'Let me put it to you, Watson, that if I were a Fenian assassin, at what better spot in London could I strike my blow? The Prime Minister of England and Lord Mayor of London assassinated practically at the confluence of the very streets named for King William and Queen Victoria — the instigator of the Penal Laws, and the 'Famine Queen' as she is known by the more extreme nationalists in Ireland. Think of the propaganda!'

'And yet it seems to me,' I said, musing over the messages I had seen, 'a rather cavalier way in which to send important messages.' Then, despite the frisson of exultation I felt at our mission, it occurred to me that we were perhaps conducting ourselves in rather too leisurely a manner for housebreakers. Wiggins's ability to keep a lookout notwithstanding, I thought that we might show greater haste to be out of the place.

Yet Holmes was clearly in no hurry. 'You must remember the Phoenix Park Murders in Dublin in '82? It is a matter of fact that the operation was co-ordinated by a series of similarly-coded messages placed in the *Irish Times* around St Patrick's Day, and yet no one was able to pick them up.'

'But what if the telegraph operator should become suspicious at such incongruity?'

'Again, that is simply one of the risks which they have to run. Do not underestimate these fellows; I have no doubt that they will have had a sympathizer planted in each of the New York and London cable offices. And besides, there are many thousands of messages passed each day; look at the agony columns in the newspapers — they are full of such apocrypha and esoteric obscurities.'

'How is this connected to our investigation at the picture gallery?'

'There you take me out of my depth, at least for the present, Watson.'

'It seems to be one of those cases where the unearthing of one clue leads to several others. It is like the multiplying heads of the Hydra.'

'I should be inclined to agree rather more with you had you said *apparent* clues: we have an overabundance of them, and I have always believed that too many is worse than too few, though there should be no permutation of effects for which it is impossible to discover a cause.'

'When the circumstances are as bizarre as

these, surely the deduction should, conversely, be simpler?'

'Always providing that one is able to identify the existence of what might be called happenstance. That is our problem here: the question of whether in investigating one felony it is purely by chance we stumbled across another one. The odds against that must be incalculable, yet it has happened before. It must be recognized that in cases which entail some degree of complication, not all of the circumstances are necessarily related causally: only some are essential; therefore, some must be mere accident and genuine coincidence. The construction of a theory which incorporates an explanation of *all* the observable phenomena is likely not only to be too cumbersome, but also to be erroneous in many of it suppositions.'

'But,' I objected, 'one cannot conduct the science of detection in a laboratory — where extraneous effect and influence are isolated with clinical certainty.'

'Of course not: the object of study will always be contaminated, so to speak, by chance and inconsequence, and it must fall entirely to the judgment of the specialist to separate mere happenstance from the chain of causality. Isolate the unnecessary, and the matter should be as simple as following the trail of a one-legged man along a muddy path.'

'Yet, that would seem quite a remarkable feat to the common man.'

'Well then, it does not take much to bewilder the common man, or the common policeman, for that matter. Consider how long it would have taken your common man to unravel the simplest cipher; for example, the one which brought us to the Birlstone business a few years ago. Until today, my instincts were to go after Thisley; however, I shall be forced to postpone that until we have sorted out the greater priority of our Irish cousins' predilection for dangerous toys. I am afraid our trail can lead only in one direction.'

'To Scotland Yard?'

'No, Watson; to Whitehall.'

'To Mycroft?'

'Yes. I should not rest easy if I were to turn this over to the official police. I have no wish to denigrate Lestrade's professional integrity, but frankly, I fear he would bungle it. The stakes are far too high and the repercussions too grave should things turn out wrong. I shall go down to the Diogenes Club this evening to seek my brother's advice.'

'Surely as the matter is urgent, it would be preferable to go straight to his office right now?'

'In theory, yes, that is correct. However, my appearance there might provoke inordinate curiosity, and in order to be permitted to speak to him in his office, I should possibly have to explain the situation to one of his subordinates, something I should want to avoid at all costs. I should prefer complete privacy. There remain three clear days before the Mansion House dinner, and I am satisfied that is ample time in which to formulate a plan.'

'Then you have made your decision?'

'Yes, albeit with great reluctance. We have done an excellent day's work thus far, so let us stand not upon the order of our going.'

7

The evening being fine and warm, we made our way on foot down through Piccadilly and St James's to the Diogenes Club in order to find Mycroft Holmes, who was usually there between five o'clock and 7.30 in the evening. As I have had occasion to remark upon more than once in my accounts of our adventures, if Holmes had one besetting sin, it was the sin of pride. But his reluctance, if it may be called that, to consult his brother Mycroft on this occasion stemmed not from his unwillingness to acknowledge the existence of anyone whose intellectual powers eclipsed his own. Far from it, for he had once stated in his typically forthright manner that not only did Mycroft possess greater powers than he, but that he also did not consider modesty to rank as a virtue. Rather it emanated from his private disinclination to share the credit for solving the case with any other individual, though he was usually happy enough to turn the culprits over to the police once they had been caught, save in the handful of cases where he exerted his private right to act as judge and jury.

'In this case, there are really three separate threads of criminal activity,' he said as we turned into Pall Mall. 'There are the murders; there is the mystery surrounding the bogus picture gallery; and there is the assassination of the Prime Minister and the Lord Mayor, and goodness knows what other atrocities. It would be the greatest triumph of my career if I could bring all three sets of evil-doers to justice. Of course, I hardly need Mycroft's assistance to track down common murderers and forgers, for despite our meagre progress thus far, I am convinced I will be able to achieve that by my own efforts. But Mycroft's personal connections with some of the high-ranking members of the club who have connections with the government will ensure that a more considered view is taken with regard to the sensitive nature of our discovery. Left to his own devices, Lestrade's likely course of action would be to surround the place with policemen and then kick the door down. The outcome would be the escape of the perpetrators, who would then simply regroup and launch another plan.'

'Well, here we are, Holmes. Let us hope we are not upsetting Mycroft's routine too much.' Knowing the rules of what Holmes had some years ago once described to me as 'the queerest club in London', I observed complete silence as we entered the club from the street. The Commissionaire led us into a room off the foyer, and having seated us in a pair of leather armchairs by a long window framed with richly-textured curtains, then departed without a word. The room was hung with richly-hued portraits of former members and by a shining walnut table against the side wall stood a finely-sculpted bust of the first president of the Diogenes, the Right Honourable Jeremy Harcourt. The whole effect would have done justice to a ducal palace. The celebrated unsociability and misanthropy of the Diogenes circle was not matched by any parsimony in its provision of comfort, even luxury. A gentleman who introduced himself as Mr Calthorpe entered a few minutes later and patiently explained to us that he was both a friend and colleague of Mycroft, who had gone to the continent on a diplomatic mission. A look of mingled disappointment and puzzlement spread across Holmes's face.

'I do not suppose you are able to state either how long Mycroft will be gone or how he may be contacted?' my friend inquired.

Calthorpe smiled indulgently and replied, 'You will understand that the mission is a delicate one and therefore of the most confidential type. It is, in fact, officially designated as secret, and I am verging on the bounds of indiscretion in telling you even this much.'

'Then we shall take up no more of your time,' said Holmes, nodding towards the door. We made our way outside again.

'Well, Watson, I have never known Mycroft to have much appetite for overseas travel, especially as it causes him to alter his rather strict routine which he delights in following with almost monastic strictness — rather to the point of obsession at times.'

'To where do you think he has gone?'

'Even such a political ignoramus as I could hardly be unaware of the young Kaiser's provocative foreign policy, therefore — '

'Germany?'

'I believe that is the most likely place. The Kaiser's alarming naval expansion has already led to the French and Russians forming a military alliance, as you know. The opening of the *Kaiser-Wilhelm-Kanal*, which now gives the German Baltic fleet access to the North Sea and the English Channel, can only exacerbate an already tense situation between our nations.'

'Yes, I read that a number of German shops in London have actually been attacked and had their windows broken.'

'I suspect Mycroft is included in the diplomatic party which has been invited to the official opening. He has complete fluency in the German language, and I assume that he has gone to act as an interpreter on behalf of the delegation whose purpose, one must suppose, is to use the occasion to intercede with the more level-headed members of the Emperor's cabinet, and perhaps also to deliver a mild warning against his plans for further expansion.'

'Still, this puts us rather back to square one, does it not?'

'Indeed it does. The matter is now becoming urgent, but I am at a loss to understand what we can do alone. Apart from any other considerations, there is grave danger to innocent people with a house full of dynamite. The Clerkenwell prison break resulted in the lives of a dozen or more bystanders being lost.'

'I should say that there was enough dynamite downstairs to bring down half the street.'

'Indeed. Despite my misgivings, I fear I shall be forced ultimately to turn the matter over to Lestrade. Still, it is a lovely evening, Watson; what do you say to a stroll through the park? Then perhaps we shall go up to that little Italian-Polish place in Bridle Lane where, if my memory serves me, their Beef Zygmunt is one of the finest in London. Or should you prefer something less exotic, we could repair to the Clarendon Supper Rooms.'

★   ★   ★

When we arrived back at Baker Street just after ten o'clock, Mrs Hudson informed us that we had a visitor waiting. A tall, languid, silver-haired figure stood up as we entered. His mode of dress was foppish and old-fashioned, and he reminded me of a caricature I had once seen of a Bond Street lounger from the days of the Regency.

'Mr Sherlock Holmes and Doctor Watson,' he bowed, 'I am delighted to make your acquaintance. I should explain that your landlady showed me in and assured me that you had no objection to visitors awaiting your return. I assume your visit to the Diogenes Club was a wasted one; however, I — '

'Who are you, Sir, and what is your business here?' Holmes barked brusquely.

'I am unable to reveal my true identity to you, but let us say that you may address me as 'M.B.' In the course of our conversa- tion — '

'I fear there will be no conversation, unless

you state your identity and the precise reason for your visit. If you require my assistance — '

'I did not exactly say that I required your assistance,' the visitor replied smoothly. 'Let us put all the cards on the table at once. I am here on a very important matter of state. I work for Sir James Cardew and I am here at his express insistence.'

'The head of the Audit Board?' Holmes asked.

'In theory, yes. In actual fact, he is head of one of those arms of the state whose activities must, by their very nature, be shielded from the public gaze. The Audit Board of Administration does not exist in reality, but is merely a convenient, and publicly credible, façade. You see, I said I would put the cards on the table, and I have done so. However, you are at perfect liberty to confirm this with Sir James if you wish — I have his private telephone number which you may call,' the visitor said, handing a card to Holmes. 'I am aware that you two gentlemen visited a certain house in Cleveland Street,' the man continued, 'and from that I was able to work out the reason for your visit to the Diogenes. You intended to report the discovery which you made there to your brother, Mycroft, in order that he could seek the advice of his fellow members. Characteristically astute, Mr

Holmes, and I applaud your judgement in avoiding turning the matter over to the police, in whom, no doubt, you have as little confidence as we do. Sir James holds you in very high regard, for I believe you were of some assistance to him in the espionage affair, which led to the unmasking of the Sussex MP who had been spying for the Germans. Something to do with a seabird trained to carry messages across the Channel, though quite why Sir James thought it necessary to involve a private detective agent in such a simple matter, I am at a loss to understand.'

'It may have been because this simple matter dragged on for months and confounded your colleagues — who had every force of the state at their backs — whereas I solved the case in forty-eight hours, single-handedly, and without any material reward.'

'Nevertheless, if the present matter had been left to me, both you and the doctor would have been arrested for breaking and entering and held incommunicado until this affair had reached its conclusion. But, as I do not have the authority — '

'You would do well, Sir, to come quickly to the point,' interjected Holmes warmly.

Our visitor looked astonished. 'I may say, Mr Holmes, that you are quite living up to

132

your reputation! I do believe you would have no compunction about throwing me down the stairs! It seems that Sir James has also not forgotten your efforts in recovering the Italian treaty, and I agree with him that both your patriotism and that of Doctor Watson are above suspicion, which is why I am here at his instigation.'

'Pray continue,' said Holmes.

'As we are, I trust, speaking openly, I must confess that I am completely at a loss to understand how you came to know about this house in the first place. To the best of our knowledge, only seven people in this country, at least on our side, were aware of what was going on — and your name does not appear on that list.'

Holmes turned over Sir James's card again before he replied.

'You put me at some disadvantage, Sir,' said Holmes. 'It is, by now, rather too late for me to go rousing Sir James's household.'

'Then I shall attempt to assuage your concern. You had no doubt worked out that the present offensive is merely a continuation from the Jubilee Plot.'

'Yes.'

'There were undoubtedly a number of agents involved in that operation, an entire cell in fact. When the plot was discovered, some escaped in the heel of the hunt, though only at the expense of leaving incriminating evidence behind, which helped convict others who went down for long spells. Their code name for the present offensive is 'Operation Red S' — after the Prime Minister's personal scarlet monogram. The very fact that such a minute detail of Lord Salisbury's private seal are known in these quarters is extremely alarming, and points to one of their agents having succeeded in infiltrating a position of trust at the very highest level. It hardly requires an encyclopaedic knowledge of political affairs to understand that were this plan to succeed in the current volatile situation, the entire Irish question would be opened up yet again in the most dramatic manner; and in the ensuing political disorder, the likely balance of forces at home and abroad, particularly in America whence this offensive emanates, would turn against our interests. However, despite all their precautions, we managed to intercept the communications by which the London cell is being commanded. To bring the matter within your own sphere of interest, I can inform you that the entire operation is being directed by General James Moriarty, who is their Chief of Staff in England, and his associate Colonel Sebastian Moran, both of whom are staunch, but covert, Irish patriots.

'*General* Moriarty?!' said Holmes.

'Indeed. That is the rank he holds in the Brotherhood.'

'This cannot be the same man, the man who fought his death struggle with me four years ago. I saw him plunge several hundred feet, strike the sharp point of a crevice, then sink in the swirling foam. He cannot possibly have come out of that gorge alive.'

'Whatever or whoever you may think you saw, Mr Holmes, I can assure you that the man whom you once described with no exaggeration as the Napoleon of Crime is living and breathing. There can be no doubt, as you suggest, that the man who fell to his death in Switzerland could not possibly have survived. But no body was ever found by the Swiss Police at Meiringen. A shoe and a cravat are all that were discovered; therefore, no identification was ever properly made. But we have never been deceived by the campaign of deliberate misinformation which had been conducted following Moriarty's apparent death. We afterwards trailed him from Geneva to Philadelphia. He returned to England last month following what was quite literally a Council of War. He is the 'A' referred to in the messages.

'Despite his Eton and Oxford background, his allegiance is to the land of his grandfather's birth. You will recall how his organization pursued John Douglas through South Africa to St Helena to dispense vengeance on behalf of the Irish Americans — that was not a business proposition for once; it was done out of political sympathy. He also managed to arrange a convenient accident to happen to our informer in the Jubilee Plot affair, his fellow General, Francis Millen. As to his second in charge, Colonel Moran, his Army service in India, we lately discovered, had long provided a valuable cover for his fraternization with the Indian Nationalists with whom his organization made common cause. There is little doubt that Moran had a hand in the murder of Mrs Stewart, in revenge for her husband testifying against one of the Land-Leaguers, and also in Pigott's carefully-arranged suicide in a Madrid hotel following the Parnell forgeries. We later discovered that the bullet which killed him did not match the gun which lay beside the body, and Moran was suspected of shooting him through the open window. We managed to hush the matter up so that they were unaware of our suspicions.

'You will recall the Adair murder last year; it was also politically motivated. The public believed otherwise, Mr Holmes, and so did you, but you were not party to the information we had. Adair came from an old

Plantation family — his father was the Earl of Maynooth. Prior to his appointment in the Colonies, the Earl had sentenced one of the Fenians to hang for a crime which he was afterwards proven not to have committed. It is of no import, for the low scoundrel had certainly committed others, but the murder of young Ronald, his father's favourite, was an act of revenge. This is the third attempt by that organization on the Mansion House; there have been several at various Whitehall offices, not to mention others in the House of Commons; there was even one at the Carlton Club. Alderman, the code-breaker, cracked the ciphers contained in the cable traffic from America, and we have had that house watched for the past three weeks. That is how we came to know that you had been there. Their ordnance operation is now complete, the dynamite and charges stored, and we have now called off our watch until the final day. On Saturday morning, two men will return to the house and bring the dynamite and charges across the city — '

'And place them in the manhole at Mansion House Lane,' said my friend.

'You had worked that out, too!'

'It needed no genius; the code was a mere variation of the A for Z, and the directions were simple to follow.'

'The bomb is meant to go off at eight o'clock in the evening, by which time the agents expect to be on a boat from Liverpool. The plan shall not, of course, come to fruition because the entire cell will be captured red-handed. There are four men in it: Thomas Allen, the man who escaped in the Jubilee Plot, has been traced to a public house — the Rock of Cashel — in Coventry Close, just off the Kilburn High Road. Desmond Corcoran, from Limerick, was followed to a shebeen in Ratcliff when he went to pick up the first message. The other two we have already spoken of. I have, with Sir James's permission, revealed to you secrets of the state of which many of our own high-ranking officials are ignorant, including those in the upper levels of the Metropolitan Police. Now I must ask you to be equally candid with me as to how you came to be at the safe house yesterday.'

'That is a fair request,' said Holmes. 'I had come to a view that the Soho Picture Gallery in Cleveland Street was a front for something nefarious, and in investigating that, I discovered the safe house. I remain undecided as to whether there is any connection between the two.'

'What exactly did you think the picture gallery is a front *for*?' our visitor asked.

'It seemed to me that the place may have been used as a sort of clearing house for forged paintings, and I had begun to think that the deliveries to number thirty-two were the stock in trade.'

'Then that is outside both my jurisdiction and my interest,' he replied with a shrug, though it seemed to me there was a quiver of relief in his answer. 'What led you to the picture gallery in the first place?'

'I had been asked by Scotland Yard to assist in their hunt for the City Murderer, as the popular press have called him,' Holmes replied. 'The trail led me straight to the gallery.'

'Ah, the City Murders,' said the man sententiously and relapsed into a brief silence. After a while, he continued, 'You place me in a great dilemma, gentlemen. Your information forces me to reveal even more than I had intended to, and I am taking a great risk upon my own head by doing so. I must swear you both to secrecy.'

'Providing what you have told me is true,' replied Holmes, 'you have my word as a man of principle that this will go no further. I must warn you, however, that I shall do all that is in my power to corroborate your story first thing tomorrow morning with Sir James.'

'I should expect no less from a man of your

integrity and intelligence, Mr Holmes. Let me explain further, then: we have uncovered evidence that the murders which you have been investigating have been carried out by the Brotherhood. The motivation for this seems to be the discovery of the safe house by a woman who either lived or worked near Cleveland Street. It seems that this discovery was made quite by chance by the second victim, Patsy Harvey, who recognized Corcoran — they came from the same town. She was down on her luck and on the street; she followed him quite innocently to the house, probably to ask him for a bit of help and surprised him there. He had been incautious enough to leave the door unlocked and she must have seen something incriminating. They determined to silence her before she could let the secret out, and they must have followed her and kept a watch on her. It is suspected that the other three victims must have been associates of hers and they have suffered the same fate. The whole paraphernalia of ritual killings has been introduced purely as a blind to throw the press and the public completely off the scent by insinuating some Masonic involvement — you recall the newspapers were full of that sort of nonsense on the last occasion. It is designed to implicate the *Quattuor Coronae* because some of the senior policemen who are members have a record of acting against the Irish who have not forgotten Bloody Sunday.'

'You are absolutely certain of this?'

'There can be no doubt.'

'But don't you think that the symbolism has been rather *overdone?*' asked Holmes. 'What with five-shilling pieces, and what was the other . . . '

'The ears of corn,' the man replied. 'Well, it has served to cover their traces thus far.'

'But why does Inspector Lestrade know nothing of this?'

'We operate completely independently of the police and have had no official communication with Scotland Yard over this matter for very good reason. Even at the higher echelons, it is not only spectacularly incompetent — look how they botched Moran's case only last year — but notoriously corrupt. Do you know how much money was stolen from banks in London last year? It is an astronomical sum — some ten per cent of it ended up in the pockets of Metropolitan Police officers. Many criminals get their information by bribing policemen. If Scotland Yard were to be appraised of our intelligence *at this present time*, it could blow our entire counter-operation apart. It is not a risk that we can possibly countenance. With

141

the public pressure which is mounting upon them to find the culprits, they would be bound to do something desperate. Consider how they handled the Addleton business — a simple operation that ended in tragedy. It is a case of sacrificing a platoon, as Doctor Watson would understand, to save a battalion.'

'I am not amongst those who would rank the lives of those four women as any less worthy than those of the Prime Minister and the Lord Mayor. Surely if you had these men followed, then you could have prevented innocent people from being killed?'

'No, we have no idea who actually carried out the murders. All we know is that it is none of the men whose every step has been dogged for the last six weeks — but they are the instigators, that is certain. I expect they have trawled the gutter to find some miserable wretch who would do this for the money. Then again, there is no shortage of hired killers amongst Moriarty's criminal associates, as you will know better than anyone.'

'These men will not meekly surrender, but will happily go down fighting. They may live by the sword, but they are resigned to dying by it. And with a house full of dynamite, who knows what may happen,' warned Holmes.

'There will be no dramatic siege. The men will be taken by surprise the minute they step across the threshold on Saturday morning. At that point we will hand them over to Scotland Yard, who will be waiting in the wings. But nothing can be allowed to jeopardize this operation, and that is why the Yard has been kept in the dark: surely you can see the logic of this, Mr Holmes. I appeal to your patriotism and that of Doctor Watson!'

'Then, what is it you want of me?' Holmes asked.

'Nothing, Mr Holmes. All I ask is that you hold off until the affair is resolved. Call off your boy who stands at the shoe-blacking stall during the day, and the one who hides himself in the workhouse grounds by night. Their continued presence there may alarm our enemies. Once we have our men under lock and key you may resume your investigation into the gallery. It will do your reputation no harm in exalted circles should it be known that — '

'I was not aware that my reputation was in need of repair, and I am as jealous of it amongst the lower orders as amongst the higher ones, but I will call the boys off immediately, as you request.'

'Thank you; my time has not been wasted then.'

No sooner had our visitor's footsteps died away on the stair, when Holmes dashed to the coat-stand and seized his coat and hat. Though taken aback by this departure, I rose expectantly, but Holmes shook his head.

'No,' said he, 'two would be one too many,' and he hurried off downstairs in pursuit. I sat silently in the sitting room till long past midnight pondering over the strange conversation I had just witnessed. Then I began to nod off and eventually decided to go up to bed, so that I never knew at what hour my friend returned.

8

When I appeared at breakfast next morning, Holmes was already draining the last dregs from the teapot. I had rarely seen him in such a vexatious and troubled state.

'You have had a busy night, by the look of it,' I ventured.

'I have not slept.'

'You followed the man, then?'

'Of course.'

'Where did he go to?'

'Exactly where I had expected him to go.'

'Which was?'

'Deanery Street.'

'Titchfield's!'

'Yes.'

'Why?'

'There you take me into the realm of speculation again, Watson, though the picture is becoming clearer. What did you think of him, by the way?'

'I must confess I was quite repelled by the noxious suavity of his speech.'

'You noticed that too, did you?'

'One could hardly fail to: there was something positively reptilian about the man.

Did you discover whether his claim to be working for Sir James was true?'

'Yes, I had not doubted that, though I did take the trouble to confirm it personally. I sent a wire first thing this morning and here is the reply. You do not seem convinced, Watson, and as usual, you are unable to conceal your scepticism; come, tell me what is troubling you.'

'I did not sleep well myself last night; I tossed and turned a bit. I noticed something else about that fellow. It may be a small point, but he seemed to contradict himself.'

'That is correct, Watson, he did so in no less than three separate instances.'

'He said that they had had no contact with Scotland Yard over the murders,' I began, 'nor did he know who the murderer was: in that case, how he could possibly know about the ears of corn, which have been kept from the public?'

'Precisely, Watson.'

'Then if his statement is true, the only possible explanation is that he committed the murders himself!'

'Very good, Watson, but slightly wide of the mark. Let me tell you what happened last night. When I went down to the street, I noticed that the man had hailed a hansom straight away. That was a blow, for I was at too great at distance to hear the address he shouted up to the jarvey, though I did get the number of the cab. However, as I was fairly certain of his destination, I merely waited for another cab to come along a few minutes behind. I got off at Park Lane and walked round the corner and there was the same cab waiting outside Titchfield's, so I waited concealed in the shadows until our man came out. I managed this time to get close enough to hear the address he shouted up: the Piccadilly Hotel. The night porter there, stimulated by some gentle right persuasion, was able to tell me that our visitor goes under the name of Edward Miller-Beach.'

'The name means nothing to me.'

'Nor me. Then I stood down our forces at Titchfield's and also at the picture gallery; I can see no further use for them now. Then I came back and sat here upon the sofa and tried to puzzle out the meaning of it all. I emptied my tobacco pouch and yours, too. I flatter myself to believe that I now understand what is going on, though I am unable to fill in quite all the gaps yet. The story he told us was a mixture of half-truths and lies, and it was not until he betrayed himself over that small detail that my suspicions were confirmed. That is the clever part: the best propaganda contains more than a kernel of veracity, so that a million lies may thus be concealed.'

'It seems to me that the people who populate these secret government departments live in such a different world from the one we inhabit; a nether world of perpetual intrigue, of deception, propaganda, and double agents, where one's allies of today are the enemies of tomorrow. The very existence of the concept of truth seems to be in doubt.'

'Sad to say, not only truth, but justice also. You suggested Miller-Beach may have committed the murders himself, but though a man in his position would rarely dirty his hands with such a task, I am convinced that he not only knows who the murderer is, but that he is the directing mind behind the murders.'

'What is his motive?'

'You recall that Titchfield was listed as having held some anonymous office in Whitehall; I am sure now that it was in the same shadowy organization as Miller-Beach. I had also checked up on the ownership of the premises at number nineteen and managed to discover that the building is owned by Titchfield, and leased to Newland. We now have all the pieces of the jigsaw: Miller-Beach, Titchfield and the gallery. Miller-Beach told us that the motive for the murders was that one or more of the victims knew about what was going on in a certain house in Cleveland Street: that is true, but it was not number thirty-two, it was the picture gallery! He also said that the paraphernalia of ritual murder were used to imply some Masonic conspiracy that was devised to throw everyone off the track. That was true also, but the trail was laid by Miller-Beach and his associates, who had found out about the Fenian plot, then decided to use the City Murders to implicate the men who had been conspiring to assassinate Lord Salisbury. I suspect that the girl Harvey was singled out for that purpose: to make the story ring true of her being eliminated for having recognized Corcoran and knowing about the safe house — they needed to have someone with an Irish connection.'

'How can you be certain about this?'

'Because, there *is* no plot involving any so-called safe house.'

'But we both saw the notes and the boxes of dynamite!'

'Pshaw! We saw what we, or rather what Miller-Beach's men were meant to see: some incriminating notes written in a code; some boxes containing explosives. I went back there again last night. What do you think those boxes in the cellar contained? Harmless fog signals for railway companies, which are labelled as explosives!'

'Incredible!'

'That whole business at number thirty-two was but a clever conjuring trick, designed to deflect attention. This so-called plot to kill the Prime Minister at the Mansion House on Saturday is a mere decoy.'

'I do not understand.'

'After what Miller-Beach had told me, last night I was forced to reconsider the entire question of the interview between myself and Moriarty a few years ago. I recalled in detail the occasion that the Professor walked into my sitting room. I can only imagine that, due to my overwrought state, my powers must have somewhat temporarily deserted me — you afterwards wrote that I seemed uncharacteristically pale, drawn, and nervous at the time. The man who visited me on that day purported to be a brilliant professor, the author of a thesis so complex and innovative that it received international recognition, and a man whose gift for organization is unequalled in the annals of crime. Consider this, Watson: this apparent genius was obliged to refer to a memorandum-book simply in order to recall four recent dates — none of which was older than three months! I had never met the man before, of course, and as he had taken me by surprise, it was all the easier for the impostor to deceive me. It is impossible now to say if that was the same man I wrestled with on the edge of that gorge in Switzerland, for he wore a hat which obscured most of his features. But there can be no doubt now, though, that it was not Moriarty.

'There is an old proverb that Abrahams, the pawnbroker, used to quote. 'Fool me once,' he would say in that forlornly comical way of his, 'shame on you: fool me twice, shame on *me!*' I was determined not to be fooled twice. Could I really imagine that this undoubted genius would have engineered such an amateurish plot as this, with notes supposedly written in a code which would not deceive a schoolboy? Could I believe that his accomplices would leave boxes of dynamite lying around for days in advance for anyone to stumble over? I could not, and I did not — for I know that Moriarty is always likely to be at least one step ahead. So I went back to Cleveland Street and opened the boxes. I also took the trouble to look amongst the papers in the drawer where we found the messages. You recall how thoroughly we searched the place at the time. According to Miller-Beach, no one from the cell had visited the house since we

151

did. In that case, how could this be explained?'

Holmes handed me the note which he had transcribed: 'Patsy Harvey, ten o'clock, Sunday evening, Haymarket'.

'This was in the drawer. It had been planted there, I am sure, by one of Miller-Beach's agents to incriminate the members of the cell.'

'I think I see now,' I said.

'Beach gave himself away by being rather too eagerly curious as to what had led me to the picture gallery in the first place — that alone aroused my suspicion. I should say there is no longer room for any doubt that he went to Titchfield's last night to warn him that we were on his track.'

'Is Sir James also implicated in this?'

'I suspect not. Miller-Beach will have been allowed free rein to pursue the case as he sees fit. I'm sure there is a lot Sir James does not get to hear about.'

'Then we must move heaven and earth to expose this deception!'

'Indeed, Watson, we must and we shall, but first we have a practical problem to solve. I told you that the real assassination has been kept a complete and genuine secret.'

'Of course! What, or rather who, is the object of their campaign then?'

'I am sure it remains the Prime Minister, all right, along with his nephew — the man tipped to become the First Lord of the Treasury.'

'Balfour?

'*Bloody* Balfour as he is known in Ireland: they have not forgotten his persecution during the Land War. Clearly this plan must go off before it becomes evident that the Bankers' Dinner is a mere subterfuge; therefore, I consulted the *Gazette* in order to ascertain which other engagements the Prime Minister has between now and Saturday.'

'Good Lord, we have only two days!'

'You are aware of Lord Salisbury's interest in foreign affairs. Tomorrow, accompanied by his nephew, he is engaged to address the Friends of the Balkans Society on the Bosnia-Serbia question. The meeting is being held at Beograd House, in Hampden Terrace adjacent to the park. I walked the entire terrace from end to end this morning, and checked the lanes to the rear for manholes, lampposts, refuse bins and so on — the sorts of places a bomb might be easily concealed or planted. I found nothing. I considered whether some of the domestic staff might be implicated, and then the solution rather jumped out at me. The park is heavily wooded and the lines of sight from there to the terrace and the house are wide open — perfect conditions for a concealed sniper. At 2.45 on Friday, then, the Prime Minister's entourage will arrive; once he alights from the carriage, he will have a twenty-five yard walk from the edge of the carriage drive to the door of the house. I believe that the finger on the trigger will belong to one of the best shots in the country.'

'Colonel Sebastian Moran?'

'And I have no doubt that the weapon he intends to use will be a replica of the silent, powerful Von Herder air-gun which currently resides in the Police Museum. For a man of Moran's ability, the two statesmen would be sitting ducks.'

'What do you intend to do now?'

'I have no intention of passing my discovery to either the official police or to our friend of last night. As Mycroft remains abroad, I am afraid there is nothing for it now but to confront the man himself, and so I intend to go around to Conduit Street this morning immediately after breakfast. It would be of great service to me, Watson, if you would accompany me.'

'I absolutely insist!'

'Then it would be as well for you to bring your service revolver as this may turn out to be the second most dangerous undertaking of my career. I have a presentiment that the Colonel will fail to be amused at what we have to say to him.'

★ ★ ★

Holmes handed his card at the door, and was shown straight into the drawing room. Presently the man himself appeared. 'I shan't bother to direct you to a seat, you shall not be staying long,' he growled.

At Holmes's mention of an assassination plot, Moran laughed loudly, a sadistic mocking snort, and rather rubbed it to my friend about his failure to secure a conviction against him on the charge of murdering Ronald Adair.

'Not another one of your trumped-up charges, Holmes,' he said scornfully. 'Really, this is becoming tedious now. You know, I rather thought that you and your Scotland Yard cronies would have learned your lesson after the last time. Should you persist in this, I must warn you that I will use every inch of the law to protect my reputation.'

'Your *reputation*, Moran? What an interesting idea!' Holmes replied. 'Are you referring to your reputation for cheating at cards in the Bagatelle Club? Or the rumour of your murder of Mrs Stewart? Oh yes, I know about that, too. And then there was the sudden disappearance of Jeremy Harcourt, apothecary, lately of Fetter Lane. Yes, my researches on your behalf have been quite thorough.'

Moran's smile was viciousness personified.

'Grasping at straws again I see, Holmes. If you had the slightest evidence in any of these, you would have sent that buffoon Lestrade to arrest me. Now, if you have nothing more important to say, Benson will show yourself and Dr Watson out,' he said, as he reached to touch the bell.

'Your sympathies are as well known to the authorities as your criminal proclivities. You see, the safe house in Soho has been discovered, along with the messages which have passed between New York and London regarding the assassination of the Prime Minister at the Mansion House.'

'I have told you that I have nothing to do with any such plot, Holmes,' said Moran with exaggerated smugness.

'No, that's right; you have told the truth for once. Actually, I had come to tell you that we soon discovered that there *is* no plot.' Moran looked up sharply, as Holmes continued. 'At least there is no plot which involves the Bankers' Dinner. Whilst I admittedly found the arrangement of the stage properties in number thirty-two rather cunning at first, they were on the whole somewhat unconvincing, not to say disappointing, especially for gentlemen — to stretch a word — of yours and Moriarty's calibre.'

Moran's demeanour seemed to change, and his cruel eyes narrowed viciously, at which warning sign I cocked my revolver in my pocket.

'It rapidly became obvious that the whole business there was intended to draw attention from the real plot, which will come to fruition when a certain statesman and his kinsman make a visit to Hampden Terrace tomorrow afternoon. I have no doubt that you had already selected your vantage point. You may have been clever enough to fool the gentlemen from Whitehall for a time, but you did not fool Sherlock Holmes.'

Moran's face suddenly turned pale with rage. I had occasion once before to observe the man's wrath at close quarters, yet that was nothing compared to his reaction now. He snarled like a wild beast and leapt for the poker, but my friend had already slipped out his own revolver and now held it openly before him. Moran halted by the fireplace, still blazing and breathing fury, and he and Holmes stood there for a moment face to face, those savage eyes burning like a brazier, the murderous hand poised to strike. I had drawn my own revolver and swear that I was quite ready to press the trigger. He realized that the game was up and flung down the poker.

'You must call it off, Moran,' Holmes said evenly. 'There is no other course of action open to you. Your every move is known, the entire area will be swarming with police, and I will be there myself to ensure that nothing goes wrong. Over a hundred plain-clothes men, armed and ready, will be patrolling the precincts of the park. At the moment the evidence against you is insufficient to justify your arrest, though a warrant to search the house for the air-gun could easily be procured. Ah, there was the flicker of what passes for a smile upon your countenance — the gun is held somewhere else. Still, you must realize that to attempt any violence tomorrow would result only in certain failure, capture, and an ignominious death upon the scaffold on a charge of high treason.'

'It is not treason to right an ancient wrong.'

'It is when you have accepted a commission in the Queen's service.'

'There will be another time, Holmes, and another again, if that fails. Now get out!' he snarled with a vicious curse.

'I almost forgot,' Holmes remarked as we

backed out of the room, 'to ask you to give my compliments to Professor . . . sorry, I mean *General* Moriarty; such a pleasure to have him back. I was just saying to Doctor Watson this morning that things have been rather dull for far too long. You had better warn him, though, that I shall be looking into the recent spate of robberies with violence that has occurred. These outrages have all carried Moriarty's signature and really cannot be allowed to continue.'

★ ★ ★

'Do you think the bluff will work?' I asked my friend on our way back to Baker Street.

'Yes. He is not to know that I have said nothing to the official authorities. He will not dare to show his face. It is but from one problem to another, though, for we still have our murderer to trap, and I mean to bring him to justice. There is really only a small number of professional killers who would touch this type of work. My informant, Mercer, had drawn up a list of four suspects: Montague Parker was the first and most obvious, but as he works for Moriarty we can certainly eliminate him; then there is Teddy Hardwick, alleged founder of the Wife-Slayers' Club, and Poldy Kratz the Bavarian

— but neither man's description matches that given by Hewlett as to the man in the back of the cab; and there is Ezra Meringer who, Mercer tells me, appears to have gone into hiding. He matches perfectly.'

'Meringer?' I asked. 'I have not heard of him.'

'You have indeed, Watson, only under a pseudonym. You will recall the name Merridew from the time of the Yiddish Music Hall murder. He began as a pickpocket in Petticoat Lane; graduated as a fence with Mossy Berg in Houndsditch, took over the Cable Street gang after Pascoe Faulkner was murdered; apparently he knifed one of the Odessans in broad daylight in revenge, but no one would testify against him, such was the fear he instilled. He went to America after that and was deported once his reputation for villainy caught up with him. But not before he escaped a shootout with the Pinkertons in Anderson County, Carolina, where he murdered a sheriff and his deputy who had tried to arrest him. Reverting to his own name of Meringer, he reappeared in Bethnal Green about a year ago; word has it that it was he who garrotted the Bessarabian Tiger Maksimienko and his henchman, Kakarinov. The bodies were never found, but I suspect that the tunnels of East London Railway would be a good place to start looking.'

'Nice character!'

'Such a job would be child's play to a man of his antecedents. According to Mercer, he has not been seen in his usual haunts since the beginning of June, which corresponds to the time of the first murder. I suspect he will have been well-paid by Miller-Beach for the job, and my concern now is that he is already halfway back to America under yet another pseudonym, for he is a master at changing his identity. There is just the slightest chance that he may have decided to lie low and may have gone to ground in London rather than make a run for it.'

'But you have Thisley, his accomplice.'

'We do not, as yet, have a complete case against Thisley to go before a jury. Of Jacobs and Hewlett, only the former could give even the most tentative identification, whereas we may be certain that Titchfield would provide his man with a sound alibi. Show me the juryman who would take the word of a jarvey over that of a peer of the realm. In any case, to have Thisley arrested now — even to show the slightest suspicion of Thisley — would endanger our chances of tracking down Meringer. That is why I have kept Lestrade in the dark so far.'

'What then?'

'We are going to have to take the long way round. It remains now to find out what goes on at the Soho Picture Gallery, which would explain such an elaborate and deadly conspiracy.'

9

'So, here is my stratagem for breaching the penetralia of the gallery, Watson. Wiggins has, as you know, reported a constant coming and going of mail and telegrams, so I had begun to think that there was an opening for us. I have arranged that Cartwright, in his role as District Messenger, will go to the gallery and ask to deliver a message into the proprietor's own hand personally. It will contain nothing more than my request to become a member of the club under the name of Harris — the one I gave to the caretaker — with a false address. Once inside, Cartwright will pretend to be unwell, and will faint; it is to be hoped they will put him down somewhere to recover. He will snoop around the place if he gets a chance, and try to pick up the scent for what is going on there.'

'Is that not rather dangerous, Holmes? What if they should see through the ruse?'

'He can say that he has recovered and is well enough to leave. In any case, young men of Cartwright's type thrive on danger, Watson; after all, he is hardly a child. His lack of height, his extremely youthful appearance and frail stature belie his real age.'

'Yes, I seem to have some recollection . . . good heavens, Holmes; has it really been six years since I first came across him? How time flies.'

'Yes, though his governor predated you by a few months. I have no doubt that Cartwright will be able to take care of himself, for the vicissitudes of his life have sharpened his wits, and I have seen him in the ring, too — he is no mean brawler. In any case, you and I shall be in the vicinity during the time he is inside. I shall loiter inconspicuously in the lane behind, and I have already made my acquaintance with the lock on the gate as well as the one on the rear door of the house. You can take the front of the building, and try to remain out of sight. I suggest the bow window of the Cumberland Arms would be a good place. Should he get himself into any trouble, he has only to give a blast on an old police whistle of Lestrade's which I gave him, and we would be at his aid within minutes. He will be there at nine o'clock sharp.'

Exactly on time, Cartwright cycled up the street, stopped outside number nineteen, propped his bicycle by the railings, and rattled the door. Presently, the man we had seen a few days earlier appeared and began to question Cartwright. The latter shook his head a couple of times and made a gesture with the envelope, which he held in his hand. Eventually the caretaker opened the door and admitted him to the house, and I settled down to wait. Five or ten minutes passed, by which time I had confess I had begun to have doubts about the wisdom of Holmes's strategy. Then Cartwright appeared at the door and with great celerity, disappeared along the passage at the side of the house which led to the lane at the rear. I followed at once. By the time I had arrived there, Cartwright was breathlessly explaining something to an ashen-faced Holmes and was gesticulating wildly towards the house.

'What the deuce is going on?' I asked.

'Something that we never dreamt of in our philosophy, Watson,' said my friend, with a gesture to Cartwright.

'I was telling Mr Holmes what happened,' Cartwright gasped. 'At first, the caretaker wouldn't allow me to deliver the letter myself to Mr Newland, then he changed his mind and let me in. I was told to wait in the hall while Mr Newland was fetched. When he came back, I asked for a glass of water and put on a bit of a faint. He loosened my jacket and put me on a bed in a room. I waited a minute or two for him to go away and just as

I was about to get up and have a poke around, in comes a very portly gentleman, a proper toff! I've seen his picture in the papers. He takes his jacket off and says to me, 'A bit early aren't you?' Then he says, 'Hang on, you're not the usual boy?' I said I didn't know anything about any other boy, but that I had come to deliver a letter to Mr Newland. He laughed and said, 'Yes, that's what they all say.' Then he looked at me a bit funny and said, 'Oh I see you do have a letter. Well, don't mind what I said, young man; there seems to have been a complete misunderstanding,' and then he left the room. Soon as he was gone, I scarpered out the front door.'

'Good Lord, Cartwright,' I expostulated, 'You don't mean — '

'Yes, Doctor, it's what they call a molly house,' he replied.

'So, that's their despicable game, is it?' I thundered.

'I'm afraid so, Watson. We have been rather dim.'

'This is atrocious, Holmes!'

'Indeed; but we have no authority to enter the premises.'

'That has never held us back before!'

'I am trying to reason this out. By now, Newland may have realized something is amiss. If we wait until Lestrade arrives with a warrant, they may have time to cover things up. On the other hand, they may simply think that Cartwright has recovered and left.'

'We must do something, and immediately!'

'You are armed?'

'Of course.'

'Then my mind is made up. Cartwright, your brave conduct will not go unremarked upon. Do you think you could do one more thing for us?'

'Certainly, Sir. I am fine now, just got a bit of a shock when I realized . . . '

'Then take a cab, go straight to Inspector Lestrade and tell him exactly what has happened — here is some money. Let him know that I am here and will hold the field until he arrives.'

In point of fact, Lestrade was on the scene within half an hour. But as I recall it, that time flashed by in an instant. We were through the rear door in no time and found ourselves in the hallway. The caretaker, no doubt alerted by our footsteps, appeared at once and uttered a cry of alarm. He fled along the hall and disappeared up the staircase bellowing a warning. We raced after him to the first-floor landing only to find a door slammed in our faces. We heard him turn the key in the lock. At the same time, the sound of someone stirring in a room at the end of the hall drew our attention. We heard two voices, then the sound of a window being opened.

'They are trying to escape,' said Holmes, 'go after them and stop them while I attend to this door. You must go alone; I have no time to lose here.'

I dashed toward the room and flung the door open to find a very corpulent, red-faced, well-dressed man attempting to leave by the open window. His companion had already reached safety: a few more seconds, it seemed, and he would be clear of my grasp; and if he should gain the passage into the lane, he would be gone for good. But with his heavy frame and ungainly limbs, he was patently finding it a great effort to locate footholds on the drain pipe. His breath came in short, throaty grunts as he panted heavily with exertion. Then, either his strength or his nerve had seemed to give out, his fingers lost their grip, and he plummeted down with a hoarse shriek. I dashed across to the window and looked. A dull groan arose from the gentleman, who was now lying semi-conscious in a dishevelled heap. Blood flowed freely from the back of his head and his left leg lay at a horrible angle. He was still breathing, however, for I could see the rise and fall of his chest. But none of these things

I noticed at first: what struck me with the most incredible astonishment was that I was staring at the face of the Right Honourable Sir Gervaise Ffitch, former Cabinet Minister and Privy Councillor!

Then I heard the crash of the door at which Holmes had been heaving. It had finally given way. I returned to find a small, sparsely-furnished room which was being used as an office. The caretaker was kneeling by the fireplace frenziedly stuffing paper torn from a ledger on the hearth into the fire. He looked round fearfully as Holmes bore down on him. Panic seized him and he made a grab for a pistol from the desk drawer, but Holmes was on top of him in an instant, and whilst they rolled on the floor, I knocked the gun out of the man's hand. I dashed to the grate and saw that the fire had only recently been kindled, and so I was able to extinguish it quickly with the hearthrug and retrieve most of the contents of the grate.

'Who the hell do you think you are?' the man gasped as Holmes knelt upon his supine form.

'I am Sherlock Holmes. Where is the proprietor of this nest of debauchery?'

'Gone. Not so smart after all, are you?' the man replied.

'I know where to find Mr Charles

Newland,' said Holmes.

The caretaker answered this with a volley of foul oaths such as would shock a guardsman.

'Take it from me, my man,' Holmes continued, 'that if anyone had harmed one hair of that boy's head, they would not have walked out of this house alive. Nonetheless, this is a serious felony and not very long ago, you would have swung for this. All the same, you will be going down for a long spell.'

'If I go down, there's many a one will be coming along with me.'

'I hope so. But for the moment, I am more interested in your part in the murders. What is your name?'

'My name is George Hanby, and I will take whatever punishment is due to me for this,' he said, 'but I had nothing to do with any murders.'

'Then you knew about them and said nothing, which makes you liable to a charge of being an accessory. One of the girls who was murdered discovered what was going on here, didn't she? Either she threatened to tell the police or she tried to blackmail one of the members; perhaps your governor, too. Who was it — Jane Smart or Carden?'

Hanby made no reply.

'The police have been sent for and will

arrive shortly,' said my friend, clapping the gun to Hanby's head, 'but it would be most unfortunate if, when they arrived, they found I had shot you in self-defence after you had drawn that pistol on me.'

'Carden used to work here,' the man said. 'She left after a row with the boss. Swore she would blow the gaff on what was happening unless someone paid her off.'

'So I had thought. Who paid her?'

The man merely shrugged.

'Then she came back for more,' said Holmes, 'and someone decided to settle the matter once and for all?'

'That was nothing to do with me.'

'Well, you'll get a few years' hard for the rest.'

'I'll be well paid when I come out.'

'How do you know that?'

Hanby leered at Holmes. 'You got the book, haven't you, or most of it. Look at the names. They'll be only too happy to purchase my silence.'

I had managed to retrieve some of the papers once the fire had cooled. There were lists with times and dates next to names which were obviously those of clients. I handed everything to Holmes.

'Good Lord, Holmes,' I said, 'this will shock you to the core. It reads like a page from *Debrett's*, supplemented by the *Military Gazette* and *Crockford's Directory*. Look here!' I pointed to one of names: a member of our reigning Monarch's close family, admittedly one whose reputation for licentiousness had already been the subject of speculation in the foreign newspapers. There came the sound of a commotion at the front door, the pounding of footsteps on the staircase and Inspector Lestrade bounded in, followed by four uniformed constables. Holmes patiently explained the situation to the Inspector, and a pair of constables handcuffed Hanby and led him away.

'There is another one in the yard,' said Holmes, 'he will need some medical attention, I'm afraid. He fell from the window when attempting to escape.'

'Who is it?'

'Sir Gervaise Ffitch.'

'The Privy Councillor?'

'Yes, and there are even bigger fish in here.' Holmes handed Lestrade the torn book and damaged sheaves. 'I look to you to do your best to see that these people are brought to justice, for I need not appear in it. Find Newland and you will have the honour of arresting the vilest man in London, for not even Moriarty would have stooped to this. No doubt Newland is at present warning his clients that their cover has been blown, so I shouldn't think he would be very far away.'

Lestrade shook his head in disbelief.

'Lord Fitzallan, the Duke of Hinton, General Sir Digby Probert, Justice Harding, the Very Reverend Thaddueus Elsworthy, dear me; and it goes on and on. I am not quite sure which surprises me most: the names in this book or how you got to know about this.'

'One name you will not find there is that of Edmund Algernon Clermont. He is the owner of these premises, better known to you perhaps as the Earl of Titchfield.'

'The Whitehall mandarin?'

'Indeed he was. I cannot go into details here and now, and I must confess I am unable to prove anything at present. But I should lose no time in getting him under lock and key, for I believe he may also have played no small part in the murders which you have been investigating.'

'It's strange that you should mention his name in connection with that. We eventually found the owner of the coach with the stripes. You were right; there weren't that many after all. We questioned the coachman and his master, but they both had unshakeable alibis. I had begun to wonder if Jacobs had been mistaken — it was dark after all, when he saw the coach. Truth to tell, Mr Holmes, we have had our eyes on the mail boys and telegraph boys for some time. You see, one of our beat constables noticed that some of the boys seemed to be spending money rather more freely than their meagre wages would allow. Naturally we suspected they were pilfering, but as we had had no complaint of money or goods going amiss, we were rather stumped. I couldn't have imagined this!'

'It is young Cartwright who deserves the praise,' said my friend.

'The messenger boy from the Devonshire case?' asked Lestrade.

'Yes.'

'How did he manage to get himself mixed up in this?'

'He was our Trojan horse. I shall explain his precise part later. You know, I have a feeling that he might make a rather good policeman.'

'Perhaps he should come down to the Yard and have a word with me some time. There's just one other thing, Mr Holmes. Now, don't get me wrong. I am very grateful for what you have done here, of course. But am I to understand that both you and Doctor Watson simply barged your way in here?'

'Yes, I see now that was rather impolite of

us. In fact, the downright barefaced discourtesy of it makes me blush with shame!' My friend smiled mischievously. 'No doubt we should have waited meekly outside for you to arrive with your warrant, by which time, of course, Hanby would have burned the client list and cleaned out the grate, Ffitch could have walked straight out through the front door, and Newlands could have sat on his hands with nothing to worry about. He would have closed down the gallery here and re-opened another one in a fortnight.'

The Inspector shook his head ruefully. 'One of these days, Mr Holmes, you will go too far in taking the law into your own hands. The depravity of the culprits cannot condone — '

'One can never, in my estimation, go too far in the interests of justice,' interrupted Holmes. 'In this case, the ends amply justify my means, however dubious.'

'And I should have been only too happy,' said I, 'to defend my part in bringing this unspeakable wickedness to light.'

'I'm sure no judge and jury would see it that way,' Lestrade persisted.

'In any case, there is no reason why the doctor or I should appear in it at all,' Holmes continued diplomatically. 'The sole credit for this lies with Scotland Yard, and the criminal classes of London must realize that they cannot hoodwink Inspector Lestrade for very long.'

★ ★ ★

The events at Hampden Terrace on the Friday afternoon passed off peacefully as Holmes had expected. The following morning, Lestrade dropped in to see us. My friend assumed an attitude of complete ignorance as to the reason for his visit.

'Why, you are up and about early today, Lestrade, has something happened?' my friend said.

'No; well, yes. I suppose I mean that something didn't happen that we had expected to. It was all very *hush-hush*, and I'm afraid that is why I could say nothing to you about it beforehand.'

'Really?'

'Security of the realm, no less.'

'As serious as that?'

'Only seven people in the country knew about this, apparently. But it was a strange one altogether. You'll remember the Jubilee Plot; well, we received information that the dynamiters had set up a safe house and it was to be used in connection with an attempt on the Prime Minister's life tonight at the

Mansion House. Where do you think it was?'

'Kilburn, or perhaps Wapping? There are a lot of Irish in those districts.'

'Wrong! Only a few doors away from the Soho Picture Gallery — in Cleveland Street!'

'What an incredible coincidence!'

'The guv'nor is furious that we weren't brought in until the very last minute. A law unto themselves, these Whitehall chaps!'

'So I have heard.'

Lestrade related to us the story of the raid on the house: how they had positioned themselves at three o'clock in the morning and waited; how no one had turned up; and how the police charged in at eight o'clock and discovered the messages in the first floor room and the boxes in the cellar.

'You'll never believe what was in those boxes which we thought had contained dynamite!'

'I'm sure I wouldn't.'

'Harmless railway fog signals.'

'That's very odd.'

'Yes. Two of the men whom the Whitehall chaps were watching, and whom they expected to turn up at the house, have disappeared too. The whole setup is puzzling: a safe house, coded messages, boxes arriving in handcarts in the middle of the night. Then it's abandoned at the last moment and we find the dynamite isn't dynamite anyway — no one knows why. I'm beginning to think there is an informer somewhere within our ranks, though perhaps the whole thing might have been a hoax.'

'A hoax?' said Holmes. 'Are you sure you don't mean a decoy?'

'A decoy for what, Mr Holmes?'

'It's just a theory I had.'

'A bit far-fetched, if you don't mind my saying so; but then your knowledge of the circumstances is somewhat different from mine.'

'Very different, indeed,' Holmes agreed.

'Now about the picture gallery affair. Hanby, of course, remains under lock and key. We eventually arrested Newland outside Fitzallan's. He had, as you say, sounded the warning, and as we feared, Titchfield has fled — we suspect to France. Fitzallan and Hinton have been arrested. Probert was out of the country, as it happened, and I fear he will be in no hurry now to return. The Reverend Elsworthy has, I am grieved to say, committed suicide — or at least that is what it looks like at first hand. His body was found hanging in the vestry at Kempshott. We have also arrested Purcell from the Telegraph Office who helped procure some of the boys, and Sir Gervaise Ffitch is recovering in the prison hospital, though I suspect his reputation is now beyond recovery. We are making further inquiries into other names on the list — gross indecency will be the charge. As for our royal friend, rumour has it that his family has finally admitted that there is something seriously amiss with the fellow and have indicated that they intend to send him to Saxe-Coburg to be treated.'

'I have not lost sight of the murder investigation,' said my friend.

'I am delighted to hear that,' Lestrade answered. 'Progress seems to have been fearfully slow.'

'Yes, well I have been rather busy as you know. However, if you will return this evening at ten o'clock,' said Holmes to my astonishment as well as Lestrade's, 'I would hope to be able to present you with information which will lead you directly to the culprit.'

After Lestrade had departed, we sat over a pipe. 'I have been thinking, Holmes, was that not rather a rash promise which you made to Lestrade?'

'Not at all; you see I reasoned it out that Titchfield would have fled. With Thisley's patron and protector gone, he is bound to be feeling rather isolated, and I felt that the time may have come for us to enlighten him on the question of his identification by Jacobs and

Hewlett. It is the one card I had been forced to hold back, but I intend to play it to full advantage now.'

'What if Thisley has gone with him?'

'My dear Watson, you obviously have no idea how that class of person operates. To have taken Thisley with him would have been to multiply his chances of being caught. There is no loyalty where self-preservation is concerned amongst those people. In fact, not only have I established that Thisley remains, but I have wired him to meet us here in Baker Street this evening.'

'What makes you think he will come?'

'This,' he said, handing me a slip of paper. 'It is the content of the message Billy took down to the telegraph office earlier.'

The message read: 'Come to 221b Baker Street tonight at eight o'clock. Say nothing to anyone, Titchfield.'

10

The audacity of Holmes's note took me by such surprise that I was reduced to a fit of laughing.

'Shrewd, and yet, simple,' I remarked.

'Yes, it was the simplicity of it that appealed to me. I have, needless to say, staked all on the very high probability that Titchfield would have disappeared without a word to anyone. Thisley will be wondering what is going to become of him. Unless I am much mistaken, he will not know that his master is on the continent by now, probably living under an assumed name.'

At the appointed time, we heard a timid knock on the door, and at a sign from Holmes, I bade the visitor enter. Hardly had the man crossed the threshold, when Holmes was behind him, turning the key in the lock.

'What the deuce — ' said the man.

'I will not waste words with you, Thisley.'

'I came here to see my employer,' the visitor said indignantly.

'You came in response to my wire. I merely used your employer's name. He has left the country, probably never to return.'

'Well, that's nothing to do with me. Open that door . . . I'll not be treated this way, it's against the law.'

'So it is. But, then, so is conspiring to commit murder. Let me tell you, there will be no Police Code niceties about not forcing a confession from you; I am not bound by any laborious process, only by my conscience and a thirst for justice.'

'I don't know what you mean.'

'I think you do. The City Murders, as they have been called.'

'I've never killed anyone.'

'No, but you drove the cab for the killer. That's a capital offence in itself if it can be proven that you knew in advance!'

'I have no idea what you are talking about.'

'I warn you that your bluff is useless. I have a number of witnesses; the first is John Jacobs, the man from whom you hired the cab. He remembered you and identified you outside the Carlton a few days ago when you dropped your employer there. Then there is PC Hewlett, upon whom you practised that little deceit with the bloody knife. As you can see, I hold all the aces in this game, Thisley, now that your patron has fled and left you to face the wrath of the law. As it happens, I believe you are innocent, but you would not be the first man who went to the scaffold for a crime he did not commit. Think of the pressure on Scotland Yard to find the culprit, consider the public clamour for a scapegoat: John Henry Thisley will do as good as any. Wouldn't it be better for everyone that they hang a jarvey rather than a belted earl?'

The man's demeanour had changed abruptly, and he cowered before Holmes's tirade. He sat for a few moments in silence.

'Why haven't you called in the police?' he asked at last in a weak voice.

'Because it is the big fish I am after, not the minnows. Tell me everything that happened from the first occasion on which you were sent by Titchfield to pick up Meringer.'

'Meringer? He told me his name was Carson.'

'I can assure you I know the fellow well. Go on.'

'M'lord said that this man, Carson, was a friend of his. I hired the cab and went to collect this gentleman. First thing he did made me a bit suspicious; he got me to slip a false number over the original one. Then we went down to the Haymarket to pick up a girl.'

'Where did you meet Meringer?'

'At Radlett's Temperance Hotel.'

'He was staying there?'

'I believe so.'

'And you chose the girl at random?'

'Meringer did it. I swear I had no idea that he was going to murder her. I thought it was . . . you know . . . twice round the park with the blinds drawn. But Meringer shouted an address to me and off we went. When we got there, he dragged her limp body out of the cab. 'What's going on?' I cried. He whipped out a pistol and shoved it in my face. 'You'll keep your mouth shut if you know what's good for you,' he said, 'now get back up there!' Then he just dumped the body in the lane and we cleared off. I could see that I was already in it up to my neck. I told m'lord about it when I got back, but he just laughed and said I had better carry on, or Carson, as he called him, would do for me, too. I was being well paid, he said, but then he said something strange: he said not to worry, for we would never be caught; he had a friend in a high place and they had already got a plan together to pin the murders on someone else. I have no idea who he meant. I could see that if I tried to back out then, and went to the police, they wouldn't believe me.'

'On the second and third occasions, however, you went looking for a specific individual, did you not?'

'I was so terrified I can scarcely remember.'

'Tell me about the episode of the knife.'

'We had turned into a quiet street about one in the morning, and I saw a copper approaching us. My hands began to shake and I was going to turn the cab round and make a bolt for it, but Meringer opened the trap door and said, 'You'll do no such thing; our flight would arouse his suspicion. Stop right here and wait for him to come up. Tell him you are taking me home to Smithfield and that there is something wrong with the catch on the door.' Then he pulls out a knife and I thought he was going to chive the copper right there and then — I began to protest. But then he cut a little nick on his forearm, smeared some of the blood on the blade of the knife, and threw it into a shop doorway. He told me to draw the constable's attention to the bloody knife. I did so, and as soon as the copper turned his back, I gave the horse a clout and away we trotted. I remembered then that we had a false number on, and there was probably nothing to worry about.'

'Did you know what was going on at the Soho Picture Gallery?'

'I never set foot inside the place, but all the servants had heard rumours.'

'And you know why your employer sent you with Meringer?'

'I began to understand after a while.'

'What do you intend to do for work, in the meantime?'

'I am going back to my old job with the railway company.'

'I am afraid, though, that you will still have to answer for your part in this. You have a choice: I can send for Inspector Lestrade from Scotland Yard and turn you over to him; or you can write down what you have just told us and sign it. I will retain this until we have Meringer safely behind bars. If I am able to track him down with the information you have provided to me, I feel sure that you will be treated leniently.'

'You mean turn Queen's evidence?'

'I cannot see that you have any choice.'

'Give me the pen,' the man said, after a pause, 'I will sign.'

'You will have to incriminate your employer as well as Meringer.'

'Why should I give a damn about *him*?! He has left me to face the music.'

Once Thisley had left, my friend said, 'I think I owe it to Lestrade to hand the entire case over to him now.'

'You are not going after Meringer yourself, then?' I asked.

'No. There is no need for any further secrecy, and I should think there would be no difficulty in finding him at Radlett's. I had been puzzled at first as to how Meringer managed to slip in and out of the hotel at all hours of the night without arousing suspicions, but it occurs to me that he would have been cunning enough to ask for a ground-floor room and could have used the window. I had thought he might have fled, too, but I now see there is no reason for him to flee — to do so would only raise suspicion. Knowing how deeply implicated Thisley is, he will not fear exposure from that quarter.'

As it happened, Lestrade called upon us just after the clock struck 9.30: no doubt he was impatient to discover what progress Holmes had made. My friend handed over Thisley's confession and patiently explained all he knew about the case, going over those points in minute detail which were confusing and complicated.

'Then all this malarkey about crowns and corn was simply a blind after all?' the Inspector asked.

'It was a kind of double bluff on the part of those who were planning the murders. I am sure they recalled the public speculation about ritual murder and Masonic conspiracies during the last case, and the sensational treatment it received in the press. No doubt they believed they could harness the idea to make good a propaganda exercise. I must allow, it was devilishly clever.'

'I think we may find it difficult to implicate this Miller-Beach character,' Lestrade said.

'I confess I am not absolutely certain as to his precise part in this triumvirate of evil, but if he was not the instigator, then he certainly had the guilty knowledge of what was going on. There is little proof against him and the only person who can incriminate him is Titchfield. Now let me warn you that this man, Meringer, is extremely dangerous, and you shall have to take him unawares. He may attempt to shoot his way out of it, for I think that he would rather go down fighting than submit to the ignominy of dying on the scaffold.'

'We shall take every precaution, as you suggest. After the Addleton raid, we have been rather more careful in dealing with this type of situation.'

Lestrade was as good as his word, for Meringer was captured with little difficulty and no violence, and was subsequently arraigned for trial on the evidence provided by the cabman who had been his accomplice.

I have already alluded elsewhere to the remarkable sequence of cases that the year 1895 brought us and so will not elaborate here. But by the beginning of July, Holmes was so often absent from Baker Street that I was forced to trawl alone through the newspapers for news of both affairs, that of the City Murders and of the Soho Scandal, as it was called.

'I do not like the look of it,' he said to me in a concerned tone one morning on his return. 'Meringer gave in without a fight; it does not sound like him at all. As for the other case, there has hardly been whisper in the press. You would have thought that scandal sheets would be having a field day.'

He bore his disappointment well, but worse was to come before very long. Lestrade visited us one morning a few weeks later. The first thing I noticed was the look of frustration which the Inspector flashed at us as he took a chair in the sitting room.

'Well, Lestrade, what is the news?' my friend asked.

'You mean you haven't heard?'

'Heard what?'

'About Thisley.'

'You don't mean he has recanted his confession?'

'You have not read the morning papers, then?'

'I was half-way through the agony column when the doorbell rang.'

'Then you had better read this,' the Inspector handed my friend a copy of the

Morning Post, 'page seven, bottom left.'

'"Man Dies Under His Own Van: Serious Head Injuries," Holmes read out. 'Listen to this, Watson. 'There occurred late last night a fatal accident to John Henry Thisley, 42, of Chichester Road, Paddington, presently employed as a freight car man by the Great Western Railway Company. There were no witnesses to the accident, which happened in Bourne Terrace, a quiet street near Westbourne Green.' I am sure there weren't!

'It continues, 'The wheel of his van seems to have clipped a high kerb, and he was thrown from the vehicle, his head crushed by the wheels of his own van and the hoofs of his horse.' Damn it! This was no accident, nor was it any coincidence.'

'We will never prove otherwise, Mr Holmes.'

'Even the least credulous conspiracist will admit that it is unusual for a cabman to be run over by his *own* cab — a few hundred yards from his front door. The article below it goes on, 'The fastest vehicles on four wheels in London — excepting the fire tenders — are the railway goods carts. Owing to the railway companies' miserly policies of paying low wages, most of the drivers begin as railway porters and have never handled a whip or rein until they are almost ready to climb upon the box.' What twaddle! Thisley came from a family of cabmen, he had been a gentleman's coachman, and he was anything but inexperienced in handling horse, cab or freight van. I detect the hand of Miller-Beach.'

'It means, of course, that I shall be obliged to release Meringer,' said Lestrade. 'I am afraid PC Hewlett's report merely mentions that he saw a foreign-looking man with dark hair and a sallow complexion — that could be almost anyone. Besides which, it was at night and Meringer was in the corner of the cab with his face turned away. We had Hewlett down at the Yard this morning to look at Meringer, he says he cannot be sure it was the same man.'

Holmes groaned.

'You had better hear it all at once,' the Inspector continued. 'When I read some of the names on that list at the Soho Picture Gallery . . . well, I knew that they would do all in their power — and some of these people possess enormous power — to stop the case coming to court. This morning, the Prime Minister told the Commissioner that he has refused application to institute extradition proceedings against Titchfield. Fitzallan and Hinton have absconded and — '

'You mean they have been allowed to abscond, perhaps even ordered to disappear,' interrupted Holmes.

'More than likely,' Lestrade nodded, 'and His Royal Highness has been packed off to a Hessian sanatorium. I have been ordered to drop the case against these four, and I am now powerless to proceed.'

Holmes's eye took on a cold, hard glitter. 'You may rest assured that even if justice cannot be done in full measure, the British public has a right to know about this, and they *shall* know the full facts. I had a premonition as to what might happen, and I have already considered what arrangements may need to be made to ensure the matter finds its way into the public realm.'

'I hardly need to remind you of the law of libel, Mr Holmes. I should not like to think of either you or Doctor Watson breaking stones in Pentonville.'

'Fear not,' my friend replied, 'I have no intention of entangling the doctor in this. I have in mind quite another method, and I also have the best possible defence against a charge of libel — *Veritas!*'

After Lestrade had gone, we sat in empty silence for some time. Finally, Holmes broke in on my thoughts.

'I have always prided myself on my superiority over the official force,' he said, 'yet I feel I have hardly risen above their level of mediocrity in the present case. It is true to say that this has undoubtedly been the most unsatisfactory point in my career; as my chronicler, you are bound to record my failures as well as my successes. If I had not been so slow off the mark, we could have taken Titchfield as well, and possibly Miller-Beach.'

'Don't be so hard on yourself, man!' I said. 'You managed to clear up two serious criminal cases which had eluded the police, and by your action, probably saved the life of the Prime Minister and another senior statesman. It is the most complicated affair I can ever recall. Such deception and intrigue; and from the beginning every hand was against us.'

'Including one of the hands of the state,' he said in a voice laden with dismay.

Epilogue:
From the Diary of Doctor John H. Watson

It may have been due to the part Holmes played in a celebrated espionage case later that year (which involved trapping a dangerous spy who had murdered a young naval architect); or it may have been that the story of Holmes's part in foiling the attempt on the Prime Minister's life at Beograd House had come to the ears of someone in authority; whatever the reason, in June the following year my friend was offered the Royal Victorian Order for his services to the realm. His egalitarian spirit was generally against such decorations and he believed, like an old soldier, that to be called upon to render service in a just and proper cause was sufficient reward in itself. He also believed, quite frankly, that the Prime Minister had irretrievably compromised the high ideals of his office in dealing with the Soho scandal and felt that, as his nomination for the Order was issued on that statesman's personal recommendation, he would have been in some way tainted by this. He had likewise, at

King Edward's coronation, refused a knight-hood, although he had accepted the *Ordre National de la Légion d'honneur* as a *Chevalier* from Monsieur Sadi Carnot out of respect for his French antecedents — much to Mycroft's great annoyance and discomfiture.

As to the scandal in Soho, however, Sherlock Holmes did indeed have one further trick up his sleeve, as he had warned Inspector Lestrade. One afternoon in July, he called upon an old university associate of his, Mr Langdale Pike, at his lair in St James's, and laid the story before him. An idealist with an ineradicable iconoclastic strain, Pike had made my acquaintance some years before. Although he had, on that occasion, been of inestimable service to Holmes in a rather complicated case, I must say frankly that I did not like the man, for I found him conceited, arrogant and affected. He was the founder of the Fellowship of the Left Ear — a coterie of writers so cynical and misanthropic, it made Mycroft's Diogenes Club cronies look gregarious — and was a celebrated society gossipmonger, whose scurrilous columns were to be found in the more salacious magazines and vulgar newspapers, a profession which I found distasteful and effeminate. My friend assured me that despite appearances, Pike often suppressed more scandal than he retailed and that he had become a society columnist largely out of abhorrence at the antics of the upper classes.

'Langdale Pike is justly famous for never having been open to any bribes or amenable to any threats,' said my friend. 'He is quite fearless, is quite immune to the vagaries of public, or any other, opinion, and embodies Wellington's own maxim about writing without fear or favour, regardless of class or status.'

He assured Holmes that the matter would receive his urgent attention and that he would not be deterred by threats of legal action from naming the parties involved. That the fellow had influence amongst the low-circulation radical newspapers was undeniable, and the following week, the story was splashed across the front page of one such paper, the *Clerkenwell Free Press*, which made comparisons to the odious days of the Hell-Fire Clubs and Beggar's Benison. The circulation of many of these newspapers quadrupled for a period following Pike's revelations. One of the Russian émigré newspapers had got hold of the story, too, as did the *Arbeter Fraint* and the *Fáinne An Lae*; and so the scandal ended up being retold in four languages. No qualms were shown about naming either the individuals concerned in the scandal or the organizations which were suspected of covering them up. The story had reached France where the press drivelled over every iota of the scandal, and revelled in the gory details of the murders that had been committed in order to prevent the scandal leaking out. One Boston newspaper leader thundered on about the inbred royal stock of Europe becoming deteriorated bodily and mentally, speculated upon the end of the monarchy, and went so far as to predict that England 'would never have another king'.

The ramifications of the affair continued for several months: there were claims and counter-claims in both the mainstream and radical press, and threats of libel abounded. The editor of the Russian journal was deported, questions were asked in Parliament and one radical member was expelled from the Lower House for calling the Prime Minister a liar. A fortnight after Holmes's visit to St James's, only a strict recluse could not have heard of the case, and I confess I was, as a result, forced to alter my view of Mr Langdale Pike. It was inevitable, however, that he would eventually become the defendant in a defamation case along with Mr Ernest Fields, the proprietor of the

Hackney Clarion. As it happened, Pike and Fields lost the defamation case and received twelve months each.

'As I recall,' said Holmes when we heard the news, 'Pike was rusticated on a number of occasions at university for producing outrageous lampoons in a university magazine, so he is no stranger to banishment. It will merely augment his reputation. I had considered raising a subscription for his benefit to take account of his loss of earnings whilst in Pentonville, but he assures me that having foreseen his fate somewhat in the latter days of the trial, he has already negotiated a healthy, large advance from his publisher to produce an account of life in prison. I am informed that *Langdale Pike's Prison Diaries* will appear next year! Did I not say what a remarkable character he was, Watson?'

The case against Meringer was dismissed due to lack of evidence and his accomplice, Titchfield, remained in France, safe from the laws of England. Miller-Beach disappeared completely from public life. The death of the earl's former coachman was, despite a number of practical objections raised by Holmes, recorded at the coroner's inquest as an unfortunate accident. When the accused were brought to trial in the Soho case, those who were convicted received between four and six months' imprisonment. There were many at the time who believed the very lenient sentences handed down to the convicted men in the dock by his Lordship represented a *quid pro quo* for keeping far more august and eminent figures out of the limelight. After the case was over, Cartwright — on Lestrade's recommendation and to Holmes's great delight — joined the ranks of the Metropolitan Police Force in H Division. There was a tragic postscript, however: the royal personage who was implicated in the scandal took his own life with a revolver whilst interned in an asylum on the banks of the Rhine.

'Twelve months for telling the truth, six months for loathsome debauchery, and a whole triumvirate of murderers walk free.' I shook my head in deep despair as I sat after dinner with Holmes one summer evening.

'One recalls Swift's epigram, Watson: 'The Law is like a cobweb which catches small harmless flies but lets the wasps and hornets through.''

The Adventure of the
Edmonton Horror

Throughout my many years of acquaintance with Sherlock Holmes I can recall, from more than a hundred of his adventures (to which he referred, with characteristic self-effacement, as 'my trifling achievements'), a small number of cases which stretched beyond the merely strange and seemed, perhaps, to have bordered on the supernatural: none more so than that which is recorded in my notes for the year 1897. It was a particular facet of Holmes's character that whenever he was presented with a problem of this sort, he would scathingly dismiss, *a priori*, any suggestion of supernatural cause or influence and seek, instead, natural explanations. He also bore a remarkable capacity for gallows humour, or what the French call *rire jaune:* 'no ghosts need apply,' he had once told me with marked sarcasm. However, once my friend had become acquainted with the details of the affair which Inspector Wills of the Middlesex Constabulary called one day in late autumn to lay before us, even *his* agnosticism towards the supernatural was at first somewhat shaken. It was undoubtedly one of the strangest beginnings to any of the cases I had ever come across, the outlandish features of which resulted in the wildest speculation in the London press at the time.

At that point in my life, I had retired from regular practice and had gone back to my old quarters in Baker Street. October had been an unusually quiet month, and the brief hiatus in my friend's consulting work allowed him to labour without interruption on the completion of a number of monographs upon which he was engaged; namely, the provincial accents and dialects of the English language, and a paper on the history of bee-keeping to be presented to the British Apiary Society. I recall that it was the first day of November and the onset of chills and fogs had arrived with perfect seasonality. Holmes was generally immune to the state of the weather, but on this occasion he was in one of his more cantankerous moods — the reason for which will soon become apparent. He could be as capricious as a woman and twice as cutting, and I should have said that I was a fair judge. We had just consumed a most excellent lunch and sat musing over the postprandial coffee. As I glanced over the newspapers, Holmes began to pore over the midday post which lay unopened whilst we had attacked the dish of devilled kidneys prepared by Mrs Hudson.

'A rather mixed bag today,' he muttered to me, as the maid finished clearing away the crockery. 'I feel like the poacher's wife in the fable; you know, the one who discovered the trout in the rabbit traps and the pheasant on the hook at the end of the fishing line. I believe this is your doing, Watson,' he continued, looking up sharply as he indicated the object of his attention. 'How often have I railed against your meretricious treatment of my *métier*? See what it has brought us to now!'

He tossed over a letter, very neatly handwritten in purple ink on lilac notepaper, on which he had underlined some of the words:

' . . . anticipate your support for our proposal to establish a London branch of the Sherlock Holmes Appreciation Society to celebrate the glittering accomplishments of your illustrious career . . . your gracious acceptance of our invitation to address the inaugural meeting which is being held in the Cordwainers' Hall, Pepys Lane on . . . '

So it went on. I looked up with a mixture of disbelief and chagrin to meet that withering gaze, which could be worse than a dozen of his wounding words — yet another characteristic he shared with womanhood.

'They seem to wish to turn me into some sort of national spectacle,' he rasped. 'Perhaps I shall end up on exhibition in a penny gaff in the Whitechapel Road, or on the bill at the Hackney Empire sandwiched between Daisy O'Malley and Conan & Doyle, guessing the occupations of the patrons in the stalls.'

'The intention is well meant, no doubt, my dear fellow,' I replied soothingly. 'I see that they go on to mention that your brilliance is especially appreciated at the palace, and indicate the possibility of securing a royal patron for the society.'

'They might at least have waited until I was dead.' He seemed in no mood to be humoured as he continued, 'Well, the matter is closed now.'

'Closed?' I asked.

'At any rate I intend to draft a reply — in the name of Doctor John H. Watson, of course, to which you will afterwards append your signature — explaining that this Sherlock Holmes person to whom they refer does not actually exist and that he is merely a literary invention of your own.'

'Very droll, Holmes,' I retorted, although my amusement was mixed with some relief in that he seemed to have somewhat recovered his acerbic wit. 'Of course, no one will believe that.'

206

'No? Well, I am sure they will take the hint. Now, from the ludicrous to the fantastic: look at this one — it *is* rather fine, is it not?' he said, shaking his head as passed me a second slip of paper. The note read:

Have you ever known of vampires in London? Will call later over Edmonton. Insp. John Norman Wills, Middx. Const.

I looked up at Holmes in surprise.

'It is certainly the time of year for troubled, restless and wandering souls,' he said with a sardonic glance at the calendar.

'I cannot recall the name Wills.'

'On the contrary, I believe we can claim the Inspector's acquaintance. You will recall the Maberley case a year or so ago. Let me see, letter postmarked 8.43, in Lower Edmonton, so our man was up and about in time to catch an early post. One would surmise that something has occurred there during the night. Now then, Watson, what have we learned about vampires since last time?'

Despite his cold, sceptical exterior and his intolerance towards superstition, Holmes was nevertheless assiduous in keeping what he called, with typical self-irony, his 'uncommonplace book.' This contained a collection of some of the strangest and most mysterious occurrences ever recorded in the capital, and a common feature of these phenomena, many of which had passed into myth, was that they had remained in some way either unexplained or unresolved. I forbore to publish such apocrypha, for whatever interest they may have held for a connoisseur of curiosities or a student of the bizarre, it seemed to me that to disclose a problem without revealing a solution amounted to a short-changing of the reading public. Of particular interest amongst the curiosities in this *index incredibilis* were: a transcription, long suppressed by official-dom, of an account by the magistrate in charge of the Ratcliff Highway Murders which named the true culprits; a deathbed confession by a witness in the celebrated Constance Kent murder case which threw light on a number of factors which had confounded Detective Inspector Whicher at the time; several reports of sightings of the giant black swine of Hampstead; an account of the London tram which vanished with its crew and passengers in a Christmas fog on Highgate Hill and was never seen again; and the discovery of the most extraordinary reliquary in an underground passage in Wellclose Square, thought to have been the site of a long-abandoned coven of Kabbalists. Of bloodsucking creatures of the night, however, there was no mention.

'Nothing under vampires,' I replied, 'though,

of course, we have since had a recent addition to our popular literature on the subject. Some Irish writer, whose brother is a fellow medical.'

'Utter balderdash, Watson! How people can be diverted by such mediaeval nonsense in this nineteenth century of ours passes all understanding!'

'Well,' I replied, feeling rather resentful at having the work dismissed so glibly when I had read that it was rather well written, 'there are people still alive today who can recall when suicides were buried at a crossroads with stakes driven through their hearts; it was not so long ago, you know.'

'Have you read the book?' he asked.

'In fact I haven't, though the reviewer in the new *Daily Mail* seems to have approved.'

'Pshaw! It is not often that I find myself sharing a viewpoint with the Prime Minister, but I must say I am forced to agree with him: vacuous phrase-mongering, gimmicks, and . . . *prizes!* He ought to have described it as 'fit for school boys' rather than 'office boys'. Well, you have seen the note, what do you make of it?'

'The 'x' in his abbreviation of 'Middlesex' is quite twice the size of the preceding letters and the writing goes off at all angles, here upwards, here downwards, sometimes sloping to the left, sometimes to the right. Going by the untidy scrawl, I should have said it had been written by some uneducated person,' I ventured, 'perhaps one of his subordinates?'

'I think not. The note displays all the hallmarks of a man unable to think in a very straight fashion and I should say that is what explains the hurried scribble. Despite the handwriting being rather awry, his punctuation, which is instinctive, is perfect. He also manages to include his middle name, an action which, you must owe, would hardly occur to a subordinate, and which has not the slightest relevance; whereas he has omitted to mention a single useful detail of the case. He has made one rather obvious error too.'

'What is that?'

'If he wished to engage my urgent attention, surely a reply-paid telegram would have reached me in a fraction of the time taken by a letter, and would not only confirm my preparedness to meet him, but possibly prevent his arriving here in my absence. I presume, therefore, he had dashed this off before he had time to gather his wits. Nothing in the papers, I suppose?'

'Nothing that could possibly be associated with this note.'

'Hm. Wills struck me as the type of policeman who embodies sound, stolid,

English common sense. He has nearly thirty years' experience in the force; that he should be so disturbed as to pen such a note must give rise to no small concern. I am afraid the dull, genteel northern suburbs are rather *terra ignota* to me, so if you would be so good as to hand me down the volume containing the 'E's. Thank you, let's see now . . . the Edge Hill Murder, the Edinburgh Poisoning, outbreak of mass hysteria in Beaumaris, Edmonton, Alberta; then there's Edmonton Street, Mayfair — you remember the infamous Tiger of San Pedro eluded the plain-clothes man there — ah, here it is: 'Edmonton: parish in Middlesex, eight and a half miles north east of Charing Cross. Ermine Street, listed in the *Domesday Book* . . . blah, blah . . . town hall built in 1884.' Listen to this, Watson: 'The chiefly rural Edmonton has held a reputation for the supernatural. Peter Fabell, known as the Devil of Edmonton, burnt at the stake in the fifteenth century; the Witch of Edmonton, Elizabeth Sawyer, burnt at the stake in 1621'; a stronghold of religious dissent and nonconformism, it seems, which is no doubt why we find an Anglican bishop describing the place as 'the head of the serpent' in that strife-torn year of 1666. Rather colourful history, is it not?'

'So much for your genteel suburb, Holmes!'

'Indeed. And it goes on: this brief history mentions the ancient fair of Edmonton 'with all its mirth and drollery, its swings and roundabouts, its spiced gingerbread, and wild-beast shows'; in 1820 a lion tamer was eaten when one of his charges went mad, 'a magnificent Barbary lion' apparently. When the parish constables arrived to investigate, the circus owner — a woman — threatened to open the cage and let loose the beast upon them!'

'Strange how the aura of maleficence seems to linger over certain places down the ages,' I said. 'I should not be surprised to find that someone has produced a theory upon it.'

'I fear it would be a rather far-fetched one, Watson, but the place is certainly living up to its reputation. Now that I come to think of it, I recall from my university theatrical days a Jacobean play about the Witch of Edmonton. The Puritans banned it in their time, of course, and it remained forgotten and unperformed for centuries until some enterprising person in the Trinity Dramatic Club discovered it amongst the relics of the *Stationers' Register*. It was as much pantomime as tragedy, for it involved a case of bigamy, a devil dog, a cat that could speak, and a bewitched codpiece.' Holmes smiled mischievously.

'Really, Holmes, your ideas of humour can be quite outlandish.'

'And not infrequently objectionable; yes, I am aware of that. Lestrade has mentioned it on a number of occasions.'

'There are times when I don't quite — '

'Ah, unless I am mistaken, here is the man now,' he interjected, as we heard the doorbell ring. Very shortly afterwards, a stocky, red-faced, bucolic man in a tweed suit, whom I recognized from Holmes's earlier reference, appeared at the sitting room door. He looked flushed and agitated, and bore the appearance of a well-dressed ploughman come to town for the day, rather than a police detective. He nodded to us both and sat down in the easy-chair which Holmes indicated to him with the stem of his pipe.

'I have just opened your letter, Inspector Wills, and was recalling to Doctor Watson the incident where we first met at Harrow Weald,' said my friend.

'Yes, we got our men in the end and it turned out we didn't need you after all. Still, it's always an education to listen to your theories, and that's why I have come. It really *is* a most extraordinary occurrence, and I'm still not quite sure if it is a case for a detective, a clergyman, or an occultist,' the Inspector said anxiously.

'Excellent,' said Holmes, rubbing his hands and looking at me with barely-concealed delight, 'we shall retain the other two professions in reserve until we have exceeded the jurisdiction of the first.'

'I'm not quite sure where to start, gentlemen,' he said with the look of a man at his wits' end, as he dug out his notebook.

'Try the beginning,' said Holmes. 'I am bound to warn you, however, that someone recently tried to convince me that they had discovered a vampire down in rural Lamberley, but upon investigation it turned out to be nothing more sinister than the resentful fury of a spoilt child. At which solution, I had arrived,' my friend continued, 'without actually having to leave Baker Street.'

'Well, I'm not so sure that you will be able to dismiss this case quite so lightly,' he went on doggedly with an emphatic shake of the head, 'no, I'll wager you will not.'

'Pray continue, then.'

'I was called out at about eight o'clock this morning to an address in Lower Edmonton, the home of a young spinster, a Miss Ruth Farnham, aged twenty-seven, who works at the library. She had been found dead in her bed by the woman who comes in to do general work for her, a Mrs Kenny, an excitable Irish widow. The sight of Miss

Farnham's corpse struck Mrs Kenny with such a complete hysteria that her frenzied screaming aroused one of the neighbours, a Mr Danvers Crane, a schoolmaster, who made his way immediately to the house. By the time he arrived there, Mrs Kenny had fallen into a faint and was lying in a heap on the floor. It wasn't simply the fact that Miss Farnham was dead . . . ' His voice trailed off as he evidently sought to marshal the correct words to describe the scene.

'Take your time,' said Holmes soothingly, 'and tell me everything in order.'

'After arriving at her normal time and finding her mistress absent from downstairs, Mrs Kenny then ascended to the first-floor bedroom. Miss Farnham was never a late riser, she was a regular churchgoer, you see, one of the type that is forever wrapped up in the work of committees for doing good works. Mrs Kenny at first thought that perhaps the woman had taken ill and had lain in a bit longer. When she opened the bedroom door she received the shock of her life, which set off in her such a sudden panic and terror.'

'One moment; was the window open or closed?'

'It was wide open . . . why do you ask that?'

'Please continue, I shall return to that point.'

'Mrs Kenny found Miss Farnham lying on the bed, on top of the counterpane, dressed in a white wedding gown as though arrayed for the bridal. On closer inspection, she turned out to be stiff and cold, with that pallor which comes only with death — Mrs Kenny was formerly a nurse and she recognized the symptoms of *rigor mortis* right away. The dead woman's neck was bare, and on the left side of it, her flesh was marked with two small very neat puncture wounds rather less than an eighth of an inch in diameter, separated by a space of about an inch and a half. The wounds are too large to have been made by the fangs of any native species of snake,' Wills looked across at me strangely and said in a voice that had dropped to a whisper, 'but the doctor here will know that the distance between the wounds approximates to the space between . . . a pair of human canine teeth.'

'Why, I suppose it is,' I said.

'The police surgeon, Dr Pardoe, made mention of it, too. Here is his note, it says: 'two punctures which penetrated the flesh and resulted in a double perforation of the external jugular vein. Likely cause of death: haemorrhage.''

'It must have been a pretty gory scene, then,' said Holmes.

'No, that's just it, Mr Holmes,' said Wills, with a shake of his head and a tremor in his voice, 'there wasn't a speck of blood anywhere in the room.'

There was a silence, as Wills looked at one, then the other of us. He continued, 'The corpse of the poor woman seemed almost to have been drained of blood!'

I must confess that I felt a creeping sensation at the man's words, and even Holmes's usual imperturbability was dispelled.

'You are certain of this?' he asked, fixing the Inspector with his gaze as he leant forward. I could see by his expression that he was deeply intrigued.

'Absolutely. The corpse lay there as white as a sheet, with those two faint pinpricks of red on her neck. I have seen plenty of murders, but her expression bore no sign of the fear or horror which you would expect to see given the fate that had overtaken her. It was as if she had submitted to her death willingly.'

'Dear me,' said Holmes shaking his head, 'this grows more mysterious.'

'There is more to tell,' Wills went on. 'Mrs Kenny noticed that a crucifix which normally hung on the wall above the woman's bed was missing.'

'Most singular.'

'The bedroom opens on to the adjacent churchyard; and the window, as I told you, was wide open in spite of the chill. There were marks on the sill which seemed to suggest that someone or *something* had effected an entrance by that means.' He paused to consult his notebook.

'What was the time of death?' asked Holmes.

'It has been impossible to tell, but Dr Pardoe confirmed that the *rigor mortis* which had set in, had not begun to dissipate.'

'That would put the time at roughly between about four to twelve hours beforehand,' I said.

'Yes, he had said he believed it was some time during the night, probably after midnight.'

'But that is purely conjecture at this stage,' interjected Holmes, 'until the official post-mortem results are to hand.'

'No, I don't believe so; you see, there is something else. This morning it had been brought to the attention of the beat constable, Jennings, who was just finishing on night duty, that one of the crypts in the graveyard seemed to have been opened during the night. On searching the area, he found the crypt door lying open and signs that it had, indeed, been disturbed. On entering the crypt, he discovered one of the old coffins with its lid removed. Jennings had passed through the churchyard before midnight the previous evening — it is his custom to make sure there are no drunks or vagrants skulking around there after the public houses have closed — he saw nothing unusual, and would certainly have noticed if the door of the crypt had been open. Do you know what was in the coffin?'

Holmes shook his head.

'Nothing, Mr Holmes; it was completely empty. Whoever, or whatever, was in it had vanished.'

'You examined it yourself *after* the discovery of the murder?'

'Yes.'

'How old was the coffin?'

'It was a very old one.'

'Then I suppose we can rule out the depredations of resurrectionists,' said Holmes with some asperity.

'I ought to mention the dead woman's diary,' Wills continued. 'Given the strange circumstances, it occurred to Sergeant Channon that Miss Farnham may have kept a diary and that there might be some clue in it. It was found in a drawer in her bedroom.'

'Excellent!' said Holmes. 'The sergeant is

to be congratulated on his presence of mind; he will go far in the service.'

'He is the youngest sergeant in the Middlesex force,' said Wills, with the genuine admiration of a teacher for his brightest pupil. 'I have the diary here — I read through it on the journey down in the cab. Some of the entries gave me a chill of horror.'

'Go on.'

'The entry for August thirteenth reads: 'We met again. A mysterious change of mood came over me, which dissipated once we parted. An hour after midnight, still I can find no rest.' Then there is September tenth: 'I felt once more that strange unearthly attraction and an excitement that quickened my pulse, though I could not say whether with fear or with longing. Another sleepless night.' Then finally, on October eighth: 'a burning sensation of welling desire mingled at the same time with the deepest revulsion.' Miss Farnham does not give a name or even the initials of the man she met on these occasions.'

'I see you have made the assumption, then, that her companion on these occasions was male,' said Holmes with a smile.

'My dear Holmes!' I ejaculated.

'I do not know what to make of it,' Wills shrugged wearily. Then he continued, 'Do you notice a correspondence between these dates?'

'Yes, they are all Fridays,' replied Holmes.

'More to the point, Mr Holmes, each date is either on or near to the day of the full moon!'

Holmes had been making some brief notes as the Inspector talked, and now he looked across at me. 'It is certainly a most intriguing problem. Wouldn't you say so, Watson?' he asked.

'*Intriguing?* Good lord, I have heard nothing quite like it!' I replied, still dazed at the Inspector's account. 'I can recall cases from the past which may have at first appeared strange or grotesque, but I cannot think of one which I could truthfully describe as *macabre.*'

'I have never come across anything like it in all my years in the force,' added Wills. 'I am at a loss to know what to do next.'

'Let us recapitulate, then. Your theory, Inspector, is that Ruth Farnham had first been visited by this person on the dates you mention, as some sort of precursor to the events which followed?'

The Inspector nodded vaguely.

'And that she was subsequently murdered by this same person, or creature, which drank her blood and which had heretofore been residing in a coffin in the adjacent graveyard, but for some reason has not returned to its lair?'

'I hesitate to put it with such certainty, but . . . the evidence, Mr Holmes.'

'I find the evidence anything but conclusive. So far, the doctor and I have restricted the foci of our inquiries to the living and the dead; we have, as yet, failed to discover any intermediate state.'

'With respect, Mr Holmes, you would perhaps not talk so lightly of the matter if you had seen what I had. Consider the facts, Sir: the nature of the woman's injuries; the absence of any bloodstains; the open window; the disappearance of the crucifix; the empty coffin; the strange talk of the attraction and repulsion of this mysterious midnight visitor who appears at the same point in the lunar cycle!'

'I'm not sure exactly what it is you want me to do. If you believe that this is beyond the bounds of nature, then it is certainly beyond Sherlock Holmes. Perhaps it is a clergyman that you ought to consult after all.'

'If you would only come out to Lower Edmonton and take a look — '

'Why not call in Scotland Yard?'

The man hesitated, 'Well . . . '

'You do not wish to seem credulous?'

'I would wish to be more certain that I had ruled out any logical explanation, and if I call in the Scotland Yarders, I should be robbed of any credit, though there is likely to be precious little of that.'

'Well, Watson, as we seem to have nothing else to do, what do you say to a vampire hunt through the suburbs?'

'Things have been rather too quiet for some time now,' I replied, eager to be gone, for the Inspector's story had kindled in me the most intense curiosity.

'Perhaps, in view of the singular features of the case,' said Holmes mordantly, as he rose to collect his coat and hat, 'we should prevail upon Mrs Hudson for a few cloves of garlic.'

Soon we were clattering up through the dreary brick-and-mortar wasteland of Holloway, with its grim castellated citadel of correction, and along the gloomy Seven Sisters Road. The journey entailed an almost constant climb, and to make matters worse, we were slowed to a crawl for the greater part of it until we reached Tottenham Green, beyond which our driver left behind the traffic-choked main road and took to the quieter byways. There was some further hold-up outside the Great Eastern Railway Company's goods depot where a cart had broken down, then the streets gradually widened and we began to make better progress. The Inspector fizzed with impatience at each fresh delay.

'Now then,' Holmes began judiciously as we sat in the four-wheeler, 'until we have completely exhausted all rational explanations, let us put aside for one moment any speculation based upon supernatural phenomena; let us forget about undead spirits rising from the grave, and confine ourselves to the plain facts. You implied that there was no sign of a struggle, Inspector Wills?'

'Absolutely none.'

'No trace of any poison?'

'There was nothing obvious, but the post-mortem will confirm that, as likely as not.'

'No smell of chloroform?'

'No, but then the window was wide open, as I told you before. What is the significance of this fact?'

'I am trying to understand how the victim was subdued sufficiently to allow these injuries to be caused. Then there was the reaction of Mrs Kenny. Both effects may have been explained by the presence some chemically poisonous atmosphere in the room. I have seen it done before. Then there is the absence of blood, which is also puzzling. You say that the corpse was drained of blood.'

'So it seemed to me,' said the Inspector, 'such a ghostly pallor as I have never seen.'

'In point of fact,' I put in helpfully, 'one would only have to lose about a third to a half of one's blood supply, depending upon circumstances, for death to occur; a surprisingly small degree of exsanguination would suffice.'

'Nevertheless,' said Holmes, shaking his head, 'if the loss of blood was sufficient to cause death, one would have thought there would be some blood-staining in the vicinity and on the victim's clothes. No doubt you have made a search of the premises?'

'I left Sergeant Channon in charge of the house. He will rake the premises from coal-hole to garret and search the garden; if there is anything else to find, he will find it.'

'I suppose nothing has been stolen?' asked Holmes.

Wills looked astounded. 'It would be a rather elaborate blind for a robbery, would it not, Mr Holmes?'

'I could tell you of stranger ones. Then there is this preposterous rigmarole of the corpse being dressed up in a bridal gown — presumably the one she was intending to be married in?'

'Yes. Both Ruth Farnham's parents were deceased. Her late father had been a clergyman and she had at one time been a member of his congregation, but she recently left that church to join another. A quite extraordinary one: it is one of these strange cults, officially known as the Divine Order of the Purple Rose, and its leader is a rather odd character. You may have heard of him; he is the Reverend Henry Staunton.'

'No, I have not.'

'He is well known locally as an eccentric. He is sixty-two years of age, but still a live wire. He apparently intended to take Miss Farnham as his next bride in a fortnight's time.'

'He was widowed then?' I asked.

'No, gentlemen, he already has a wife: several in fact.'

'*Several?*' I repeated in astonishment.

Holmes smiled. 'As Doctor Watson would tell you, Inspector, the idea of taking one wife seems to me preposterous enough, but to take two or more . . . well, you have presumably arrested him on a charge of bigamy under the Offences Against the Persons Act?'

The Inspector shook his head ruefully. 'Not exactly. You see, he is not legally married to any of them — *spiritual* brides they are called in the Divine Order of the Purple Rose. They have a bit of hocus-pocus which they call a marriage ceremony, but it has no legal standing.'

'*Hieros gamos*,' said Holmes, 'Greek: ritual marriage.'

'I am sure you are right,' said Wills dubiously. 'The Order has its premises in the old Church of All Souls, which became vacant when the parishes of Upper and Lower Edmonton were merged some time ago. The Reverend Staunton bought it — or rather it was bought with one of his former wives' money — and they all live in what was once the old vicarage: the '*Aion Erospiti*' as they call it.'

'*Aion Erospiti?*' my friend repeated. 'The abode of — '

'Heavenly bliss and eternal love, according to Staunton — harem I would call it. As it happens, some of his younger *spiritual* brides seem to have brought forth a perplexing number of progeny; however, there is nothing illegal in that. They are an isolated little group, quite self-sufficient. They grow most of their own food in the vicarage garden, keep a few chickens, and have little to do with the outside world except for their evangelizing. Miss Farnham lived close to the church, but it was planned that after the wedding she would go and live at the . . . at the old vicarage, with the others. I have their names here: Anne Evans, forty-eight years of age; Rebecca Crouch, thirty-three years of age

— she is the sister of one of his pastors; and Drusilla Jane Ellis, twenty-two.'

'I suppose you do not know what will happen to the dead woman's estate?'

'It was a simple matter to contact the woman's solicitor at Waltham Cross, and we should have the answer to that by the time we arrive at the house. We already had some background information on the Reverend Staunton. Prior to his ordination, as you might call it, he managed a string of unsuccessful enterprises: a scriptural book-shop and then a provincial theatre catering for biblical productions, which burnt down about two years ago. In this latter, he was suspected of insurance fraud, but nothing was ever proven. Then there was the spiritual centre, as it was called, which was at the heart of a financial scandal before it was closed down about a year or so ago. Of his present wives, the youngest one is of considerable means and, although she seems to have put those means at the disposal of the Order, none of the women have legally transferred any of their property or money into his name.'

'It would certainly give our investigation some direction if it were known that the Reverend Staunton should benefit in some way from the death. What were Miss Farnham's movements on the night that she died?'

'According to Staunton, she had been to the church for Sunday evening service, went to the vicarage for about half an hour, took a cup of tea, and then went home. A Miss Collins, who has a dressmaker's shop in the town and who lives a few doors away, saw Miss Farnham arriving home about 7.30 in the evening. None of the neighbours we questioned saw anyone entering or leaving her house after that time until Mrs Kenny came around this morning. Miss Farnham seems to have had supper after she returned from church, for the remains of some food — a roast lamb joint — were discovered in the kitchen. The joint had been carved and had been partly eaten. It has now been removed and sent for analysis.'

'Who made the tea which Miss Farnham drank at the vicarage?' Holmes asked.

'Miss Crouch made it.'

'And all the occupants of the house drank it?'

'So they said.'

'Tell me about this crypt which appears to have been disturbed during the night.'

'Both the crypt and the coffin were very old and the inscription is withered away, therefore it is not known to whom they belonged.'

'But the crypt could, of course, have been disturbed at some other time and yet not been noticed until this morning?' said Holmes.

'It is possible, but the constable's evidence is that it was not.'

'And no one knows whose remains were in it?'

'I have sent a man off to check the burial records for the churchyard, but I am not hopeful. One would have thought that there would have been nothing more than a pile of old bones.'

'A pile of old bones . . . ' repeated Holmes thoughtfully, 'yes, of course, very likely a pile of bones.'

'But after this morning's discovery, I am not so sure what may have been lurking in there,' the Inspector said. 'Well, we are almost there now, Mr Holmes, and you will be able to see all for yourself.'

We had turned by the pleasantly rural Edmonton Green, with its colourful stalls and live chickens and geese. Crossing under the railway bridge, we made our way along a bustling street with shops and cafés, and then turned off to the right just before the tram terminus. We alighted at the house in Church Avenue, one of a line of neat, comfortable-looking, semi-detached, suburban villas with tidy gardens. A uniformed constable stood on the pavement outside number 27, where a small knot of curious neighbours had begun to gather around to exchange gossip and to try to peer across the garden into the brightly-curtained windows on the lower floor. A short, dark, stocky fellow in uniform, who was introduced to us as Sergeant Channon, hailed us as we entered the house.

'You may speak freely before these two gentlemen,' said the Inspector, 'this is Mr Sherlock Holmes and Doctor Watson.'

'I am honoured to meet you both,' said the young man earnestly. 'I have assiduously read the accounts of all your cases. I have most of the information you have been waiting for, Sir,' he said briskly to Wills, waving a sheaf of papers, 'I opened them all as you directed. Miss Farnham's solicitor, Mr Herbert Lloyd, confirms that she is intestate. She had inherited some property from her father, which has been in the family for generations, and also some investments. The estate, therefore, is quite considerable — several thousand pounds. She had interest on the investments and with her salary as a librarian, she must have been quite comfortable. Then there is the house, which is certainly worth a few hundred pounds. Mr Lloyd is presently trying to trace any relatives which the dead woman may have. There are no brothers or sisters, though one of the neighbours said he thought she had an old aunt in Hampshire whom she used to visit occasionally.'

'Surely the housekeeper would know?' asked Holmes.

'Mrs Kenny is under sedation at her daughter's house presently, Mr Holmes,' said the sergeant. 'She is a tough old creature, though, and I hope she will be able to speak to us before too long. Once I have finished here, I shall go round to see her. I'm afraid, Sir, that the burial records have not been found, so we are unable to say to whom the crypt and coffin belongs or how old they are.'

'Some of the older folk are very superstitious about it,' Wills added. 'They talk of an old legend that goes back to when Edmonton was a village. It had belonged to a family whose son had been put to death in the witchcraft trials several centuries ago.'

'It is no mere legend, Sir,' said Channon. 'When I went round to see the sexton about the matter, he let me see a fragment of an old manuscript he had amongst the records. It is dated 1631, and entitled *Funerall Monuments of Edmundton*. It says: 'Here lieth interred under a seemelie tomb without inscription the body of one ingenious conceited gentleman that, by his wittie devices beguiled the devill, and who did live and die in the raigne of Henry VII.' There is no record of who this refers to, but on closer inspection this morning, I ascertained that there had never been any inscription on the tomb.'

'Well done, Sergeant!' said Wills. 'What else have you discovered?'

'Constable Parkins and I have searched the house, the garden, and the outhouses and found nothing incriminating. Parkins spoke to the neighbour, Mr Crane, but he could add nothing to what we already know — he was the gentleman who informed us of the dead woman's elderly aunt. Here is a wire from the police surgeon, too, which arrived just before you did.'

Wills quickly ran over the contents. 'As I suspected, Mr Holmes, no trace of poison, and no other injuries. Time of death, between ten o'clock at night and two o'clock in the morning.'

'Well, I think you have done as much as you can,' said Holmes. 'Let us have a look at the room where the body was found.'

Channon went off to speak to the housekeeper and Wills led the way upstairs. I deduced from Holmes's manner rather than his words that he had found little to excite his suspicions in the room. He examined the bed, the wardrobe, and the windowsill, the state of which seemed to corroborate the Inspector's suspicions that it had recently been used as a means of access or egress. The window opened out on the rear garden, beyond which could be seen the churchyard, the church, and the first-floor windows of the vicarage. The Inspector pointed out to us where a path led from the street, between two of the villas, and skirted the churchyard. This had been Miss Farnham's usual route to and from the church.

'Then the dead woman's movements could easily have been anticipated by any assailant?' Holmes asked.

'Yes.'

'And watched, too, from the upper windows of the houses in this row, or by anyone at the vicarage?'

'Undoubtedly,' replied Wills. 'In the main, Miss Farnham spent most of her time either at the library or at the church and vicarage. According to the neighbours, she rarely varied her routine. Church at seven o'clock, then back home to breakfast, which Mrs Kenny would have ready for her. She would come home from the library at one o'clock for lunch, then Mrs Kenny would lay out something for tea and be gone by the time Miss Farnham returned at six o'clock.'

We returned to the lower floor and then went into the rear garden. On examining the shrubbery under the bedroom window, Holmes pointed to the soft, damp ground. 'I suppose this vampire can fly as well, Inspector,' he muttered acerbically. 'There is no evidence of any footprints which would indicate someone gaining entry from here; neither is there any means of accessing the bedroom window from here — no drainpipe, for instance. I think I have seen enough; let us proceed to the vicarage.'

The church itself seemed conventional enough, though Staunton had removed the name 'All Souls' from the pediment and had had it replaced with 'Ekklesia Rhodon Porphura'. The grounds had been liberally planted with purple roses, and at the base of the steeple, on an elevated plinth supported by naked caryatids, were four figures cast in bronze: a bow, a quiver of arrows, a spear, and a fiery chariot. As we approached the vicarage, I noticed a man wearing a long, flowing white robe with a purple stole secured about the waist by a silk cincture, whom I took to be Staunton. He was conversing in the porch with a member of his congregation, an elderly woman whose gaze he held. Once he saw us approach the house, he terminated the conversation with a bow and a gesture towards us and made his way down the path. The pastor was a tall, bespectacled, bearded fellow with a florid face, high ruddy cheekbones, and long grey locks of hair. His drooping jowls and his affectation of unctuous piety gave him a slightly comic air, though I seemed to detect a hardness about the mouth. Holmes and I had stopped to look at the notice board outside the church, which contained a bold summary of evangelical success: 'Tracts distributed — 1728; Visits to the sick and dying — 87; Persons led to church for the first time — 56; Drunkards reclaimed — 35; Fallen females rescued from vice and debauchery — 12; Persons living in sin induced to marry — 10.'

'No doubt, gentlemen, you were admiring the good work of our Order,' said Staunton with an ingratiating manner, 'of which, surely, no decent, upstanding Christian person could disapprove.'

'No. I was pondering the proposition that virtue was intended to be its own reward, rather than to be reckoned up on a board like cricket scores,' Holmes replied coolly. 'Perhaps we had better go inside.'

The vicarage was very richly furnished, lacking in no creature comfort. Staunton told us that the Order did not normally permit visitors from the outside world, but, as he emphasized none too subtly for our benefit, in this case he was more than happy to make the exception 'twice in one day'. He seemed remarkably calm for someone who had just lost a prospective wife, yet there was still something in his manner which appeared to be a forced show of fortitude. He introduced the rest of his household, who were all dressed in mourning, the severe funereal appearance of the inhabitants contrasting starkly with the sumptuous surroundings. Miss Evans was a tall, dark-haired, sharp-eyed, buxom woman who, like Staunton, seemed very composed. Miss Crouch appeared like a younger version of Evans; but the youngest one, Drusilla Jane Ellis, thin, fair-haired, and highly strung, appeared distraught, with red-ringed eyes and an unnatural pallor that told me she had not slept during the night.

'This must have come as a very great shock to you all,' Holmes began once Wills had introduced us, 'and I must apologize for intruding upon your grief.'

Staunton nodded gravely, 'Yes, we are all immeasurably saddened by the news, especially Sister Ellis. She and Sister Farnham were very close. Just as the rose is surrounded by thorns, so now is our very own little rose now surrounded by sorrows. We had all looked forward to the joyful times we would share here in the *Aion Erospiti*.'

'Yes, I am sure you did,' replied Holmes drily. 'I hesitate to go over what might seem like old ground, but I must inquire about some of your movements.'

'Last night?'

'No, not last night, as it happens. On these dates,' said Holmes, passing across the note with the dates from Miss Farnham's diary. Staunton looked bemused.

'Did you visit Miss Farnham late at night on any of those dates?' asked Holmes.

'I had already told the Inspector,' replied Staunton, 'that I had never been in Sister Farnham's home at any time, and certainly not alone with her. I would not countenance such impropriety. The colours of our Order, Mr Holmes, purple and white, signify humility and purity, and for — '

'Yes, of course,' Holmes interrupted the flow of the man's insufferable homily. 'Premises such as these — this enormous church, the house, the large gardens — must require a substantial amount of upkeep, Mr Staunton. How do you manage it?'

'*Brother* Staunton, if you please,' he replied to my friend. 'We are fortunate in having within our congregation a number of persons who are more than happy to assist in defraying the necessary running costs. This household, I may say, contributes more than its fair share. We produce much of our own food, and as we do not indulge in the sin of gluttony, our wants are rather modest.'

'Then you have no financial difficulties?'

'We are not running a business enterprise, Mr Holmes; all that you see here is but a material means to a spiritual end, which is salvation; we have displayed the fruits of our labour for all to see and judge; hence, I was distressed to find you casting aspersions upon it.'

'I was merely wondering what had happened to the idea of doing good by stealth, as opposed to trumpeting it. Where is Mr Crouch at the moment, and what position does he hold in your Order?'

'*Brother* Crouch holds no position, because there *are* no positions. We have neither rank nor title, Mr Holmes, we have no need for bishops or cardinals, dames or knights; we are all brothers and sisters in, and all equal before, our Saviour. Ephraim Crouch is in America at the moment, helping to spread the gospel and gathering souls for salvation.'

'Can you tell me exactly where he has gone and on what date he left?'

'Yes, he is with the Goshen Congregation in Arkansas — a kindred chapter. He has been gone for two months. I have a letter from him which he posted upon his arrival, if you would care to see it.'

'No, that will not be necessary. I don't suppose Miss Farnham is the type that would have made any enemies?'

'*Enemies?* Of course she had an enemy, Mr Holmes. Every righteous person under heaven has an implacable enemy — Satan!'

'I had in mind someone of more terrestrial connections,' Holmes replied with ill-concealed derision.

'You know of the manner of this poor girl's death?' asked Staunton hotly.

'Inspector Wills has apprised me of the relevant facts. He has, however, asked me for, as it were, a second opinion.'

'What need is there for any second opinion,' Staunton interrupted my friend, 'when there can be no doubt as to what has happened? The untainted blood drunk from the girl's chaste young body; the marks of the beast left upon her; the empty coffin. It is the work of Satan!' his melancholy voice boomed as little flakes of sputum fell upon his beard, at which point the youngest girl gave a piercing shriek and burst into a flood of tears.

'Yes, I have seen and heard it all, and as you see, I remain quite unconvinced,' replied Holmes in his most tranquil manner.

'The evil thing which has done this is still at large. How will you go about finding it? With your magnifying glass and your chemical analyses? I have heard of your great, and no doubt well-deserved, reputation, Mr Holmes, but you are wasting your time here ... 'for we are not fighting against flesh-and-blood enemies, but against evil rulers of the unseen world, against mighty powers in this dark world, and against evil spirits!''

'Ephesians six, twelve,' said Holmes coolly, as he stood up and made for the door. 'Let me be perfectly honest with you: when a woman is murdered under *any* circumstances — yes, even circumstances as apparently singular as these, the first suspicion falls upon the husband, or the prospective husband. Experience teaches us that this is often the correct solution. I will now take a walk outside and inspect the gardens and out-houses. I may return with some further questions for you.' Staunton glared icily at Holmes as we departed.

'What do you expect to find?' I asked my friend at length, as we walked outside with the Inspector.

Holmes replied with a gesture of futility. 'Look at the size of this place,' he said. The vicarage gardens were quite large, and there was a small orchard and a row of greenhouses. 'I have no intention of searching for anything. It was pure bluff in order to gauge his reaction. I must confess it had little effect; either he has nerves of steel or there is indeed nothing to find here. Had there been some guilty secret to discover, I thought I might have provoked him into some indiscretion. I should at least have expected him to watch us through the window, but he has not cast a single nervous glance in our direction. We shall leave him to stew a bit longer before we return. A bigger fraud I've scarcely seen, though.'

'Yes, he has drawn a storm of charges in charlatanism,' said Wills. 'His first, legal, wife was a wealthy, elderly friend of his mother whom he appears to have simply married for her money; she left him a quite phenomenal sum which allowed him to buy the old parish church and all that went with it. There was, and is, absolutely no suspicion that her death was anything but natural; she was, after all, eighty-nine. Within three months of his first wife's death, he had married, so to speak, the Evans woman. Six months later he attached himself to Crouch's sister and then finally to this Ellis girl. Ruth Farnham was to be the next.'

'I can see him mesmerizing a gullible congregation with little effort. You know,

242

Watson, I had a vague idea that his face was familiar to me, yet I cannot place it. The voice, too.'

'I am afraid I cannot recall him, Holmes. I am sure I detected a hint of the colonial in the accent,' I said.

'He explained to me that he had once run a Gospel Mission in one of the Australian gold field towns on the Yarrowee River,' said Wills.

'I should wire to South Australia to check the story if I were you,' said Holmes.

'They have taken the whole thing remarkably calmly, though I could not help noticing that the younger girl seemed very upset by it,' I said.

'Yes, that was a more natural reaction than the stony-faced stoicism of the others,' replied Holmes.

'One must allow that their story was fairly solid all round, though,' said Wills.

'But corroborated only by themselves,' I persisted.

'True, Doctor, but what other alibi *could* they have other than that provided by the members of their own, admittedly extraordinary, household?' answered Wills.

'I remain convinced that a simple murder has been committed here,' said Holmes. 'I am unable to say how it was done, or by whom at this point, but the most likely explanation for the absence of bloodstaining is that the murder was committed somewhere else, the body brought into the house and placed in the bedroom, and everything was arranged to be found by the housekeeper in the morning. This neighbour, Miss Collins, may not have seen the victim leaving her house after she arrived at 7.30, but that does not mean she did *not* leave.'

'She is a bit of a busybody by all accounts, perpetually peering out from behind the chintz curtains and aspidistra,' said Wills.

'But, if time of death was midnight or later, how many neighbours would be up and about at that time? I see you are not convinced, Wills.'

'I am keeping an open mind and noting everything you say,' the Inspector replied noncommittally. 'You do not subscribe to the theory that those wounds were made by teeth?' he asked.

'Frankly, I do not.'

'But the surgeon's report . . . '

'The surgeon's note merely confirmed the spacing of the wounds; the idea of teeth marks had been put into his head,' replied Holmes with a sidelong glance at the Inspector.

'But what sort of weapon could produce such wounds?' Wills asked.

'A bradawl perhaps or something of that nature,' I suggested.

'Too narrow a point,' argued the Inspector. 'And there were two identical wounds, remember, side by side. It is impossible to imagine such a weapon having been used, for it would require a fair aim to pick out the jugular vein, and then to strike again a second time.'

'Let us leave that question aside for the moment, and consider the motive,' said Holmes. 'It is pretty obvious, is it not, that Miss Farnham was worth more to Staunton alive than dead? Therefore, if he committed the crime, it could not have been for material gain, and I doubt whether he is a cold-blooded, calculating murderer. All the same, I want to have a parting shot at him.'

On our return to the morning room, Holmes indicated that he wished to speak to each of the residents privately. The Ellis girl, however, had since been put to bed with a sleeping draught. Without any preamble he asked the others, one by one, what Miss Farnham had been wearing when they had last seen her alive. Staunton replied airily that he took no notice of such worldly details, but the two women gave the precisely same answer calmly and unhesitatingly: a light grey woollen skirt, a plain white cotton blouse, and dark grey overcoat. With that, we left the strange household of the *Aion Erospiti*.

'If we could discover what happened to those clothes Miss Farnham had been wearing, it would be a great help. However, I suspect they have been destroyed, probably burnt,' said Holmes.

'We could apply for a warrant to search the house.'

'No, it should be a waste of time. Now for the neighbour, Mr Danvers Crane,' said Holmes.

Sergeant Channon was making his way briskly up the path through the churchyard, his face flushed with excitement. 'Some further important information has come to light,' he said. 'I have just come back from speaking to Mrs Kenny. She has quite come round now, though she is still very upset, but she was able to tell me something that may change your view of the case. Apparently there was some dalliance between Miss Farnham and one of the neighbours, this Danvers Crane chap, the schoolmaster — the one who was at the house this morning. It turns out that he did not go to school today as a result of the shock of the news.'

'Most interesting,' said Holmes.

'He made no mention of this to me when I questioned him earlier,' replied Channon. 'He had courted Miss Farnham quite ardently for some time by all accounts, and Mrs Kenny thought that she seemed to be flattered by his attentions at first. But she broke off their relationship not long after she joined Staunton's Order. First of all, he has practically no alibi, for he maintains that he was alone on Sunday evening at home, reading by the fireside, and that he never left the house. Secondly, he plainly lied to me earlier when I asked him how well he knew the dead woman.'

'He has the motive then — jealousy!' said Wills. 'There is no doubt that he seemed very cut up about what had happened, but whether it was grief or remorse . . . '

'Then, you at least have come round to a theory of natural causes?' asked Holmes.

'Who is to say that his mind had not become unhinged by his separation from Miss Farnham, and that he turned to the darker powers?' the Inspector replied.

'Don't go sharpening your wooden stake just yet, Inspector,' laughed Holmes. 'It is obvious that if Crane had designs upon Miss Farnham's little fortune, he would also have a more material motive, and that is a rather powerful combination. My suspicions are aroused, too, by the fact that he was first on the scene. Does he live next door?' asked Holmes.

'No, two doors away.'

'Then his hearing must be of the first order, if he heard Mrs Kenny screaming.'

'He says he was in the garden at the time, and heard the commotion through the open bedroom window.'

'How very natural, don't you think, to wander around the garden first thing on a foggy, chilly November morning? Let us speak to him without further delay.'

Danvers was a respectable-looking fellow of middle age. Bearded and thin, almost pinched-looking, nervous and slightly ingratiating, but slow to take offence. He certainly bore the dazed and stricken aspect of someone lately bereft as he led us wearily into the house. He was adamant that after he had come back from bell-ringing practice on Sunday evening at nine o'clock, he did not afterwards leave the house.

'It seems you did not trouble yourself to mention to Sergeant Channon about your former engagement to Miss Farnham,' said Wills.

'I did not think it was of any importance since it ended so long ago.'

'When did you and Miss Farnham break off your engagement?' asked Holmes.

'We did not break it off; Ruth broke it off under the influence of that degenerate,

248

depraved satyr,' he said, concluding with a torrent of unprintable insults.

'You did not answer my question.'

'In June,' he said, adding with pathetic bitterness, 'the nineteenth, to be exact.'

'And you did not meet her again?'

'No.'

'Dear me, that's very strange, because you see, Miss Farnham distinctly mentions in her diary that — '

'Her *diary*?' A rictus of alarm crossed the features of Mr Danvers Crane. Holmes pressed home his advantage.

'Amongst her personal effects was a diary in which she records meeting with a certain person on these dates,' said Holmes, passing Crane the same slip of paper he had shown Staunton.

The man turned pale. 'Yes, that was me,' he stammered. 'I realize now that I ought to have told the Sergeant. It was very foolish of me not to. We met a few times in secret, late at night so that the neighbours would not know. I had hoped that she might reconsider. I tried to make her see sense. I flattered myself to think that I had begun to have some influence over her and tried to reason with her. I pointed out to her how many other young women Staunton had ensnared. This swine is unfitted to use the word *Christian*; it is a hideous blasphemy. I couldn't bear to think of Ruth as one of his *heifers*!'

'And so you put her beyond his reach?' asked Holmes.

'No! I could never have harmed a hair of her head.'

'You have lied in your answers to the police, you have no alibi for the time of the murder, and you have at least two motives for committing it.'

'Are you suggesting that I did it? How can you possibly imagine that any human hand was behind this? You must know what happened.'

'I know what was placed in the house for Inspector Wills to find when he arrived.'

'What do you mean?' he retorted.

'That whoever committed this murder would have had all the time in the world to dispose of the real evidence and arrange this theatrical farce. Was it by chance alone that you happened to be in the garden at the time that Mrs Kenny arrived?'

'No, I was tending the hives. I am a keen apiarist — '

'Tending the hives in November?'

'Yes, there is still work to be done.'

'Such as?'

'These are not native bees; they require some feeding and the queen is still laying worker brood. And the hives still have to be hefted throughout the winter.'

'And you chose first thing in the morning to do that?'

'It is too dark by the time I arrive home from school.'

'You went to meet her on the evening she was murdered, did you not?'

'No.'

'Come, Sir, it is obvious that a meal was prepared for two people — Ruth Farnham was going to share it with you, was she not?'

'Yes. But I did not go. I swear I didn't. We were to have dinner together. Ruth wanted us to carry on as friends, but I just couldn't face that. I knew that it was too late for her to change her mind.'

'How did you know that?'

'Because Miss Collins, who has the dressmaker's shop, told me on Saturday evening that she delivered the wedding gown to Miss Farnham. I knew at that point it would be futile to try to dissuade her. I never kept the appointment; I swear this is true!'

Wills had been following this exchange with alacrity and signalled to Holmes to step outside. The Inspector made it clear that he was for arresting Danvers Crane on the spot.

'No, I should not do that, Inspector, for at present you only have evidence of the most circumstantial kind. Any half-decent counsel would tear it to pieces. You may have the opportunity and the motive on your side, but you lack the corroborating evidence, that one piece of unshakable, incontrovertible, damning proof which will have the jury nodding in agreement and will send your killer to the scaffold. Could you demonstrate how this man committed the crime? No, you cannot. What was the weapon and where is it now? How did he dispose of Miss Farnham's bloody clothes and so on?'

'But the man has told us a pack of lies — he continued to meet the dead woman and we now find he was invited to her house on the evening of her death. That's misleading the police for one thing.'

'Indeed, but it is not necessarily material to a charge of murder. I exhort you, Inspector, to have some patience. I cannot say yet if Crane is the murderer, but a vague idea is beginning to form in my mind. If you must do something, then charge him with giving you false information and leave it at that. I should much prefer it if you implied that you accepted his story, subject to your further inquiries. But I shall have to leave you to make up your own mind upon it.'

'Does that mean you are returning to Baker Street already?' asked Wills despondently.

'Not immediately. I have a desire to stretch my legs. Doctor Watson will tell you that I like to soak myself in the atmosphere of the place; I find it helps to be in empathy with the surroundings of the events, especially ones as dramatic as these; and then again, one never knows what one might discover.'

At these words, the Inspector glanced at my friend strangely. I had caught that look on the faces of many people from time to time. It seemed to say: 'These very clever people all have a touch of madness.'

'The doctor and I shall take a train back to town, so if you would meet me at, say, five o'clock, I expect to have some advice for you by then. Shall we say . . . yes, why not that cheery-looking little café at the tramway terminus?'

We left the Inspector looking rather glum, and then we rambled for a couple of hours through the pleasant neighbourhood. We began by walking along the rippling Salmon's Brook, which separated the churchyard from the cricket ground, followed it down to the riverbank by Cook's Ferry, and returning by a green lane adjacent to the railway. I said barely a word to Holmes during this time and made no attempt to interrupt his thoughts, for I sensed that he was turning over the facts of the case in his mind. Finally, we went into the café and obtained no little diversion by reading the press reports of the affair, for by now the news-vendors were shouting the headlines of the 'Edmonton Horror' from the street corners.

Some accounts of the case were exaggerated beyond belief. The *Middlesex Chronicle* led with 'Churchyard Vampire Strikes' whilst the *North London Advertiser* called it 'The Bloodsucker Murder'; the *Eastern Argus*, which had produced a special feature for the evening edition, referred to 'grave robbery and blood sacrifices'. The *Pall Mall Gazette* mentioned the victim's connection with the Divine Order of the Purple Rose — or the *Erospites* as they called them — and lampooned Staunton as the 'Brimsdown Messiah'. The *Standard* made a wide sweep which included mention of the Rosicrucians, messianic cults, millenarian sects, and the prophecies of Joanna Southcott — although the writer managed to comically mix up the words 'gravely' and 'gravelly' in one passage, which somewhat spoilt the solemn effect. The *Evening Post* was generally more sceptical and reported the incident only as a 'mysterious death' and avoided mention of the empty crypt and coffin. The *Globe* article deplored the credulity of the populace, blamed the public hysteria which attended the case on the influence of the shilling shockers, and excoriated the author of a recent sensational work on the subject. The *Telegraph* fulminated against what it saw as one of the drawbacks of mass literacy.

'It seems to have become the habit,' I remarked, 'to ascribe a goodly proportion of crime to the influence of cheap literature.'

'Indeed,' said Holmes, laughing and tossing the papers aside with a smile of contempt, 'it is a view which is surprisingly prominent amongst the magistracy. If only it were so simple, Watson. Rather, it has always struck me that the attraction of such literature to the lower classes lies precisely in its *contrast* with their own dreary lives, not in its similarity to them.'

Wills and Channon arrived promptly at the hour, the former bearing an air of frustration and impatience.

'You won't stay for tea, then?' Holmes asked.

'No, thank you. I really just wanted to ask if you had discovered anything.'

'Yes, I discovered that the brook was far too shallow.'

'For what?'

'Come along, surely it is not difficult to conjecture.'

'You said you might have some advice for

me,' Wills persevered.

'Try to find out if either Staunton or Crane has lit a fire outdoors since Sunday night. You know the sort of thing, burning twigs or bits of garden rubbish. I think it unlikely, but let me know immediately by telegram if you find out that either of them has.'

'You're thinking of the dead woman's missing clothes, I suppose, that they may have been burnt.'

'As it happens, I was not. They could be very easily disposed of. In fact, something hasn't turned up which I had expected to turn up.'

'Is there anything in particular to which you would direct my attention?' said Wills as he turned to go.

'Yes, the empty coffin — that is what holds, or rather held — the key to this entire affair.'

'The empty coffin! Are you serious?'

'Perfectly so.'

'But you have ridiculed my theory that anything had come out of the coffin!'

'The coffin, Inspector,' replied Holmes mysteriously, 'and we have until Friday, then all may be lost.'

'But why Friday?'

'Think of the date, Inspector.'

'You mean the pattern of the dates in Miss Farnham's diary?'

'I have given you a number of suggestions: you really must use your own faculties of reasoning,' was all he would say to the bemused Inspector, who eventually departed with a look of frustration. We wandered down to the low-level station where our four-carriage train arrived punctually. Holmes had deliberately chosen the quieter line by which to return, in order that we could be undisturbed, though it was a longer journey and meant a change at Shoreditch. We found an empty carriage in the deserted train easily enough, then the level crossing gates swung across, the signal cleared, and the whistle screamed. As we chugged on slowly, I looked out upon the cemetery with its mysterious headstones and exotic inscriptions, and remarked to my friend that our case must surely be unique in the history of crime.

'Hardly that, Watson, hardly that,' he replied to my surprise. 'On the contrary, during our perambulations I was guided towards my preliminary conclusions largely by recalling the precedents.'

'Precedents! You mean this has happened before?'

'Of course, you are well aware of my conviction that there is nothing new. A similar case occurred in Forfarshire some years ago, and farther back in Quimper in the days of the Second Empire.'

'You told Wills that the coffin held the key,' I said in an attempt to draw him out. 'What did you mean?'

'Only that he should pay attention to apparently trifling details — and I noticed that young Channon's ears pricked up when I mentioned that. Something came out of that coffin, Watson, and has not returned. If my view of the case is correct, it shall, nay, *must* return.'

'Something came out . . . you cannot possibly believe this!'

'Can't I?' He smiled mischievously.

'Really, Holmes, you are a most trying individual at times.'

'If you would apply your own powers of analysis — powers which you habitually underestimate — then you would no doubt reach the same conclusion as I. Tell me, Watson, there have been recent medical advances in what might be called the artificial reconstruction of the human form, have there not?'

'Why, yes,' I replied, somewhat taken aback at the direction which his thoughts now seemed to be taking. 'There have been a number of articles in the *Lancet* on successful applications of such techniques. Developments in both rhinoplasty and otoplasty have been the subject of some recent remarkable expositions based on the seminal work by Herr Dieffenbach. It is not a subject that I thought would have held your interest.'

'You would be surprised, then.'

'Some theorists have gone so far as to postulate the novel idea that given the requisite evolution and refinement of present practice, an entire human being could be manufactured from — '

'Novel! Why that idea is as old as the *Book of Psalms*,' he said. 'In point of fact though, Watson, I think you have just provided me with the final piece of the jigsaw. I believe that the case is almost complete now.'

I said no more, for my friend was staring absorbedly out of the window. I sat for the rest of the journey, mystified by the implications of his words.

As it transpired, we were summoned back to Edmonton sooner than we had planned. The arrival of Inspector Stanley Hopkins at Baker Street the following afternoon gave me an awful presentiment, and I began to have a vision of some dreadful repetition of the events at Church Avenue. Hopkins was one of the youngest of the Inspectors at Scotland Yard, and due to his qualities of acuity and tenacity, was something of a favourite with Holmes. He had already shared in a number of our adventures, and on this occasion, he briskly explained to us the reason for his visit. At 10.30 the previous evening, two young women returning home late from a meeting of the Guild of St John, had taken a short cut by the churchyard path. Their attention had been alerted by a rustling in the shrubbery, and as they looked in the direction of the noise they saw the shadow of a hooded, cloaked figure creeping between the gravestones in the dark, near to the disturbed, unnamed crypt. They immediately took to their heels and their violent screaming aroused some of the neighbours, who, their nerves already strained by the events, turned out with hatchets and pokers to discover the cause of the disturbance. Wills had been summoned immediately, and although a search of the graveyard had been undertaken, nothing had been found. Neither of the women had any known connection to the Divine Order of the Purple Rose or with any of the other people of the saga so far.

'I received the wire just before midnight last night, but by then the excitement was over,' said Hopkins. 'I understand that you had already been informed of the case.'

'Yes, I have examined all the evidence and become acquainted with the principal *dramatis personae*.'

'And you have formed some opinion?'

'Which I have communicated to the local constabulary. And you?'

'I have read the official documents including the surgeon's report, and I am on my way out to Lower Edmonton now. I stopped by to ask if you would care to join me.'

'Yes, I should be happy to do so, for I now feel slightly guilty about having left Wills to his own devices. Heaven knows, I threw out enough hints to him and to that bright young sergeant of his, that they really ought to have cleared the matter up themselves by now. Perhaps I am becoming lazy, though, for I suppose I might have expected this.'

'Expected it?' Hopkins looked surprised.

'Of course.'

'Then, this latest incident doesn't change your view of the case?'

'On the contrary, it reinforces it. You do not, by any chance, incline to the supernatural explanation yourself?'

Hopkins looked more confused than ever I had seen him. 'I should be relieved to hear a more convincing explanation, but you won't get anyone in Edmonton to believe any other at present. The rumour of what happened last night spread like wildfire throughout the neighbourhood; the entire district, which had already been in a fair panic, is now in complete hysteria. We have had to send reinforcements up there to help the local constabulary keep the peace, though ostensibly they are there to assist in the search.'

'You will find nothing,' said Holmes.

'We have already found something! Wills discovered fresh footprints in the vicinity of the crypt.'

'And what conclusions do you draw from that?'

'Inspector Wills, who is one of the most experienced men in the provincial constabulary, believes that this fiend, or whatever it is, had been making it way back to its lair when it was disturbed.'

'But the coffin remains empty,' said Holmes wearily.

'Indeed. Goodness knows where it is lurking now!'

'Come, Hopkins, you are a trained police officer.'

'Mr Holmes, you cannot deny that there is something or someone which is terrorizing the community and has already claimed one woman's life. Whether it is human or otherwise remains to be discovered, but who knows what the fate of those two young women might have been last night, had they not run away?'

'Then, you believe this corpse has come back to life?'

'I didn't exactly say I did . . . I haven't yet examined the scene of the crime,' the young Inspector continued defensively, 'and you yourself have often told me that it is a mistake to theorize in advance.'

'*Touché!*' Holmes smiled as he stood up to collect his overcoat and hat, though I detected a touch of mockery in it. Within the hour we met with Inspector Wills at the old churchyard gate. He was pale and haggard with fatigue and his expression was more eloquent than his words.

'Well, Mr Holmes,' he said, 'so much for your scepticism and elegant theories. It seems that this demon has returned and two people are prepared to swear that they saw it last night.'

'I know exactly what they saw,' said Holmes. 'Incidentally, did you wire to Australia yet? No? Well, Inspector Hopkins knows me rather better than you do, and he will tell you all about the importance which I attach to apparently unimportant details.'

'What has it to do with the case?'

'It may have everything or nothing to do with it. It is the first task of the professional to gather every piece of data he can, and then sift the crucial from the irrelevant by trial and error. Indeed, did not someone say that all the business of life was an endeavour to find out what one doesn't know by what one does? I have no doubt that there are a good many people basking in the district's notoriety, but had I been a bit quicker off the mark, I might have saved the neighbourhood from descending into a pandemonium.'

'What do you mean?' asked Wills. 'If you know something, Mr Holmes, please enlighten us.'

'I will not only enlighten you, I will make you a present of the person you are looking for.'

'How?'

'By playing along with this ridiculous charade for a little longer. Inspector Wills, I should like you to send a few of your constables round the immediate neighbourhood and warn the residents against the perils of going into the churchyard until a capture is made. Say that it is out of bounds for the present.'

'There is no need for that, Sir, for there is not a grown man in the district who will go near the place now!'

'Nevertheless, make it quite clear that it is considered the most dangerous folly to go anywhere near the crypt, and tell them that you are going to close the footpath through — '

'Impossible,' Hopkins shook his head, 'we have no power to do that.'

'My colleague is correct,' added Wills, 'a right of way has existed there through the parish since the time of the Conqueror. As guardians of the law we should be laughed at for our ignorance.'

'I did not exactly say that you should *do* it, merely imply very forcefully that you intend to. Make sure that the public know also that the constables are being called off at dusk, as you consider it futile to continue any search after dark.'

'What!' said Wills. 'Why, the district is almost in a state of siege; the constables are the only protection that they have.'

'Do you not recall the case of the Hampstead dog walker last year, Mr Holmes?' asked Hopkins. 'There was a very ugly scene when we withdrew the auxiliaries after forty-eight hours. There was almost a riot, in fact. It ended with four of the residents being charged with affray after taking the law into their own hands.'

'You can say that you intend to resume the search at first light tomorrow. It is but a ruse to draw our fox from the covert.'

Hopkins considered for a moment. 'What do you think, Wills, can we chance it?'

'If you think it will have the desired effect,

we shall do as you say,' said Wills resignedly.

'Excellent. The next part is the easier one: meet me here outside these gates tonight, but it is vital that no one knows about this — say nothing, even to your own men. We four shall suffice.'

'I am far from convinced,' said Wills. 'I think it is perfectly ridiculous, but . . . ' His voice tailed off and he shrugged.

'Prepare for a long vigil, though I think a nine o'clock start will be sufficient for our purposes.'

'What *are* our purposes?' asked Wills.

'Unless I am much mistaken the culprit will walk straight into your arms, and you will obtain precisely the evidence you require to get your conviction. Doctor Watson and I shall repair to the Stag and Hounds for the rest of the day. Before I return tonight, I must pay one final visit to the house in Church Avenue, if you would be so good as to give me the key. There is something I wish to examine.'

'In the chamber of death?' asked Wills.

'No, in the pantry as it happens,' Holmes replied to our utter astonishment.

'The pantry?!'

'Yes, I have been rather obtuse, for it occurs to me that it possibly holds the other key to the solution of this remarkable, but by no means unique, case.'

'Come, Mr Holmes, you have been playing games with us, dishing out a veiled allusion here and throwing in a suggestion there,' said Wills.

'Yes,' said Hopkins, 'it seems to me if we are to share this danger with you tonight, then you ought, at least, to answer one question.'

'I suppose that is not an unreasonable request,' my friend replied.

'Then whom do you suspect as the murderer,' asked Wills with a glance at Hopkins, 'Staunton or Crane?'

'Neither,' my friend replied with an enigmatic smile, and off he marched. We stopped at the house in Church Avenue and Holmes went inside. He returned in a very short time with just the faintest smile of satisfaction upon his face, but he would say nothing more of the case. On the contrary, he deployed his customary power of detachment from the affair in hand and we enjoyed a most hearty repast in the dining room of the Stag and Hounds that evening. The tavern was an admirable exemplar of our rural hostelries: oak-beamed, cosy, with a roaring fire and a welcoming host. Mounted on the walls were some very fine specimens of stuffed coarse fish with their titles displayed above in Latin.

'How much more homely the Anglo-Saxon names are,' he said, musing on the inscriptions above the glass cases. 'I should prefer a pike to *esox lucius* any day.'

'That reminds me,' I replied, 'I was appalled by the state to which the River Lea has degenerated.'

'Yes, it would be impossible to imagine Walton's Piscator hauling carp and tench for his table out of that sewer we saw today.'

'Yes, I suppose our dash for progress is never without a cost.'

'Now, Watson, before we go out, let me lay a few details of the case before you. The events of last night showed me that the perpetrator — or more likely, the perpetrator's accomplice — felt we were getting too close. They acted hastily to try to put an end to the affair, and unfortunately for them, the plan misfired.'

'I think I can follow your deduction, Holmes. The killer either went about dressed in a hooded cloak to try to create the impression that the creature was still at large, or he sent someone to do that.'

'No, I'm afraid that is not correct. There was a far more material purpose than that, and it is inconceivable that another attempt would not be made again this evening. The difference is that this time, we will be there to capture that person. I am willing to bet that you will all be astonished when the identity of the murderer is revealed.'

We met Wills and Hopkins at the gate just as the distant church bell of All Saints rang out.

'' *Tis nine a clocke, and time to ring curfew,*' said Holmes good-humouredly, 'and yet the streets seem so empty of people that any curfew would be quite unnecessary.'

'After last night, there is hardly a soul to be found who will venture abroad after dark,' said Wills.

'You have warned the residents?'

'Yes, we have. Where to now?'

'To the crypt where the empty coffin lies.'

Wills led us through the lichen-covered gates, and we immediately branched off the main path to where the most ancient-looking of the headstones stood. There was little light; indeed, the nearest gas lamp was fifty yards away, and it was not difficult to understand how the sight of a figure creeping amongst the gravestones in the dark might have induced hysterics. The stones glistened in the dank air, and an ethereal vapour rose off the brook behind the cemetery wall. It was a dismal, eerie atmosphere punctuated only by the crunch of our footsteps on the gravel.

We eventually found the square-looking

mass of stone with an ancient wooden relic of a door. It creaked noisily as we swung it open, and rasped loudly again as we shut it behind us. Wills lit his pocket lantern on the stygian scene. A single unadorned coffin lay against one of the walls, its lid askew. The sepulchral odour from the crypt clung to one's throat, and I was glad that I had remembered to bring my hip flask. Holmes turned to whisper to Hopkins, but hardly had he got the first words out when the door began to creak again. Wills snapped out the lantern and we had to shrink back to the wall as quickly as possible, for there was no time to stumble through the dark to our hiding places in the corner. Slowly the door edged open, and it was just possible to see the outline of a short, stocky man, with a hat pulled down over his face. He closed the door briskly and then a match flared in his hand; I felt a thrill of shock and horror as I distinguished the swarthy features of Sergeant Channon!

He remained unaware of our presence for a moment, and in that infinitesimal split second of time I could think only of the scandal which would ensue following the exposure of the Inspector's protégé as the murderer, and my overwhelming sentiment was one of heartfelt sympathy for Wills. The match had briefly thrown enough illumination for the young man to realize suddenly that he was not alone in the crypt. He started violently and then, to my continuing astonishment and confusion, an expression of embarrassed amusement crossed his features, and he began to laugh noiselessly.

'False alarm,' said Holmes, and I am sure each one of us breathed a deep sigh of relief.

'Yes, Mr Holmes,' the young man said sheepishly, as he took in the situation, 'I picked up your hint and thought I was the only person who had read the clues right, but I see now that I wasn't the only clever one.'

'We were almost arresting you as the murderer,' said my friend.

'You ought to have reported your suspicions to your superior officer,' said Wills sternly to the young man.

'Yes, I know, Sir, and apologize frankly. However, I thought you would have dismissed my suspicions as ridiculous.'

'You cannot possibly think that we would have come out here at this time of night on some ridiculous suspicion,' replied Wills imperiously.

Holmes smiled, a touch sarcastically. 'You can see now why I described Sergeant Channon to you as one of the cleverest young men I had met in uniform,' he said diplomatically to Hopkins.

'I suppose you may as well remain with us now that you are here, and we will discuss the matter of your indiscipline in the morning,' said Wills.

'We had better take up our stations now,' said Hopkins. Wills relit his lantern and we managed to get ourselves into positions of concealment at the rear of the crypt. Then the lantern snapped out, and we waited and listened for a lengthy time. More than once I nodded off and had to jerk myself awake. A few minutes after the church bell rang out midnight, we heard a crunch of gravel on the path outside. I stiffened with anticipation and fingered my revolver as I recalled Holmes's words: if it were not Staunton or Crane, who could it be?

The door creaked once or twice and it was just possible to make out the silhouette of a thin, cloaked figure creeping inside. A candle was lit and we saw the figure bend down in order to slide the lid of the coffin. From the folds of the cloak I saw a human skull appear, hideous in aspect; it seemed to hover in the air for a second then disappear again into the darkness; then the skeletal remains of a human torso materialized. I felt my pulse quicken and then, in an instant, I had grasped that the visitor had taken these relics from a hessian bag under the cloak and was placing them carefully into the coffin; at the very same instant, Holmes made his move. He motioned me forward with a touch on the elbow, and as we broke our cover, a terrified, high-pitched squeal emitted from under the figure's cowl. My friend pulled back the hood to reveal long blonde locks of hair and the terrified face of a young woman: Drusilla Jane Ellis.

'Quick, Watson, before she falls!' cried Holmes as the girl collapsed, senseless with shock and fear.

'Well, your fox turned out to be a vixen!' said Hopkins.

'Yes, but we caught it nevertheless,' replied Holmes.

'What are these?' asked Wills, shining the yellow light of his lantern into the coffin.

'Those are the bones which were in the coffin before it was disturbed,' said Holmes. 'They were taken out when the whole charade was set up. It was pretty obvious to me that they would have to be returned at some point. You have your murderer, and now you have your principal exhibit. I shall explain all to you in a moment. First, though, I think that we ought to agree upon a fair division of the spoils.'

'The credit is really all yours,' said Wills. Hopkins nodded in agreement.

'Not at all,' Holmes waved away the suggestion. 'To you, Inspector Wills, can go the praise for capturing the murderer of Ruth Farnham. As you might suspect, this young woman did not act alone — she was aided and abetted by the man who calls himself Staunton. So, to Scotland Yard, and Stanley Hopkins, goes the credit for finally catching up with the man they have been after for two years — the attempted murderer of Lady Frances Carfax — better known to you as Holy Peters.'

'No, I think you are mistaken there, Mr Holmes,' said Hopkins. 'I have seen his picture at the Yard; Peters, or Shlessinger as he was last known, is a bald man with a torn left ear.'

'He was until he acquired a wig, a pair of spectacles, and had some reconstructive surgery done upon his left lobe.'

'Then Miss Evans must be Annie Fraser!' said Hopkins.

'Indeed. I am afraid I entirely failed to recognize her at first, for I merely recalled her as a tall woman from our brief meeting in Brixton. It is far simpler, of course, for a woman to alter her appearance than it is for a man. But once I realized who she was, I must confess that is who my money was on, for I read the whole affair as the jealousy of the older woman towards the younger wife.'

I had been trying to bring the young woman round with an application of the hip flask, and a tinge of colour had come back into her cheeks. Eventually she at up and looked around at us with a terrified expression.

'What will they do to me?' she asked between her sobs.

'I fancy,' said Holmes, 'that the death of Miss Farnham was by no means a wilful, cold-blooded, premeditated murder?'

'No, I did not mean to kill her,' the girl blubbered, 'it happened almost by accident.'

'I think I will be able to show, Miss Ellis, that you did not go to Miss Farnham's house with the intent of murdering her. Let me put it to you that on the night Miss Farnham died, there had arisen some bitter jealousy between yourselves, which resulted in a violent quarrel. As I observed from her diary, Miss Farnham is somewhat given to self-dramatizing, and I can guess that your meeting was an explosive one.'

'Yes, we had an argument, and I followed Ruth into the kitchen. I screamed something at her, something I would not repeat in front of you gentlemen, and she turned on me violently. I wish to God I had not said it, for if I had not, she might be alive today. She picked up a knife from the table, and then . . . ' The girl burst into a paroxysm of weeping.

'And you defended yourself with the only weapon to hand.'

'What was it?' asked Hopkins.

'Use your imagination,' said Holmes. 'Which kitchen implement could cause two small punctures spaced an inch and a half apart — why, a carving fork.'

'A carving fork?' repeated Hopkins.

'As she lashed out at you, you struck her on the neck and were probably instantly astonished to see how much blood you had drawn. By chance you had struck an artery and within a short time, Miss Farnham became unconscious through loss of blood. You rushed home and told all of this to Staunton, as you know him. By the time he returned with you to the house in Church Avenue, Ruth Farnham was already gone and he had his plan carefully worked out. Along with the other inmates of the house, he cleaned up the mess and decided to set up the charade which Mrs Kenny saw when she arrived in the morning. He burnt the bloodied clothing, then he went to the graveyard and opened an old crypt — all the better that it was one which had attached to it a legend of necromancy — and removed the bones from the coffin to suggest some undead spirit having been disturbed. I am afraid to say that it was good enough to take some of you in.

'However, whilst this investigation was going on, this placed him in a dilemma: the longer he held on to the bones, the greater the chance was that the house and gardens might be searched and your guilt would be established. The brook was too shallow — I established that on my walk, therefore I suspect that he decided at first to burn them. As Doctor Watson will confirm, though, human bones, even old bones, are unfortunately very difficult to get rid of by burning. It takes a long time and requires a tremendous amount of heat. However, there was a chance that if he waited until Friday — '

'Why Friday?' asked Hopkins.

'Come, Hopkins, every schoolboy knows what happens on the fifth of November! In time-honoured fashion there would be bonfires all around the town and it would be easy to put the bones at the bottom of the piles which have been accumulating for weeks and the evidence of his guilt would be gone. You know, I have often thought that it was the best time, apart possibly from Christmas Day, to commit a certain type of murder. I reasoned that Staunton would probably have buried them in the grounds rather than keep them in the house, which might be searched.'

'Then why didn't he wait until Friday?'

'Because a better idea had come to him — he would return the bones to the coffin rather than take his chance with a bonfire. It was probably safer than holding on to evidence which would incriminate him. Miss Ellis came down to do that last night, but she was surprised by the two women. I suspect she was more frightened than they were. My stratagem was devised to make it look as though the coast would be clear tonight, and I'm afraid he rather took the bait too. He will go down for a very long time, Miss Ellis.'

'It is I who deserve to be punished; neither he nor any of the others did anything to harm Sister Farnham.'

'Perhaps, but tampering with the evidence in a murder case is serious matter and I am willing to stake my reputation on the supposition that you wanted to make a clean breast of the matter but were talked out of it or, more likely, terrified out of it.'

The girl said nothing.

'Besides, this gentleman's colleagues,' he indicated Hopkins, 'have been looking for the man you know as Staunton for some time. His real name is Henry Peters and I am sorry to say that he is wanted for attempted murder. I'm afraid your husband, as you would have it, is unlikely to see the outside of a prison again for the rest of his natural life. As to yourself, Miss Ellis, I think you will find that the law will treat you fairly, and I shall be happy to render any assistance I can when the trial comes up.'

'Sergeant Channon will take you down to the station,' said Wills quietly.

'I would lose no time in quietly surrounding the vicarage with your men, Inspector, for Peters is a most devious character, and by now he may have become suspicious about Miss Ellis's delay in returning. He has the distinction of being one of the very few men to have escaped my clutches after I had cornered him.'

On this occasion, though, half a dozen burly constables stood between him and his escape, and we heard later that he and Annie Fraser had gone along quietly with Wills and Hopkins.

'When I considered the evidence,' said Holmes later, 'I was fairly certain that it was the sort of crime which a woman would commit; it was impulsive and inopportune. I had often thought that the most difficult murder to solve would be one committed by, or indeed upon, a pillar of the community, particularly some churchgoing spinster noted for her charitable work. I never thought I should see one.'

'You mentioned a precedent; two, in fact.'

'That was how the woman in Forfarshire was murdered: I believe she was killed by her maid, who, after putting up with her insults and degrading treatment for years, one day flew into a dreadful rage and lunged at her. The maid fled immediately afterwards, however, and was never seen again. The Society for Vampirism Research gave great publicity to the incident at the time, and recalled as proof the Breton case to which I also referred, where the nature of the injuries had given rise to a corresponding moral panic.'

'And a humble carving fork was to blame.'

'Have I not always said that the dreary conventionalities of existence often conceal the most outré circumstances?'

'And they did not even take the trouble to hide it.'

'No, for its absence would have been more remarkable than its presence. It was simply cleaned and replaced in Miss Farnham's kitchen drawer where it remained ever since. I gave both Hopkins and Wills the hint at the time, but they refused to take it.'

'And at what point did you realize this man was Holy Peters?'

'As I have said before, Watson, you are a great conductor of enlightenment. I was sure I recognized the man's features and that set me thinking about previous cases, but when you pointed out his colonial accent, then that narrowed the field considerably. When you mentioned the developments in otoplasty, my suspicion became a certainty. Attaching himself to gullible females under the guise of religious ministry was this man's hallmark. The last time he sailed very close to murder and was almost caught. Though I cannot believe that he has completely divested himself of his murderous tendencies, I think he may have learned his lesson in the Carfax case and he no doubt pledged himself to avoid such dangerous tactics in future. I had known that it would not be long before we made his acquaintance once more. He was a trifle unfortunate in that, once the bones were back in the coffin, it would have been difficult to prove anything. The matter would have remained, perhaps, as one of our many unexplained occurrences.'

'He could have thrown Ellis to the mercy of the court, and justly have claimed complete innocence.'

'Yes, but he would still have been called upon to give evidence in court. In that event he could not be absolutely certain that his real identity would not come to light, and he had his previous exploits to consider.'

Henry Peters was sentenced to fifteen years for his part in the Carfax and Farnham cases, and Fraser received ten years as an accomplice. Rebecca Crouch was fortunate in that the judge took a more lenient view of her association with Peters and she escaped with an eighteen-month sentence. Drusilla Jane Ellis was acquitted on the basis of the evidence submitted by Holmes to the effect that she had acted purely in self-defence. Holmes received a letter from her some weeks after her acquittal to say that she had left the Order and was going out to India to work as a missionary. Ephraim Crouch returned to England for the trial, which received the most sensational coverage in the popular press. Afterwards, he made various attempts to shore up the Order of the Purple Rose, but after the scandal and exposure of Peters as a potential murderer, even its most deluded adherents abandoned it in droves. It failed miserably, and both the church building and the *Aion Erospiti* have now fallen into sad ruin.

The Adventure of the
Rotherhithe Ship-Breakers

The reading public has long been aware of my association with Sherlock Holmes through the publication of his numerous adventures over the last two decades. During that time, I have been greatly privileged to share in his myriad celebrated successes as well as a small number of his professional failures. Nonetheless, there remain a few cases of greater or lesser interest which have never been subject to public disclosure for various reasons, and which have been buried away at the bottom of my dispatch box in anticipation of the day when their publication should be considered appropriate. In the natural course of events, the details of some of those cases had, in one way or another, already entered the public realm, occasionally through newspaper reports of the arrest of the culprit, or more commonly, of the proceedings at the Assizes. In such instances, there was no lawful reason for my withholding the particulars of the case once the jury had delivered its judgement, and often it was little more than the combination of forgetfulness and indolence upon my own part which held things back.

I was reminded of one such case whilst drowsing over a copy of the *Gentleman's Magazine* one autumn evening in the comfortable stupor of the bar of my club. The article in question had praised the charitable work of a well-known banking heiress on behalf of the East End poor, and had also referred to the ceaseless campaigning of the Reverend Osborne of Holy Trinity to have the worst slum tenements in the metropolis demolished and replaced by more salubrious dwellings. This set off a train of thought which brought to my mind some of the notorious rookeries which had been swept away in the last years of the old century, the sorts of places which were Holmes's natural hunting ground.

Friar's Mount north of Shoreditch, built on a burial pit and better known as the Old Nichol, had been cleared; Tiger Bay in the Ratcliff Highway remained only in the memories of nostalgic writers of wharfside fiction; the infamous shanties of St Giles and the labyrinthine alleyways of Seven Dials in the West End had long since fallen to the demolishers. But, the march of progress being somewhat slower south of the river, there lingered another of these criminal plague-spots near the point where the low-lying ground between Bermondsey and Deptford makes a peninsula, of which I was reminded when reading the article. This particular quarter of the parish of St Barnabas, which stands in the shadow of the mercantile fortress of the great Greenland Dock, was a warren of impoverished streets and courts of ill repute, and which the *Morning Chronicle* had once described as 'the Venice of Drains', so badly was the place riven by open and noxious sewers. The area around the Deptford Lower Road was known locally as 'the Four Corners of Hell', due chiefly to the disorderly and disreputable dockside taverns straggled around its skewed crossroads. It was in this colourful locality, reached through the archway of a narrow vennel off Chilton Close, where Holmes kept one of the hideouts whither he would occasionally disappear, and in which vicinity occurred some years ago a remarkable series of events which I now lay before the public for the first time.

Holmes and I had read of the incident in the morning paper during a lull following one of Mrs Hudson's ample breakfasts. My friend had picked up the paper, glanced desultorily at the heading — 'Shot Fired At Surrey Wharfinger' — and then, having cast his eye over the first few lines, tossed the paper aside muttering that, as usual, there was nothing in it deserving his serious attention. It was only when the sturdy, florid-faced figure of Inspector Baynes of the Surrey Constabulary, one of the few police detectives for whom Holmes had a genuinely high regard, appeared in our sitting room some half an hour later, that my friend rekindled his interest in the matter.

'It must be three or four years since we first met, Mr Holmes,' said Baynes by way of introducing himself, 'but I trust you still recall me from the Oxshott case.'

'Yes, I remember both you and the case well. Doctor Watson may correct me if he wishes, but I am sure certain that it is the only narrative he has yet produced which has included a case of voodoo!'

'I notice that your reputation has continued to expand,' said Baynes.

'You have not done so badly yourself,' Holmes continued heartily, 'for if I recall correctly, you managed to put away the Randall brothers for a long spell after the raid on the gambling club in Peckham, and caught the entire Spencer John gang red-handed in Camberwell. I also read that you trailed Woodhouse all the way from Norfolk to Liverpool and took him just as he was about to step on the boat to America.'

'Well, as he had sworn your life away, I

suppose you had more than a passing interest in that case,' said Baynes, whose bright eyes twinkled with unconcealed pleasure at my friend's words of praise. 'I see you have been studying form,' he continued, with a gesture to the newspaper.

'Oh, the business at Rotherhithe, yes. But surely it is an open and shut case to a man of your calibre? Find this Donovan character and you have your culprit,' said Holmes.

'So I had thought at first, but I recalled the importance that you attached to minor details, and there are some aspects of the case which have puzzled me; just a few small things that have given me cause to be cautious about jumping to obvious conclusions. I like to keep to my own methods as you know, but you have a knack of turning over apparent trivialities until you can see something that isn't always apparent to the rest of us. The press got some of the incidental details wrong — they mixed up the Christian names of the Donovans, father and son — and as usual, they give only the sensational stuff and omit the important details.'

'Such as?' I asked, for I had read the report myself and had come to a similar conclusion as had Holmes.

'Well, I'll start at the beginning, gentlemen.

Late last night, I received a report that a shot had been fired through the window of the house of a Mr Elias Burdock, a ship-breaker who owns a small wharf at Rotherhithe, which as you may know, is a rough and ready sort of place. Sailors get knifed or robbed there with monotonous regularity, and the stevedores and the fish-porters knock merry hell out of one another in the street once they've had a few. But a pistol shooting: now, that's very rare. So I went down immediately, and when I arrived there, I discovered that the man for whom the bullet appears to have been intended — Elias Burdock, the proprietor — had left the house earlier on the day in question and had not returned. In fact, he had decided to visit his wife in Margate that morning on the spur of the moment and had left at about midday to catch a train. It was therefore a good many hours later, just after darkness had begun to close in, that someone fired a pistol shot through a window at the rear of the house — presumably intended to kill this Mr Burdock. As I said, he was gone by then, but his foreman, a Mr Richard Parlow who lives on the premises, had remained behind and just missed being hit by the bullet. The assailant escaped in the darkness and unfortunately was seen by no one.'

'And you think the assailant mistook one man for the other?' asked Holmes.

'I am not quite sure about that. You see, it is complicated by the fact that the window shutters were closed at the time.'

'You do not mean that the assailant fired through closed shutters?'

'As far as I can ascertain, the bullet was fired through the left-hand shutter, shattered the window, and lodged in the kitchen dresser.'

'Rather odd, surely, to take a shot through a closed shutter in the hope that your bullet will find the target. Do you know if this assailant had taken the trouble to ascertain whether his quarry was present in the room?'

'It is difficult to say,' Baynes replied. 'Apparently the two men would often sit at the kitchen table at the end of the day with the books, making out the gains or losses to the firm. So unless the assailant knew who was in the room, it would be pot luck as to which man he would hit,' said Baynes. 'That was what inclined me to think at first that it was not a professional assassin at work, or even a serious attempt at murder; more the sort of thing some reckless young lad might attempt.'

'Young Donovan, for instance?'

'Exactly.'

'What makes you certain that it was not the foreman, Parlow, who was the intended victim?'

'Because there was some history of animosity between Burdock and the Donovan family. Some months ago, Burdock accused one of the Donovans, who runs a rival ship-breaking business, of stealing his timber. It resulted in one of my men arresting young Donovan and carrying out a search of his father's yard. Nothing was found, but Burdock remained adamant that he had seen Tadhg Donovan hanging around outside the yard just before the timber went missing. Personally, I believe it was Donovan who did it, but as we had no proof, the matter went no further. Anyhow, the Donovans apparently vowed vengeance on Burdock — the son, who is a wild one by all accounts, declared he would knife him. According to the foreman, Parlow, they had been on their guard at Burdock's Wharf ever since the incident. It seems that young Donovan has been missing for a few days and his family have told us they don't know where he is. Went off to find a boat in the Downs, his father said. He also swears that no one in the house owns a pistol. The old man, Peter, has a record, too; mostly minor offences admittedly — petty theft and brawling in the taverns — and the boy seems to be growing up in his father's image.'

'It sounds reasonably credible to me,' I said, 'that this lad might have gone there in a moment of hot-headeness and, knowing nothing about the movements of the household and being unaware that Burdock was absent, might have fired the shot as a warning and then disappeared. There is now an attempt to cover up for him by pretending that he has gone down to the coast to find a ship, which seems an obvious cock-and-bull story, for a twenty-minute walk would take him to the Pool of London, which has more boats than any other port in the world.'

'Precisely, Watson,' said Holmes. 'What is it that has caused you to think otherwise?'

Baynes laughed. 'Admittedly, it is nothing more than a vague suspicion, but there are a surprising number of small coincidences. The incident happened about eight o'clock last night, just a few minutes after the maid went out to buy some oysters. After the shot was fired, Parlow ran straight out on to the wharf, and although there were a number of people in the vicinity, neither he nor the others saw the assailant, whoever he was, make his getaway. The only escape routes are along Grove Street by the oyster stall, or along the river path; the maid and the stallholder swore they saw no one, and a man and woman who had been standing on the river path said the same. So there was the coincidence of Burdock having left the house earlier, on what seems to have been a sudden whim; there was the coincidence of Parlow being left alone just a few minutes before the shot was fired; then there was the coincidence of not one of five possible witnesses having seen this man escape.'

'You are certain that a shot *was* fired?' asked Holmes.

'Yes, the window shutter bore the hole where the bullet had gone through. The wood was clean around the hole, showing it had been done recently.'

'It could not have been fired from inside the room?'

Baynes smiled. 'I see you are as sharp as ever, Mr Holmes! Most of the broken glass had fallen inwards and we found the bullet in the kitchen dresser. Then we fetched down Perrins, our small-arms specialist, to look at it. There is little doubt that the shot came from outside, for the hole in the shutter matches the bullet found in the dresser.'

'And both bullet holes were fresh?'

'Undoubtedly. Perrins also detected some staining around the shutter, but he was unable to say whether or not it was from powder blackening. Parlow says he remembered thinking that the explosion was fairly loud and that it must have been fired by someone standing close to the window.'

'Is it not possible that the intention was to kill Parlow rather than Burdock?' I ventured.

'It seems no less likely under the circumstances,' said Holmes, 'in which case, it would point very strongly to the maid as a possible accomplice of the assailant.'

'That occurred to me, too; after all, the maid was the only person who knew for certain that Parlow was alone in the room, sitting at that very table. However, when I spoke to Parlow, he laughed and said that he had no enemies in the world. He seemed not to have the slightest concern for his own safety — rather more for his master's; he scorned the suggestions of his neighbours that one of them should come and stay with him. He refused the offer of a pistol and said it would be useless as he had never handled one before, though he did somewhat reluctantly take a handsome heavy stick to his quarters, which was pressed upon him by an acquaintance, Nathaniel Wright, who owns a nearby public house.'

'Have you been able to confirm whether Burdock was at home when this happened?' asked Holmes.

'Yes, we have already done that. I wired to Inspector Hescott of the Kent Police, who spoke to the railway porter at Margate. The porters all know Mr Burdock by sight as he travels frequently from there, and the man who spoke to Hescott confirmed that Burdock arrived at a time which would have been consistent with his leaving the Deptford Road station on the 12.38 train. The man who was on duty last night also confirmed that Burdock did not leave again before the station closed at night. Hescott questioned Mrs Burdock's maidservant, who also attests that her master was at home all night.'

'A solid, but by no means unshakable, alibi,' said Holmes. 'After all, Burdock could have slipped out of the house without the maid's knowledge and then taken a train from a different station on the line.'

'Indeed, but why?' asked Baynes.

'That, of course, is one of a number of things which we shall have to discover for ourselves. Well, Watson, how does a trip to the Surrey side strike you?' Holmes asked.

'It is a fine day for a drive downriver,' I replied as I looked out of the bow window of the sitting room. 'I see that friend Baynes has taken the liberty of keeping his four-wheeler waiting.'

'I shall fill you in with some more details *en*

route,' said Baynes, drawing out his notebook as the cab set off down Baker Street. 'Elias Burdock is fifty-nine years of age and was formerly the manager for Seldovich's, the Baltic timber merchant in Bermondsey. Some years ago, having made enough money from a bit of speculation, he left the import trade and decided to buy a breaker's yard just upriver of the Earl's Sluice at Rotherhithe. This is a rough plan I have made of Burdock's Wharf,' he said, drawing out a cylinder of paper and passing it across to us. Holmes unrolled it and spread it out on his knee.

Baynes continued, 'The premises consist of a yard for storing the dismantled parts, mainly timber, ships' components and scrap iron, and there is a short wharf where the hulks are actually broken up. There is also a narrow slipway for smaller craft. The wharf house is a two-storied building with an outhouse which is used for keeping coal and oil, and there is a shed in which the tools are kept. As you can see, the subjects are enclosed by a nine-and-a-half-foot-high fence surmounted by barbed wire to the north and west; to the east is the river; and to the south there is the sheer wall of the disused naval victualling yard. There is a main gate in front of the house, which is always kept locked except on the rare occasions when wheeled traffic has to come in or out, and a small front gate to the side of this which is the usual means of entry for the labourers in the yard. There is a rear gate to the yard set into the palings by the riverside which opens on to a path in the close vicinity of the Dog and Duck public house, kept by the aforesaid Mr Nathaniel Wright; a few of the labourers from the Rotherhithe Street area come in this way. Both pedestrian gates are opened about eight o'clock in the morning to allow the labourers in and are then locked again at night after the last man has gone home. Only the three people in the wharf house have keys to the gates. They are Burdock, the proprietor, Parlow, the foreman, who is some twenty years younger than his master and Esther Cromley, the maid, who comes in during the day to do the cooking, cleaning, and provisioning. She is normally at the house from 8.30 in the morning until about the same time at night, with a three-hour break in the afternoon from two o'clock until five o'clock. The two men live on the premises, and Burdock goes home to Margate on a Friday afternoon and returns on a Monday morning by the first train. Parlow lives permanently at the wharf house. Mrs Burdock rarely visits the wharf, and never stays at the wharf house overnight. Burdock has taken recently to going home in the middle of the week if business is slack enough to leave in the hands of his foreman.'

'Therefore his departure at midday yesterday, whilst rather sudden, was not without precedent,' interjected Holmes.

'That is correct.'

'One moment; did Burdock send a wire to his wife to say that he was coming home?'

'No, he did not.'

'Do you know at which point Burdock actually decided to leave the wharf?'

'Yes, apparently he intimated his intention to Parlow the previous evening, and the following morning both men agreed that Burdock should return home as things were quiet.'

'We are justified, are we not,' said Holmes, 'in inferring from this that there must be some considerable degree of trust between the two men? Especially as the trade in used timber and small scrap iron is conducted largely on the basis of on-the-spot cash.'

'Yes. In fact, Parlow obtained the post through his sister, who was Esther Cromley's predecessor, some two years ago. He worked at first as a general hand purely for board and lodgings, then Burdock offered him the foreman's job at thirty pounds a year when the previous one left. Parlow said he later obtained an increase in his wages to a hundred a year, though with some adjustments in his duties and in his boarding arrangements to take account of the extra salary; all this was confirmed with Burdock. From that point onwards it seems that Parlow has been running the business from day-to-day. The new arrangement seemed to suit both parties, for according to the maid, they rub along pretty well.

'Yesterday seems to have been a fairly uneventful day at the wharf. Business was slack, as I have said, and a number of the labourers had been laid off, so Burdock departed to catch the train from Deptford Road station which entailed one further change en route to Margate. At about eight o'clock in the evening, the maid asked Parlow if he was hungry, and upon receiving a reply that he was, she went out to fetch him a dozen oysters. His intention was that when he had finished making up the books for the day, he would walk across to the Dog and Duck to bring home a jug of porter to wash down the oysters. The maid had left on her errand, and Parlow had just sat down at the table in the sitting room at the rear of the house when a shot rang out. He suddenly realized that a bullet had come through the window frame and lodged itself in the dresser opposite to where he was sitting. He immediately sprang up and dashed out on to the wharf, but in the dark, and what with a slight mist drifting in from the river, he could see no one. Then he ran round to the front gate only to find Esther, who had left the gate open, coming back. If the attacker had escaped that way, she must have seen him, but she had, she said, seen no one, nor had she heard the shot. Now, as you see, there are only two ways in or out of the wharf by foot — through the front gate or through the side gate that leads by the river path to the Dog and Duck, which was by that time locked. The man and woman whom I mentioned were conversing outside the tavern, and they said that although they had heard the shot, they were certain that no one passed that way. I was puzzled at first as to why neither the maid nor the oyster woman heard the shot, but the report may have been muffled by the bulk of the house, whereas the river path is open and has nothing to block the sound.'

'It is possible, though, that the culprit got away over the palings is it not?' I asked.

'In theory, yes. But Parlow says he was on the wharf within a very short time after the shot was fired, and it would be no easy job for someone to shin up the palings without being seen. Even so, once the escaping man has come down on the other side of the fence he still has, for practical purposes, only two means of escape — the river path or Grove Street. I think we can rule out the sheer twenty-foot wall of the dockyard.'

'What about the yard itself; surely with piles of timber and scrap iron, a fugitive could easily conceal himself there?' Holmes said, pointing to the plan. 'There are sheds and piles of timber and there is the crane too.'

'Yes, you could hide a regiment in that yard in the dark, and there is the old boat which is being broken up at the wharf. We searched them all and found nothing.'

'Then there is the roof of the house,' Holmes interjected.

'We sent a man up there, too. However, even if the culprit could somehow have concealed himself in any of these places, he would still have to escape from the yard at some point. Now, the whole neighbourhood was turned out in the street and on the river path within minutes, and soon the yard itself was swarming with police. People had brought torches and dogs, and I can assure you that my men turned the place upside down, but found nothing. If the assailant had been hiding in the wharf, it is inconceivable that he would not have been discovered.'

'But you have only the maid's word for it that the assailant did not pass onto the street through the gate she had left open?'

'The maid and the oyster woman. However the constables took some trouble to make enquiries at all of the neighbouring houses and no one reported seeing anyone suspicious at the time. The gate of the yard is within sight of the oyster stall, and they spoke to the owner, a Mrs Taylor, who says she saw no one. However, I feel that there remains just the slightest chance that the assailant could somehow have got himself quickly out of the street gate whilst the attention of the maid and the fishwife were distracted — after all they did not hear the shot and so there was nothing to alert them to the fact that there was anything amiss. The assailant could possibly have hidden somewhere in the badly-lit surrounding area, and then could have slipped away unseen before we arrived at the scene. The difficulty is that Parlow is adamant that when he reached the gate, the maid was already returning, and she *must* have seen anyone leaving. Of course, she may be lying,' said Baynes.

'Let us consider all the points,' said Holmes. 'If this assailant was after Burdock, he was well enough acquainted with the ways of the house to know where his quarry would normally be sitting; on the other hand, he appears not to have known that Burdock had suddenly gone home to Kent. That would suggest he was acting alone. If, however, he was after Parlow, then it would favour the theory that the maid is implicated. And if the maid is lying — that is to say she has deliberately misled you and is not simply mistaken — then it can only be because she is either in league with the assailant or is in fact the assailant herself, which would explain why no one was seen escaping. It would also suggest that the oyster woman is part of the conspiracy, too, which is beginning to stretch credulity, and so the entire accomplice theory begins to fall apart. Even if we assume, then, for one moment that the maid is in league with this person and that the target is Parlow, she lets the killer into the yard and somehow manages to distract the fishwife's attention long enough for him to escape. Why then did he, the assassin, not simply walk into the kitchen and blow Parlow's brains out? Why did he fire through a closed window?'

Baynes shrugged. 'A warning shot, perhaps, as Doctor Watson suggested? To frighten him.'

'Surely not,' Holmes said, 'for the tendency would be to fire a warning into the air where it would do the least harm, whereas by firing through a closed shutter one could not be certain that it would not be fatal to the occupant.'

'I suppose it is highly unlikely that girl could have been the target?' I asked.

'I should think so, though I would not entirely rule that out until I have spoken to her,' replied Holmes. 'Now, let us address the possibility of the assailant having some other means of escape: what about the river, for instance? Could he have left by boat? After all, there is both a wharf and a slipway; surely a small boat could easily have been launched very quickly from the slipway?'

'The letter 'A' on the plan marks the window through which the shot was fired,' said Baynes. 'Parlow swears that as he ran out of the house through the main door — at 'B' — in the direction from which the shot came, he came immediately within sight of the slipway, and he saw no sign of anyone.'

'Well, that seems certain enough. It is a most interesting problem, and we have summed up all the difficulties and inconsistencies,' said my friend. 'I am afraid that I must reserve further judgement until I have more data.'

Holmes sat absorbed in the corner of the cab as we trundled on in silence over London Bridge and then eastwards through the riverside districts where the swirling Thames could be glimpsed only here and there through a dock gate, or at the end of a small jetty which ran down to the murky water's edge; occasionally a subterranean culvert revealed the ghost of an ancient forgotten tributary. The river could be smelt, though, for the incoming tide had brought with it the salty tang of the marshes and the clammy air of our sultry Indian summer was thick with coal smoke, tar, and wet rope. The roads by the canals and docks were busy and cramped, and we passed by what seemed like miles of timber basins, railway sidings and the blind, high walls of dock warehouses where the smell of raw timber and acrid reek of creosote assaulted our senses. In the narrow dock-side streets where small dingy shops supplied the wants of the riverine populations, the masts and funnels of ships seemed to sprout from the roofs of the low, dilapidated weather-boarded houses huddled together at odd angles. Foreign sailors of every sort — Malays, Lascars and Chinese — abounded, but the Nordic types were most numerous, and there were enough rough dock-side taverns to supply the wants of half of London, for every second building, it seemed, was an alehouse or gin shop. In the back alleys lurked opium dens as numerous and as vile as their counterparts in Ratcliff or Limehouse. Holmes, attentive as ever to the peculiarities of the populace, would here point out a deal porter by his headgear, or there declare a workman to be a cooper or a stevedore by the tools he carried. Each deduction was invariably followed by an explanation of his reasoning to an appreciative Baynes.

'A gift you have been born with,' said the Inspector in admiration.

'I do not believe so,' began Holmes. 'On the contrary, I have come to the conclusion that like any branch of science, it may be studied and, in time, mastered. It requires the most assiduous attention to the minutiae of dress and demeanour, and diligent observation of the most infinitesimal peculiarities of anatomy. I confess I once mistook a tripe-dresser for a cheesemonger, though I would plead the feeble illumination from the gas-flares in the Borough Market in my partial defence.'

The district certainly gave every appearance of living up to its treacherous reputation, and yet, grim as it seemed to me in broad daylight, I dreaded to imagine its alleys and courts under the meagre glow of the sparse street lamps on a night where the fog was drifting in off the river. With the foul vapours from the ditches and open sewers, it seemed an even chance as to whether a traveller who strayed within its bourn would expire from typhoid or by having his throat cut. Once we had passed Southwark Gas Works and crossed the narrow hump-backed wooden bascule over the Surrey Canal, the landscape opened up. There was an almost rural feel here, and the neat cottages in Windmill Lane were spaced well apart. After a sharp turning by the cooper-age, we came to Burdock's Wharf, a gloomy, untidy-looking yard with a drab, dun-coloured, brick-built house looking across a muddy fore-shore towards the bleak Isle of Dogs.

We rang a bell and waited for some minutes for the maid to admit us. She was a tall, gaunt-looking girl with strands of colourless lank hair tied untidily back, and she seemed to take an age to understand why we had come. Eventually she admitted us, and then went off at an ungainly amble to fetch Parlow from the wharf. The interior of the wharf house was in a somewhat begrimed condition; a row of empty rum bottles in the kitchen, and a cracked mirror by the coat-stand in the hall showed how badly the place lacked the discipline of a mistress. Baynes introduced us to the foreman, who was a big, brawny, blue-eyed, fair-haired fellow, as tall as Holmes and as broad-chested as the Inspector himself. He greeted us with the apologetic air of someone who had caused unnecessary trouble.

'The guv'nor should be back any minute now,' he drawled with a trace of West Country accent. 'I'm only glad he wasn't here last night when this happened. The ole fellow would have died of the shock. I warned him a while ago that young barn-shoot was boastin' about how he'd get his revenge. I said to him at the time, you'd better bring them pistols of yours down an' keep 'em handy.'

'You seem fairly certain that you know who it was,' said Holmes.

'Well, it stands to reason. Mr Burdock hasn't another enemy in these parts. He's an honest man an' what's more a trustin' gen'lman, as I've reason to know. As I told the Inspector here last night, he took me in when I had nothin', gave me a job, an' now I have the runnin' of the place. He was kind to my sister, too, when she worked here. The only person to have had cross words him with was that thievin' rogue.'

'But you did not actually see the young man?' Holmes asked.

'No, Mr Holmes, I won't perjure myself. I didn't actually see him; he was off his mark in an instant. When the shot went off just outside the window, it took me a second or two to collect my wits, an' by the time I got outside, he was gone without a trace. I'd wager it was him all the same. Most likely got away over the fence.'

'It occurred to me that the bullet might not have been intended for Mr Burdock, but for yourself,' said Holmes.

Parlow smiled ingratiatingly and shook his head in a dogged fashion. 'No, I can't think of no one who'd want to do me any harm. Why, some of the neighbours offered to come and stay here with me! I was offered pistols an' sticks an' all. No, t'was the master Donovan was after, not a doubt of it. I only wish as he would stay at home until this is all over an' done with. I can keep things runnin' along until you have the fellow under lock an' key.'

Holmes signalled to Baynes, who asked Parlow to show us the room in which he had been sitting when the shot was fired. We observed the broken window and the hole in the dresser where the bullet had lodged. Holmes pondered aloud whether it might be possible to determine the point from which the pistol was actually fired and so we walked round to the side of the building. As Baynes had said, there was ample scope for concealment: a crane with a platform, numerous woodpiles, and heaps of scrap metal as well as the wreck of an old boat, half-stripped, lying at the wharfside.

'The ground is bone dry and hard,' Holmes said, 'so there is nothing much to go on here.' He went over to the edge of the wharf and looked over the hulk, which was moored there, then he came back and strolled down the short slipway.

'Let us take a closer look at the bullet hole in the shutter,' said Holmes, retracing his steps to the window. 'You can work out the trajectory from the angle of entry, and a reasonable inference is that the person holding the pistol must have fired from a point almost level with the window. The platform of the crane is several feet higher than the window and lies to the side, which rules out any possibility that the gun may have been fired from there.'

'But if he fired the shot whilst standing outside the window, he would surely have been seen by anyone standing on the river path. Very audacious,' said Baynes.

'He might be seen, but not necessarily identified; after all it was dark by then, and the yard is not lit,' replied Holmes.

'What's this fellow's game, I wonder?' said I. 'Why would he be prepared to take such risks?'

'It is pure speculation at this stage, but who knows what went on in the house?' replied Holmes with a shrug. 'Many a pretty game of fox-and-goose is played amongst the servants when the master is not at home. Oh, such things are well known, Watson! I merely offer it as a conjecture at this stage, but if such an intrigue were going on here and a relative — her father or brother or a suitor — had come to avenge her honour . . . '

'She is no Helen of Troy!' laughed Baynes.

'What is it, Holmes?' I asked as my friend began to stare intently across the wharf towards the river. From the water's edge, there was a broad open view through the wharves and landing stages right down the Thames until it curved away to the left at Greenwich Reach.

'Just an idea,' he said. 'One must explore every theoretical possibility. I had thought at first that it was possible for a man to have escaped by a boat from the slipway, but it occurs to me that it is equally possible that the shot may have been fired from a boat. How often do the river police patrol this area?'

'They start every two hours from the station at Wapping: one boat goes upstream, one downstream,' answered Baynes.

'I may or may not decide to follow up such a thread. Now, let us have a word with Esther.'

The girl made every appearance of trying

to answer Holmes's questions as helpfully as possible, but she was certainly not quick on the uptake. Yes, Mr Burdock was a good master, she said, and she got on well with Mr Parlow too. The two men were friendly beyond the normal master and servant relations. After the books were done, they would sit at night playing a game of cribbage over a glass or two of grog. No, she couldn't imagine who would do such a thing, not even the Donovan boy she said; as for the idea that someone might be after Mr Parlow, she couldn't think of any reason why. She hadn't heard any shot, and was quietly adamant that she saw no one either on her way to get the oysters or on her return.

'Whose idea was it that you should go out for the oysters?' said Holmes.

'Well, I suppose it must have been mine,' said the girl. 'I thought Mr Parlow might be hungry — he often has a dozen and a pot once he gets the books done. So I asked him did he want any before the stall closed. At first he said 'no' then he changed his mind.'

'Are you not afraid to come to work here after what has happened?' Holmes asked. 'After all, your master may have been killed.'

'Oh, no. At least, not as long as I'm not left here on my own. I can't think as anyone is after me. And it's a good post I have here, for the gentlemen's wants is easy met and there is no mistress in the house to make a fuss about trifles or chide me over a few farthings. But here is Mr Burdock now I believe,' she said, as the sound of two men having a conversation floated in through the open window. Presently the kitchen door opened and the white-haired proprietor stepped inside. The man looked much older than I had expected, and his excessive leanness made him seem rather frail. He had a pair of sharp, yet kindly, eyes and his first concern was for the girl's well-being. He bid her go home immediately till she had recovered from the shock. Holmes asked the man outright what he thought of the matter.

'A private grudge, yes, undoubtedly and bitter one too it would seem,' Burdock replied, 'and yet I can hardly bring myself to believe that even that thieving band of tinkers would go as far as this.'

'The Donovans?'

'Yes. As you know, Inspector, I had reason enough to set the law on them before, but for them to make an attempt on my life is scarcely credible. But then, I suppose, there is the evidence . . . '

'We have no evidence that any of the Donovans were involved,' replied Baynes evenly.

'Yet it can hardly have been anyone else,' said Burdock.

'You have had no other quarrels with neighbours or your labourers?' asked Holmes.

'Nothing beyond the usual disputes with tradesmen, for everyone is out to fleece you in this game, of course, but nothing of a personal nature comes to mind. The labourers and porters are casual and come and go by the day or the week, depending on the exigencies of the business. No, I really cannot think of anyone else who would hold such deep rancour against me. I did begin to wonder if there has not been some dreadful error, some possibility of mistaken identity, but that does not seem very likely either.'

'Meaning that Mr Parlow may have been the target?' asked Holmes.

'The possibility had occurred to me,' replied Burdock, 'but I dismissed it.'

'You cannot think of anyone who may have such a grudge against him as to be prepared to kill him?' asked Holmes.

'Good Lord, no! He is a most conscientious man, honest and fair in his dealings with the tradesmen and the labourers. If it were not so, any complaint that arose from the business would come directly to me, and I have received none. If this persecution is aimed at Mr Parlow, it can have no connection with the wharf.'

'How much do you know of his private life?' Holmes asked.

'Very little. He came up from Gloucestershire three years ago. He had ·sold a smallholding there but did not invest the capital too wisely and so lost the money in the City through an ill-advised business venture. Such is the nature of speculation, but his loss was my gain, for I soon found him to be a diligent general hand, and though he knows little of boats, he has a good head for business. His sister had worked for me before her marriage to a merchant seaman, after which she moved away to Liverpool. She was a most conscientious girl, and upon introducing her brother to me, I seemed to perceive similar qualities and so I took him on. I have had no reason to regret such an appointment. Far from it.'

'Whose idea was it that you should leave for Margate yesterday?' asked Holmes.

'Why, I suppose it must have been mine.'

'But you discussed it with your foreman the previous evening, did you not?'

'I seem to recall that I did, and he assured me that he could carry out the day's business, which consisted mainly of supervising the tradesmen, on his own. He is perfectly reliable and honest.'

'What precautions do you intend to take for your safety?' asked Baynes.

'I have brought a pair of pistols with me,' replied Burdock, flourishing the two small firearms, which he had drawn from his pocket. 'Inspector Hescott examined them when he came to my house last night. I shall carry them with me in future until this danger is past.'

'Even so, I do not think it is altogether wise to remain in the very place where an attempt has already been made on your life,' Baynes went on. 'Surely it would be far safer for you to return to Margate where, at least, some precautions could be taken for your protection. The wharf is rather isolated, and if this man returns and catches you unawares, you would be an easy target.'

'Nothing will keep me away from here. I won't be frightened off my own property. I had just that very argument with my wife this morning, which is the reason I was delayed somewhat. No, a man needs to show courage at times like this. I will say this to you, though, if one of the Donovans so much as sets foot in these premises, I'll not be responsible for my actions!'

'I'm not entirely at ease about leaving you here without a guard,' said Holmes. 'If I may make a recommendation, I am sure Doctor

Watson here would be only too happy to — '

'I won't hear of it,' said the old man, 'though I am grateful to you for the offer. In any case, I have Mr Parlow here with me at all times.'

'But Mr Parlow must attend to the business, and besides, he has said that he cannot handle a pistol,' said Holmes.

'I am afraid I must insist,' said Burdock with a shake of the head.

'Then, should you have any cause for concern whatever, wire immediately to me at 221b Baker Street.'

'I am inclined to believe the girl's testimony,' said Holmes, as we rattled back across the river, 'for she appears to possess neither the imagination to make the story up, nor the bravado to brazen out a lie. Let us try to reconstruct the incident: the intruder must have come in during the day and concealed himself until an opportunity presented itself, for it is surely too much to imagine that he both entered the yard *and* escaped whilst the girl was out at the stall. Did he or didn't he know that Parlow was sitting alone at the table in the kitchen? If he had been concealed in the yard, then he must surely have noticed that Burdock was missing. When the maid went out, he took his chance by firing through the window, because if he entered

318

the house, it is possible that the maid will have returned by then and he would be trapped. If it was Donovan, she would be able to identify him. He fired the shot then — and this may be of the utmost importance — how long would it have taken for Parlow to appear on the wharf? Parlow said he rushed out quickly, but this is a point which is continually coming up in criminal cases. The fact is that people are generally not very good at reckoning the passage of time when there has been some dramatic incident such as this. Parlow admits that he took a second or two to recover from the shock, then he would have decided to investigate. He knew from which direction the shot came, so he ran out of the kitchen into the hall, across the passageway and out of the front door and round to the window facing the wharf. Now, he said that he was there within seconds — but how many seconds? In all likelihood, probably nearer ten to twenty. If we accept Esther's story as true, then the balance of probabilities is that the man concealed himself in the yard and made his getaway when the gates were unlocked in the morning.'

The Inspector demurred.

'I know that your men searched the place from top to bottom, Baynes, but anyone can make a mistake, and as you saw, the yard was a perfect wilderness. The other possibilities are either that the shot was fired from a boat that was in the river, or that he made his escape by the river,' said Holmes. 'I think I should like to take a trip along by the wharf with the river police, if that could be arranged.'

'Then we shall go over to Wapping straight away,' replied Baynes. 'You know, it is a mystery to me,' he continued, 'why the man didn't simply wait another ten minutes until the girl had gone, then he would have had Parlow at his mercy.'

'Which would tend to favour any theory that the assailant could not anticipate the movements of the household, and therefore did not know that the maid was due to leave,' answered Holmes.

A vague notion had been gnawing at me. 'Who is to say that Parlow didn't fire the shot himself?' I asked.

'Excellent, Watson! That was the very first thing that occurred to me,' replied Holmes. 'It is not only an admirable theory, but a seductive one too, for it would solve almost, I say *almost*, every difficulty. It would certainly explain away the mystery of the assailant's invisibility and of his miraculous escape, too. But to what end? Give me the ghost of a reason as to why he should do such a thing. If he wished to insinuate that there was some vendetta against him, why does he afterwards laugh to scorn the very idea of it? Why does he not accept his publican friend's offer of a pistol and a man to protect him instead of remaining in that house alone during the night? Why does he not name his aggressor or suggest some pretext for his persecution? He does none of these things; he merely plods on doggedly as though nothing had happened.'

'It could be a ploy to keep Burdock away from the wharf,' I said. 'After all, you heard him suggest that his master should remain at Margate until the intruder is caught.'

'I have been involved in a number of cases where the purpose of some subterfuge was simply to get someone out of the way for a time — the cases of the Red-headed League and the Hyde Park Somnambulist spring to mind — but in this instance, Burdock is gone from Friday until Monday, and often in the middle of the week, too. If Parlow were involved in some underhand knavery which requires Burdock to be absent, he already has ample time to carry it out.'

We reached the Wapping quayside within the hour, where Baynes spoke to Inspector Colquhoun of the Thames River Police and explained what we intended to do and why. Soon we had climbed aboard the *Gabriel*

Franks and were cruising down through the crowded Pool. Once we had cleared Limehouse Reach and had slid past the Millwall Pier, Holmes shouted to Inspector Colquhoun, 'Ask the skipper to take us down until we reach the old naval yard, then turn and come back upstream very slowly.'

After the engines had eased back, we hove to in the stream some way off the wharf. Due to the position of the crane and the woodpiles, the window of the house could only be glimpsed intermittently through gaps; it would require a crack shot to pick it out from that distance. Holmes called across to the river inspector.

'How much water would there be by the wharf and slipway at low tide?' he asked.

'It is completely dry, Sir.'

'For how long?'

'For at least an hour or two.'

'Therefore the slipway would be inaccessible by boat?'

'Yes.'

'How far from the wharf to the navigable channel at low water?'

'Thirty or forty yards.'

'And in what state is the foreshore?'

'It silts up quite heavily. There is some gravel at the top of the bank, but beyond that it is mostly soft clay and mud.'

'How difficult would it be for someone to make his way from the slipway to, say, a boat lying off in the stream?'

'Impossible, Sir; not at low tide. You'd sink in it up to your waist.'

'What was the state of the tide at about eight o'clock on Monday night?'

'Let me see, now, it would be an hour or two before slack water.'

'Then there was enough water to reach the wharf in a boat?'

'Just enough for a very small boat, or at least one with a shallow draught.'

'Then again, a man could have swum out to a boat waiting in the channel, could he not?'

'By the sluice? I doubt anyone would do that, but it's possible, I suppose.'

'Thank you; I think we have seen enough.'

'I have thought from the beginning,' said Baynes when we had stepped ashore, 'that the motive may not have been revenge, but private gain. As far as I can make out, Mrs Burdock is the only person who is likely to benefit directly from her husband's death and she was the only person who did not know that he had left the wharf. I have already set one of my men on her track and I am going back down there now. I have told him to speak to the neighbours and find out what

Mrs Burdock does when she is left on her own all day. The Burdocks are childless and she must have a lot of time on her hands.'

'There is someone else who might benefit,' said Holmes, 'if a successful rival of theirs were to be put out of business.'

'Yes, the Donovans,' replied Baynes. 'I have not completely eliminated them yet. I suppose in the event of Burdock's death, they might buy up his stock, his land — perhaps the entire business. Esther Cromley and Richard Parlow, of course, both stand to lose an easy berth if anything were to happen to Burdock and the business were sold.'

'Surely the motive of material gain on Mrs Burdock's part is too obvious,' I said.

'Often it is the rather too obvious suspect who turns out to be the culprit. Criminals can have an exaggerated belief in their power to delude the police,' replied Baynes.

'It may be useful to confirm Parlow's story about selling up the land and the subsequent failure of his investment,' said Holmes.

'He has no criminal record. Do you suspect him?' asked Baynes.

'No more than anyone else, but if this persecution is aimed at him, it may arise from the circumstances of this business investment which failed; there may have been some fallout amongst the partners.'

Holmes sat with brows drawn as we made the journey back to Baker Street in a stony silence. He went out at four o'clock and returned without saying a word. He was in no better mood the next morning, where irritation and frustration ravaged his features, and an untouched breakfast spoke of his spoiled appetite. Finally, he sat down and lit a pipe.

'I have turned the case over and over in my mind, Watson,' he said. 'As Baynes put it, the chief difficulty with the stories that we have been told is in the cumulative effect of a number of minor inconsistencies; those small, but invariably significant, awkward facts which tell you that something is not quite right. Why, for example, is no one at Burdock's Wharf afraid for their lives? Parlow refuses the offer of a pistol and a bodyguard, despite having missed a killer's bullet by a few feet; the maid comes in to work the next day and carries on as though nothing has happened, although she herself must know that she may have passed within a few yards of the assassin; and Burdock himself, perhaps most astonishingly of all considering he was the likely target, refuses to leave the lonely wharf where he could, as was pointed out to him, be picked off at ease.'

'It begins to look as though they are all

engaged in some elaborate deception.'

'That's just it, Watson! You have put your finger on it. I always look for consistency: where there is a want of it, we must suspect deception. There is no consistency, therefore all is deception. But it's the question of motive, Watson, that's the singular problem here. No one, apart possibly from Mrs Burdock, has one. As to Parlow, I have failed to find a single reason why anyone would want to kill him. Yesterday I sent a couple of wires to the land and company registration agencies: the replies confirmed that Parlow did sell a parcel of land in the district of Lampern from which he made three-hundred pounds; he then invested it in the Aerated Bread Company. The company failed for twenty-thousand in the autumn of last year, and as you may recall, the crash left quite a few investors licking their wounds. In the absence of any other suspect, only the Donovans remain, but frankly there are a number of objections to that, for I cannot believe that they would go so far as to commit murder either to eliminate a rival or to gain revenge.'

We had a flicker of hope later that afternoon, when Inspector Baynes returned from Margate. 'I told you I had intended to go down to see Mrs Burdock again and I had sent the woman a wire earlier in the day to let her know that I was coming. I now believe that was a mistake. I had already decided to visit the family solicitor first, as I wanted to be clear about the position regarding any possible inheritance in the event of Burdock's death. However when Sergeant Cox and I got to the office of her solicitor in Union Row, Mrs Burdock was just leaving. It seemed a staggering coincidence, so I went straight back to the house with her, and had to drag it out of her as to why she had gone there. She was absolutely adamant that her visit was nothing to do with the shooting at the wharf. She repeated to me that her husband had not left the house on the night of the attempt on Parlow's life, and reminded me both her maid and a manservant had already sworn a statement to the effect that they were both present until after the last train for London had departed on the night. Yet I thought that she was protesting rather too much, as though by emphasizing these points in her defence of her husband, she was drawing my attention from her own possible involvement in the episode. I felt she was playing cat-and-mouse with me.

'When I went back to speak to the solicitor, Perry, I asked him about the reason for her visit, but he refused to disclose what he called his client's private business. I pointed out to him that an attempted murder was police business and that his client had come under reasonable suspicion; when I also warned him that if he wished to risk prosecution for obstructing the law he was going the right way about it, he changed his tack a little. He said that he was prepared to swear on oath that the conversation he had with Mrs Burdock concerned a purely civil matter relating to the commercial aspects of the business at the wharf and had nothing whatever to do with the events of Monday night.'

'I cannot believe that,' replied Holmes.

'Nor can I. However, without application to a magistrate, I can do no more. Perry did confirm to me that Burdock's entire estate is willed to his wife. It amounts to several thousand pounds. By Burdock's own account, his wife was insistent that he should not return to the wharf — that could be read as a wife's natural concern, but there could be another reason for her not wanting Burdock to go back to the Wharf: forewarned is forearmed; therefore, Burdock would be on his guard there and had even taken a couple of pistols with him. In Margate perhaps he would not be quite so careful.'

'A reasonable inference,' said Holmes. 'Anything else to report?'

'I found the villa at Margate to be tastefully furnished and elegantly decorated. Mrs Burdock is clearly a woman of taste and discernment who appears to have married well below her class, and it was not difficult to appreciate her distaste with the hovel at Rotherhithe. As she is almost twenty years younger than her husband, it occurs to me that if we were looking for a motive, we may not have to look very far.'

'Indeed. One question — when you met her at the solicitor's office, did you notice if she had any powder on her nose?' asked Holmes.

Baynes burst out laughing heartily. 'Oh, I'm sure I couldn't say.'

'I am perfectly serious,' Holmes continued.

'In that case, now that you come to mention it, I am quite sure that she had none — but what could you possibly deduce from that?'

'The strong likelihood that she had not made any prior appointment with the solicitor and had dashed round to see him unannounced. It must have been a very pressing matter, and I have no doubt that it was your wire which set off some alarm in her.'

'One wonders what it is she has to hide.'

'Have you left anyone to watch her?'

'There seemed little point, for she is a very sharp woman and my visit to her solicitor will have shown her that she is already under suspicion. If she is in any way implicated in this, I think it is unlikely that she would do anything incriminating. However, I have asked the postmistress to let me know if she sends anything from the Post Office and to make a note of any unusual letters or packages received by her.'

'Excellent.'

'The first thing I did once I left Perry's office was to go to the Pegwell & Cliftonville Bank, where Burdock has an account. I checked whether there had been any money passing from Burdock's account to Parlow's — nothing suspicious at all, only the three pounds, sixteen shillings odd, paid in fortnightly, which corresponds to the man's wages. Then I looked into Parlow's account at Deptford and again found no suspicious payments or receipts. Finally, I have had the report from Perrins, our gun specialist, who confirmed that the bullet found in the dresser was a very small bore, probably fired from a Webley's No. 2, which is the most common make of small pistol. That may explain why Esther did not hear the gun go off. Burdock, incidentally, owns a pair of Adams centre-fire models Mark III. We searched but found no firearms either in the wharf house at Rotherhithe or in the villa at Margate.'

'We have done all we can for the present,' said Holmes with a shrug. 'I have a few ideas of my own which I may decide to follow up. I shall let you know immediately if I make any progress.'

Half an hour later, my friend turned up in the sitting room dressed in an old, tightly-buttoned pea jacket, a muffler and peaked cap. The whole effect was set off by a clay pipe, but despite the bushy eyebrows and the long side-whiskers, those keen eyes shone through.

'Well, Watson, will I pass?'

'As Coleridge's Ancient Mariner!'

'If anything turns up, a note to Cap'n Basil at the Fighting Téméraire, Rotherhithe, should reach me.'

'Good Lord, not that disreputable dive we passed yesterday?'

'The very same place, Watson,' he chuckled. 'I am afraid to say that is the best of the bunch. I suppose the district must have seemed quite forbidding to you, and indeed it may be dangerous to those who know little of its ways, but I am able to wander its darkest alleys and back courts without fear.'

'All the same, I am not sure that I shouldn't insist on accompanying you.'

'There would be little point, Watson. The sudden appearance of two strange faces would, I fear, only draw unwanted attention and would not fail to be remarked upon.'

'Shall you be gone long?'

'I think not. A couple of days at the utmost. The malicious gossip of neighbours is often a most useful, if occasionally mildly exaggerated, source of information. Open any correspondence which may arrive and be prepared to act upon it as you see fit.'

One of the most amusing facets of Holmes's character was the almost childlike delight which he took in his various incognitos. Apart from his adopted persona as Captain Basil, as he was known in the riverside districts on both banks of the river, I knew that he often mixed with the ne'er-do-wells of Whitechapel and Bethnal Green under the cognomen of Solly Hyams, and was occasionally to be found circulating amongst the more sophisticated artistic cliques in the west end as Sigmund Holmqvist, the landscape painter. He must have struck a vein almost immediately for the next morning I received a note from him as follows: 'A long shot, Watson — can you check the bankruptcy notices during the past year. Look for Burdock's name. Captain Basil.'

Whether he had at last alighted on some definite line of inquiry or was simply grasping at straws was impossible for me to tell, but it was a simple matter for me to browse the back copies of the *London Gazette*. I delved into the pile, and to my utter astonishment, I discovered the following notice had been published in the previous year:

THE BANKRUPTCY ACT, 1869.

In the County Court of Kent, holden at Rochester.

In the Matter of Proceedings for Liquidation by Arrangement or Composition with Creditors, instituted by Elias Burdock, of 27, Imperial Villas, Margate in the county of Kent, Ship-breaker at Burdock's Wharf, Rotherhithe, in the county of Surrey.

NOTICE is hereby given, that a First General Meeting of the creditors of the above-named person has been summoned to be held at the King's Head Hotel, High Street, Rochester, in the county of Kent, on the 13th day of August, 1895, at three o'clock in the afternoon precisely.

Dated this 30th day of July, 1895.
J. H. Perry, 117 Union Row, Margate, Kent,
Solicitor for the said Debtor.

I tried to apply Holmes's own method to determine the best course of action. Should I go to Perry himself and ask him why he had kept this from Inspector Baynes, or should I be better off going to the company records office and try to ascertain whether the ownership of the business and the property at Rotherhithe had changed in the last year? I chose the latter course. The clerk at the counter confirmed that no change had been registered, but took some time to explain patiently to me that the insolvency proceedings may never have been enforced. He added that, depending upon the disposition of the creditors, it was not impossible for bankruptcy to have been avoided even after the insolvency notice had been issued, providing certain guarantees were made in favour of the bankrupt by a guarantor or similar. He had, however, no record of this and I must confess that I left the office more confused than ever. I returned to Baker Street in a welter of indecision as to what I should do next.

Fortunately, Holmes had returned in my absence: embarrassment and annoyance were inscribed upon his features, and he was not long in explaining the reason.

'I had gone down to the four corners,' he said, 'to put an ear to the ground. First I tried the Prince of Orange and the Armada Beacon and had drawn blanks there. Then I went into the Colleen Bawn, which is one of the rougher dives even by the standards of the dockside. On making my way into the snug, I had an accidental collision with one of the denizens — a fish porter, I should say from the smell. Nothing drastic, he had spilled some beer over me and then made a fuss of apologizing and cleaning it up. At least, I had thought the collision was accidental, but on later reaching my lodgings, I discovered that not only was I a few sovereigns lighter than when I had entered the tavern, but that my silver watch had disappeared along with my pocketbook.'

'The fish porter?' I asked.

'Most likely one of his accomplices when my attention was diverted. I returned afterwards, but both the fish porter and the pocketbook had gone to ground. The silver watch I managed to retrieve from an ancient pawnbroker on the corner of Trident Street who swore blind not only that he had never set eyes before on the man who pledged the watch, but that he had not the slightest idea that it was stolen property when he bought it. He was also unable to give me a very clear description of the man who pawned it.'

'Who lies with dogs shall rise with fleas!' I remarked for it was seldom that I had the opportunity to chide my friend for his folly. 'Have you reported the theft to the police?'

Holmes burst into a hearty laugh. 'Not if it had contained my last penny,' he said, as he began removing the last of his disguise, 'for I could not suffer Lestrade's or Gregson's sarcasm on the matter. Still, Watson, should I ever fail as a consulting detective, I think I have amassed enough information now to set up as a reasonably proficient ship-breaker. Buy an old boat for two-thousand guineas, engage a few rough labourers and deal porters to break it up and store it, a marine engineer to dismantle the movable parts, and in six months you will have it sold for a clear profit of five-hundred. Easy money, providing you have premises on the river and a steady supply of labour. The vessel which presently lies at Burdock's moorings, the collier *Strangford Lough*, is being broken up following a case of barratry for which the master and first mate are now doing time. The Cromleys seem to be a very decent, if rather impoverished, family; the mother is a permanent invalid whom both the father and Esther look after. As far as Burdock is concerned, that frail exterior hides a sharp business mind. He picked the wharf up for a trifling sum from the previous owner, whose inclination to strong drink and disposition to choleric temper ruined his business prospects and hastened his death. I also discovered that when he was in the timber business at Seldovich's he refused to take a few of the men back after the big dock strike. Some threats were made at the time, but that was over five years ago and I can hardly think that the rancour has lasted this long. The old fellow is generally liked, and the two men are thought to be on good terms. Parlow appears to have no strong vices; he neither drinks heavily nor gambles. Tahdg Donovan, it seems, did indeed go to look for a ship on the Downs. He left on the *Northern Cross* of the Blue Anchor Line from Dover two days before the shooting at the wharf. The story is that he got a girl into trouble and took the usual way out — via the merchant service.'

I showed Holmes the copy of the bankruptcy notice and told him of my visit to the records office.

'Excellent, Watson, you have not been idle. My visit to Colleen Bawn was well worth the loss of the pocketbook in the long run, for it contained only a few ten-shilling notes, and I picked up the scent in the saloon bar there. An old acquaintance of mine, or rather of Cap'n Basil's, furnished me with the rumour that Burdock almost went bankrupt about a year ago; he managed to get out of the trouble

337

by some means or other. How exactly is not known, though as you may imagine, the speculation was rife, and in some quarters, quite imaginative. Nevertheless, I was inclined to think there was no smoke without fire, and this notice confirms it in every respect. It throws up some interesting questions, does it not?'

'I am completely at a loss.'

'Yes, I should say, if anything, this rather multiplies our complications. I began to wonder if there was perhaps a sleeping partner — some third party — of whom and of whose interest we know nothing. From the outset, I had just the vaguest feeling that Mrs Burdock may have known more than she was letting on. Perry, the lawyer, can hardly have been ignorant of his client's bankruptcy either, and if Baynes can show that Perry's failure to disclose his knowledge of this was material to an attempted murder, he will not only face a criminal charge but in all likelihood be struck off too. But why has no one alluded to this bankruptcy? Surely Parlow must have known about it too? And who was the mysterious guarantor who averted the insolvency? Our suspicion that there has been a deliberate deception at the heart of this matter has been amply confirmed.'

'What course of action do you intend?'

'No more beating about the bush, Watson; I mean to have the whole thing out in the open. Tomorrow morning I shall wire to Baynes, then we shall go straight down to Rotherhithe, confront both men with this notice, and ask them straight out for an explanation. There is nothing else for it.'

Alas, the wire was never sent. At nine o'clock that evening we were the ones to be summoned by Baynes. The page had brought us in an urgent message: 'Come at once. The murderer returned this evening to the wharf and the old man is very critical. Have touched nothing, will await your arrival, Baynes.'

'Dear me,' said Holmes shaking his head, 'well, we did try to warn the old fellow, but he refused to listen. Your coat and hat, Watson, and I'll send Billy for a cab. I think I am beginning to understand it now. Before we go, though, there is one thing I must check, if you would be so good as hand me down the almanac,' he said, to my complete puzzlement.

'The almanac?'

'Never underestimate the prime necessity for exercising the faculty of imagination, Watson.'

'But what can the almanac tell you?'

'It can tell me something about the influence of the moon on terrestrial affairs,' answered Holmes with an impish smile.

'You jest, surely?'

'It is the literal truth, my dear fellow.'

'You do not mean — '

'No, Watson, not a case of lunacy. Let us say rather a combination of the influence of the moon and a little unpropitious timing. All shall be explained presently.'

By the time we arrived at the Wharf, Baynes greeted us with a grim look. 'It is too late, gentleman, Mr Burdock passed away about twenty minutes ago. He died in his partner's arms. The doctor has just left, and Mr Parlow has remained with the body in the sitting room until it is removed to the mortuary.'

'How did it happen?' asked Holmes

'Whoever it was must have come in during the day and concealed himself somewhere in the house, for the gates were shut at five, and the door of the house closed and locked from the inside. The two men were sitting at the kitchen table talking over a glass of grog and at one point Parlow stood up to go to the privy. Esther said that on his way to the privy, Parlow entered the scullery, asked for another two glasses of rum and water, and told her that she could go home when she had poured them. Parlow left the scullery and a few seconds later she heard the privy door slam behind him; it is some way down at the end of the passage. I questioned her very closely on this point: almost immediately after the door slammed she says she heard the sound of a pistol shot going off. She hesitated for a moment or two, then crept out into the hall. She heard a groaning sound and looked into the sitting room only to find Elias Burdock lying in a pool of blood on the floor, barely conscious. He had been hit in the back and was bleeding profusely. On her way to the sitting room, she noticed the main door lying ajar — the assailant, who must have waited until Burdock was alone then seized his chance, had left it open when he made his escape. Parlow had heard the pistol shot as well, and ordering his clothes, he rushed out of the privy and up the passage; for a moment he was torn between going to Burdock's aid and giving chase to the murderer. Seeing that the girl was attending to her master, he dashed out onto the wharf only to see a man running down the slipway.'

'But the slipway is at the rear of the house. How did he know which way the assailant had gone?' asked Holmes.

'As all the gates were locked, he assumed that the murderer would use the only means

341

of escape possible — the river. He gave chase but found that the delay owing to his few seconds' indecision meant that the man had a good start on him. On this occasion, he was able to give us a fair description of the man.'

'Really?' said Holmes rubbing his hands. 'That is quite remarkable: I should like to hear it.'

'Yes, he did very well. I have had it wired out to all stations. It was neither of the Donovans.'

'I'm sure. Did Parlow take Burdock's pistol with him?'

'I made a point of asking him; in fact he did not.'

'He goes in pursuit of an armed man who had just seriously, possibly fatally, wounded his friend and omits to take with him the only weapon there is.'

'He explains that by the fact that he does not know how to use one.'

'It was a remarkable show of bravery all the same. What happened next?'

'Parlow pursued the man in the darkness but then the attacker ran down the slipway and managed to get away in a boat that was lying off in the stream. I recall you alluded to that possibility after the first incident. Do you wish me to call Parlow in then?'

'No, I should rather speak to Esther first.'

The girl was pale and upset, with red-ringed eyes. She was still shaking with fear and shock. She confirmed that Parlow had been ill most of the day. Three times since dinner he had had to visit the privy. It was on the third occasion that the incident happened just as she was clearing up for the night.

'And you heard the privy door slam on each of these three occasions?' Holmes asked.

'Yes.'

'How much time elapsed between Mr Parlow leaving the scullery and the door slamming?'

'About seven or eight seconds, I think.'

'And on each occasion the time lapse was the same?'

'Yes, I think so.'

'Think very carefully now, Esther: on the third occasion that Mr Parlow went down the passage, how much time elapsed between hearing the door slam and hearing the pistol go off?'

'I heard the pistol go off almost immediately.'

'And you are sure that it was the same door which slammed on all three occasions?'

'Whatever do you mean, Sir?' she said, shaking her head in puzzlement and gazing at Holmes as though he were mad. 'Why should

343

Mr Parlow slam any door other than the privy door if that's where he was going?'

'Esther, let us come in to the scullery and we shall conduct a little experiment: first, we shall leave the scullery door open; then, I am going to ask Doctor Watson to walk down the corridor and slam the privy door.'

I did as requested and slammed the door as hard as I could, then returned to the scullery.

'Well, Esther, was that the sound you heard?'

'Yes, but it was much louder than that,' said the girl looking a picture of confusion. 'May I take my leave now, sir? I am very tired and must go home to my mother,' she said.

'Providing Inspector Baynes has no further need for you, yes, you may go,' replied Holmes. 'I have one final question: after the murder of your master, did you have any conversation with Mr Parlow?'

'Yes. He asked me about what I had heard and then told me that we would have to go to court. He reminded me that I must tell the truth no matter what anyone said. 'Just tell the truth exactly as you have told it to me,' he said, 'and no harm will come to you.' I don't know whatever he meant. I should never tell any lies.'

'What do you think?' Baynes asked, when the girl left.

'I think she is a most suggestible girl,' Holmes replied.

'Would you care to examine the rest of the premises?' said the Inspector.

'No, that will not be necessary, for there is nothing to be learnt from it. I rather think we should proceed directly to arrest the culprit.'

'Arrest the culprit!' asked Baynes. 'You know who is responsible?'

'Oh yes, I should have thought there was no great difficulty in working that out,' he replied enigmatically to the astonished Inspector.

'And you know where to find him?' asked Baynes.

'Certainly. However, there remains one minor detail I should like to clear up with Mr Parlow first, if you would lead the way.'

Parlow was in sitting the room with the curtains drawn, the very image of grief. Burdock's corpse, covered with a bloodied sheet, was laid out on the table awaiting the arrival of the undertakers. The foreman stood up as we entered.

'I expected that you would want to ask me some questions, Mr Holmes,' he said meekly.

'No. In fact, I have only one question to ask you, Mr Parlow.'

'Yes, Sir, what is that?'

'What you have done with the pistol?' said Holmes coolly.

'The pistol!' he cried, a spasm of surprise contorted his features.

'Yes, I am referring to the Webley's No. 2 with which you murdered Elias Burdock: the very same pistol which you used several days ago to fire the shot through the shutters of the empty sitting-room to create the impression of a vendetta against Mr Burdock. I suppose it is now lying in somewhere in the Thames mud?'

'I've no idea what you are talkin' about,' the man replied.

'Then let me recount the entire episode to you. This evening, you pretended to have a disorder of the lower abdomen in order to justify your repeated visits to the privy; on each occasion you deliberately slammed not the privy door, but the bedroom door, which is much closer to the scullery in order that Esther would hear it. Then you walked quietly to the privy at the end of the passage. The purpose of ruse this was to inculcate in her the expectation that she would hear the door slamming a short time after you had passed by the scullery. On the third occasion, Esther saw you leave the scullery, then there was the expected delay of a few seconds before she heard the door slam. This time, instead of walking quietly to the privy, you first stopped and silently opened the main door to make it look as though someone had escaped; and then you slammed the bedroom door, the one next to the sitting room. Almost immediately afterwards you shot Elias Burdock in the back; then you fled stealthily down the corridor to the privy, noiselessly opened the door, and went in. At Esther's screaming, you came running up the corridor, then pretended to go in pursuit of the imaginary assailant; in fact this is what gave you the opportunity to dispose of the murder weapon in the most convenient place — at the bottom of the river.'

'Is this how you achieve your results, Mr Holmes? By bluffin' and browbeatin' your suspects, and dazzlin' them with your wild theories! Esther has already told the Inspector here that I was in the privy when the shot was fired; therefore, it was quite impossible for me to have killed Mr Burdock. She will swear to that in court.'

'I can assure you that this is no bluff. Esther may have said that she heard a door slam, but I have just conducted an experiment in the presence of the Inspector which suggests very strongly that it was not the privy door which the girl heard, and I think I can show that she has made a very simple mistake. I am afraid it is no use, Parlow. It is low water on the river, and I had already established from the river police a few days ago that it is quite impossible to reach a boat in the channel from the slipway under these conditions, for there is a slough of impenetrable mud to cross. I have no need to examine the slipway to know that I will not find a single footprint in the mud there. Too bad you are a landlubber, Parlow, for had you picked a high tide on both occasions you might just have got away with it. Though I will grant your ruse last week was a rather clever one. It certainly took me in for a while.'

'I'm afraid you have got it wrong, mister detective. What possible reason could I have for killing my employer? I stand to lose everything I have here.'

'On the contrary,' interrupted Holmes, 'I believe I can show that you stand to gain quite a bit. Your motive for killing Mr Burdock is concerned with his bankruptcy last year, of that I have no doubt. I freely admit that I am not absolutely sure how the crash was averted, or what part you played in it, but it seems a most improbable coincidence that Mr Burdock suddenly trebled your salary at the time. It is simply a matter of searching the house until the papers are found.'

A spasm of alarm crossed his features, but the bluster remained. 'I don't know what papers you're talkin' about.'

'I am sure you will find exactly what you are looking for somewhere in the house,' Holmes said to Baynes, 'though you may have to take the place apart. You are looking for a set of deeds which relate to the wharf and probably this property as well. It is my belief that you will find that the deeds are in the name of Richard Parlow, not Elias Burdock, and they will provide you with the motive for the murder.' Holmes gazed after Parlow with an odd expression as the two Surrey constables led him off.

'A quite remarkable fellow in many ways,' he remarked to us at length. 'He is no ordinary murderer. He managed to delude two of the brightest men in the profession. I am afraid that I completely failed, at first, to grasp the significance of that very subtle opening gambit, whose purpose was to sow the wildest confusion and throw us all off the trail. Incidentally, this should also clear up the mystery of Mrs Burdock's sudden visit to her solicitor. She may have known about this transaction. The Inspector's wire exacerbated her fears that another attempt might be made on her husband's life, and so she hastened there to ask the hypothetical question of the legal validity of this prior, but secret, agreement. She is a clever woman, as you said, and may possibly have suspected the course of events; however, her husband's complicity in the deception to avoid bankruptcy probably prevented her from saying anything to you. If she had taken you into her confidence, it is possible that her husband would be alive today.'

'The registered owner of the business had not changed,' said Baynes in slight puzzlement. 'I checked it myself; it remains in the name of Elias Burdock.'

'That is correct,' said Holmes, 'but Burdock had been in financial trouble of some sort. I assume that he managed to hold off his creditors by the facade of bringing Parlow in as the new owner. In order to do that, a false set of papers would be needed making the business out to Parlow, duly signed and witnessed but — this is the important part — never lodged. Of course, the entire scheme was nothing more than a mere subterfuge aimed at mollifying the creditors at the time. It gave Burdock enough time to get out of whatever difficulty he was in and put the business back on its feet. Once the creditors were paid, the heat was off and the change of ownership postponed. Yet, no matter how counterfeit the intention, the papers, I believe, would have been signed by Burdock in the presence of witnesses, and therefore it could be argued that they had the full force of law. It occurred to me that Parlow might have kept the original copy. In the event of Burdock's death, the widow would not have been able to show that Burdock signed the papers under duress from the purchaser. It only wanted the papers to be lodged, and the business and the house were Parlow's. No doubt it was his intention to do this after the funeral.'

'But surely,' I said, 'the agreement could not stand?'

'Morally no; legally perhaps yes. It could only be declared void if there were duress or deliberate deception, or one of the signatories could be proven not to be of sound mind.'

The following day, Holmes received a note from the Inspector to say that the deeds had been discovered in a false cavity of a chest in Parlow's room at the wharf house. Burdock had indeed at the time of his difficulty signed a paper transferring the business and premises to Parlow for a sum of two-thousand pounds. It seemed incontrovertible that the foreman had coldly plotted his master's death whilst engaged in the sham of being the old man's friend and partner.

'Rank ingratitude,' I muttered on reading the Inspector's note.

'Indeed, Watson, 'A man's worst enemies

are those of his own house.' The moral of this tale is the strength of appearances and the suggestibility of human nature. It is certain that Parlow possessed this power of suggestion in abundance. Esther is one of the most suggestible females I have ever met; she treated her presumptions as facts when they were not. Her unshakeable belief in Parlow's innocence was founded on appearances. The three things that stuck in Esther's mind were: the two men sitting over a glass of grog together like a couple of old shipmates; the slamming of the bedroom door followed immediately by the gunshot; and the sight of her master's life ebbing away as he was held in Parlow's arms. She is a simple girl, yet no counsel in the world would have shaken her had the case depended upon her evidence. Parlow knew this. Hence my question as to whether she and Parlow had discussed the matter — 'Just tell the truth exactly as you have told it to me.' What he really meant, of course, was 'tell the police what you thought you saw and heard, and I shall have nothing to worry about.' Again and again throughout the case, I am sure that it was Parlow who made subtle insinuations: the idea of supplying false papers to the creditors; he will have spread the rumour in the Dog and Duck about the Donovans' sworn revenge, too; no doubt he suggested to Burdock that he go home on the day of the first shooting, and managed, by the same means, to get the girl to propose that she go out for oysters.'

'There is no surer way of getting someone to do something than to get someone to appear to suggest it themselves.'

'Indeed, Watson, it's quite an art in the Civil Service you know: Mycroft calls it 'Tidbury Syndrome' after one of the ostensibly meek, mild-mannered, bumbling clerks in his department who rules his superiors with an iron rod of pure suggestion. Norbert Tidbury never forgets the deferential shake of the head when he tells them how amazed he is at their ability to come up with such clever stratagems.'

'But why did Parlow shoot Burdock in the back? A bullet in the brain would have been a surer, and more humane, way of killing him. How was Parlow to know that the old man would not recover?'

'That is the strange part, and I have come to the conclusion that Parlow was partly telling the truth when he said he could not handle a gun. His nerve may have failed at the last moment and perhaps his aim went awry. Still, even if the old man recovered, there would always be another opportunity once Parlow had established the general belief in some bizarre vendetta against Burdock.'

'Baynes will no doubt be kicking himself for having gone after the wrong suspect.'

'To be fair, he had established the correct motive right from the beginning, and he was pretty quick to realize the possible significance of the ownership of the Wharf. What he lacked, however, was a Watson for a trusty auxiliary!'

On the evidence produced by Holmes and presented by the prosecution, the jury took less than half an hour to find Richard Parlow guilty of wilful murder when the case came up for trial. The night before Parlow was hanged at Wandsworth Prison, Inspector Baynes upheld an old and venerable tradition by visiting him in the condemned cell. At the end of the visit, the man asked Baynes to convey to Holmes his regards to 'a very fine specimen of the detective profession,' and expressed the hope that they would meet again in the hereafter. Not for the first time in our long association did Holmes shake his head in wonder at the kaleidoscopic disposition of the human soul.

'It occurred to me,' he remarked at length, 'that the affair has encompassed all the symbolic elements of the classical tragedies of antiquity: the discontent; the temptation and the dream of owning *Parlow's* Wharf; the opportunity; the tragedy of the murder and the fixing of his guilt and finally, repentance and death.'

In the same week, the *Southwark Observer* reported on the first of the demolitions of the slum dwellings in the Rotherhithe and Bermondsey districts.

'A cleaner, better London,' I said, 'will arise from the dust.'

'I must confess,' my friend replied, 'I did permit myself a slight chuckle at your portrayal of the place as a kind of Tartarus. Rough, dirty, and dangerous as it may have been, I really think it wasn't half as bad as you made it out to be. The four corners of hell,' he mused, 'yes, that could almost be a metaphor for criminal London.'

We do hope that you have enjoyed reading
this large print book.

Did you know that all of our titles
are available for purchase?

We publish a wide range of high quality
large print books including:
**Romances, Mysteries, Classics
General Fiction
Non Fiction and Westerns**

Special interest titles available in
large print are:
**The Little Oxford Dictionary
Music Book
Song Book
Hymn Book
Service Book**

Also available from us courtesy of
Oxford University Press:
**Young Readers' Dictionary
(large print edition)
Young Readers' Thesaurus
(large print edition)**

For further information or a free
brochure, please contact us at:
**Ulverscroft Large Print Books Ltd.,
The Green, Bradgate Road, Anstey,
Leicester, LE7 7FU, England.
Tel:** (00 44) 0116 236 4325
Fax: (00 44) 0116 234 0205